Finding Infinity

Susan Kiernan-Lewis

Published by San Marco Press

Other books by Susan Kiernan-Lewis:
Free Falling
Murder on the Côte d'Azur
Murder à la Carte
Murder in Provence
Murder à la Mode (January 2013)
The French Women's Diet
Horse Crazy
Air Force Brat
Grave Mistake
Walk Trot Die
The Heidelberg Effect

Finding Infinity

Chapter 1

It is a truth universally accepted that no matter how carefully you plan your life, you can always count on it to go totally to crap just when you need it to hold together.

Liddy sat at the gate in the Atlanta International terminal and felt the delicious butterflies in her stomach that matched her memory of how she felt when she first moved to Paris as a very young woman. It had been twenty years since she had first boarded the Air France flight from Atlanta to begin her life—her adventure—in the City of Light. In many ways, nothing had ever been the same for her since. The intervening years had seen her obsess over all things Parisian. She'd decorated her Atlanta house to mimic a Parisian salon, she'd learned how to bake French pastries that would make a patisserie chef weep. She'd kept her French language skills sharp and alive with French clubs and novels. She'd lobbied to spend nearly every annual vacation taken in Paris with her husband and son.

She pulled out her boarding pass just to see the words again: *ATL to Paris-Charles de Gaulle Airport.* Twenty years, one marriage and a child, now grown and gone, and she was going back to the city of her heart, the city of her youth. Liddy smiled to herself and glanced around at the other people waiting to board the flight. She thought they looked French. One woman sat and squinted at her smartphone in a seat across from Liddy. She was dressed in casual elegance, as if she had just thrown herself together but she wore her clothes with a grace and style that most women would have labored to achieve. She's Parisian, Liddy thought. It's all so effortless for her. And soon, for her, too.

She planned to stay the summer but she was open to staying longer if things worked out. If, after three months of sipping café crèmes in neighborhood cafes and strolling the museums, the quaint, cobblestone streets and waking up to the City of Light outside her balcony window every morning, she felt she must stay, then she would. A year, perhaps forever. Her schedule, her time, belonged to instinct and serendipity now. There was no husband, no office, and no child to influence or dictate how she spent her time.

For better or for worse, her life was her own again. And now, it was time to claim it.

The gate official broke into her thoughts by announcing that they were ready to board the airplane and Liddy felt her stomach lurch with anticipation and excitement. She looked at the French woman on the smartphone and noticed that she appeared oblivious to the fact that they were all about to begin their journey.

Does she make this transatlantic trip so frequently that it really is all just *de rigeur* to her? Liddy wondered. She gathered her purse and her carry-on and walked to the line that was forming in front of the gate desk. She held her passport and boarding pass in her hand and felt her butterflies go into hyper drive.

I'm really finally going.

Suddenly, she felt her cellphone vibrate in her jacket pocket. She was several people back in line and so pulled the phone out and looked at the screen. Her first thought was that it might be Ben. He was taking a summer session at the University of Georgia but he normally texted not called. The screen had a phone number on it she didn't recognize. But an area code she did.

With her stomach now evolving from delicious butterflies to a growing uneasiness, Liddy edged out of line and let the other travelers go ahead.

It was the area code from the part of South Georgia where her mother lived.

"Hello?" she said into the phone, holding her breath.

"Is this Lydia James?"

Liddy's stomach dropped. The voice sounded official, not friendly.

"Yes," Liddy said. "Is this about my mother? Is she okay?"

"Ms. James," the voice said, "I'm afraid your mother has had a bad fall. My name is Rita Swanson and I'm the charge nurse at the Hospital here in Infinity?"

Liddy nodded, and watched the column of fashionably dressed gate travelers move past her and disappear one by one into the hallway that would take them to the airplane that was leaving for Paris within the hour.

"Is she okay?" Liddy asked.

"She *will* be," the nurse said. "But right now she's pretty upset and confused. She's been asking for you."

"Of course," Liddy said, shaking her head at the gate official who gave her a questioning look. "Tell her, please, that I'm on my way."

Liddy disconnected and turned away from the gate, still clutching her passport, her boarding pass and her cellphone. She walked back to her seat in the now empty gate area and sat down heavily. She stared out the window at the airplane parked on the tarmac and at the other planes taking off and landing. She looked down at the boarding pass in her hand as if surprised to see it there.

Infinity, Georgia.

A sleepy little southern town two hundred miles southeast of Atlanta. Liddy drove there straight from the airport. Her bags had been checked through to Paris but she had her carry on with enough clothes to last her a few nights. Once she found out what the situation in Infinity was she'd be able to determine when she could rebook her flight to Paris. No point even in having her things sent back to Atlanta, Liddy decided. She'd arrange to have them stored at Charles de Gaulle until she could personally retrieve them.

She tried to remember the last time she had driven to Infinity. Her visits to her mother "down there" had been few and far between over the years. There had been nothing for Ben to do as a boy in Infinity, no summer camps, a community pool that looked like it hadn't been shocked since the summer before, no decent restaurants, no nearby golf courses for Bill, and no comfortable place for the three of them to stay. It was always easier to have her mother to come up to Atlanta—something that, admittedly, she had chosen to do less and less.

Liddy arrived at the little hospital in Infinity midafternoon and rushed in, tired and emotionally drained from the five-hour drive. One of the nurses at the nursing station told her that her mother had broken her right leg in the fall. Her doctor felt that if things went well she would be moved to the adjoining rehabilitation and assisted living center by the weekend. The nurse, a stout African-American woman with a nearly incomprehensible southern accent, indicated by her facial expression alone (with the dramatic use of an eyebrow arch) that she assumed Liddy would be staying at least until then. She led the way to her mother's room.

Liddy went to her mother's bedside and felt a sick pang of fear. Her mother had always been a beautiful woman, even as she aged, but now she looked wan and ancient. Her leg was in a cast and elevated by pulleys above the bed. The right side of her face was still dark and bruised from where she had hit the front of her bathroom sink the night before. Her eyes were closed but her face did not look restful.

Liddy reached out and touch her mother's hand that lay on top of the covers. "Hey, Mama, how you feeling?"

Her mother opened her eyes and frowned. "How the Sam Hill does it look like I'm feeling?"

"Sorry, Mama." Liddy looked around the little room. She tried to breathe out of her mouth to diminish the smell of urine in the room. "I know it's bad. But you've got a private room anyway."

"Liddy, honey…" her mother said. Her face was twisted into a grimace of pain. Her fingers clutched the hospital sheets. "You're here to stay, aren't you? Promise me you're here to stay."

Liddy stepped out into the hallway to see if there were any nurses she could flag down. She was sure some kind of pain medication was in order. She'd never seen her mother so needy before.

"I'm here, Mama," Liddy said, returning to her bedside. She picked up one of her mother's hands and gently eased the tension out of the tightly gripping fingers. "I'm here for as long as you need me."

An hour later, her mother was resting more peacefully. Liddy sat by her bed and watched her. Her mother had kept her thick auburn hair in spite of her age and was very proud of the fact. She had been a true beauty in her day and her life had been lived turning on that coin in every way, from the many boyfriends she had to the husbands she'd eventually ended up with. Her mother's beauty had walked in the door first.

"Why you so hell bent on running off to live in Paris where you don't know anyone?"

Liddy looked at her in surprise. She thought her mother had been sleeping.

"Paris has 60,000 Americans living there."

"60,000 people you don't know. People need *community*."

Liddy straightened out her mother's blanket. "I'm not convinced community is what's necessary for a happy life, Mama."

"Shows what you know." Her mother closed her eyes for a moment and then snapped them open as if suddenly alert. "Will you move on down?" she asked.

"Move to Infinity?" Liddy asked. "Mama, my life is in Atlanta, if not Paris."

"What life?" Her mother screwed up her face. "Bill gone, Ben gone. You sell the house?"

"Last week."

"So the house is gone…"

"Mama, I can't move here." Liddy could see her mother was getting upset again. She plucked at her cover and turned away from Liddy. "Come on, Mama," Liddy said. "Let's don't do this. Okay? Let's just get you well first and take it from there."

Two long hours later, Liddy stood in the center of the small gas station beside three petrol pumps with her credit card in hand. She was looking for a place to swipe it. She peered over the tops of the pumps again at the office but saw no movement inside. A dirty and peeled sign hung on the door window read

"Open." She pushed the buttons on the pumps and clicked the handle of the gas nozzle sticking in the side of her ancient Toyota Highlander, hoping this might trigger some alert to someone inside that a customer needed assistance. Nothing.

She looked down the main street of the little town. It was Sunday at six o'clock and there was no sign of life anywhere.

She looked down the quiet main road in front of the gas station again.

Stuck in Infinity, she thought. *Nothing behind me, nothing ahead of me. Is everybody still in church? Or is the town really so small that if someone takes an afternoon nap the population noticeably reduces?*

"Can I help you?"

She had not seen him walk up.

She whirled around and began talking before she was even sure he wasn't a mugger of some kind. "Oh, thank goodness!" she said. "You startled me."

She smiled at him. He was a handsome in a rugged, outdoor-living kind of way. He was dressed like he had just been to a church. His hair was thick, brown with a little gray around the temples. She guessed him to be about fifty.

"I can't get the machine to take my credit card," she said, waving a hand at the pumps. "And there's nobody here to do it for me."

"I'm Tucker Jones," he said, taking the nozzle from her hand.

"Oh, I'm sorry," she said. "I'm Liddy James. I'm here seeing my mother at the hospital. Mary Ann Mears?"

He was nodding before she finished speaking and she wondered for a moment if he already knew what she was telling him. That wouldn't have been a surprise in these little towns.

"Jessie's at dinner, I imagine," he said. "He wouldn't expect much trade today. It's a small town, I guess you noticed."

Liddy laughed.

"Your mama okay?" Jones flipped a switch on the side of the pump and began to fill her car for her. "Heard she had a fall."

"Yes, thank you for asking," Liddy said. "She broke her leg. But the doctor thinks she'll be able to get around with a cane. She's only eighty."

"We haven't seen much of your family down here," Jones said, smiling to take any criticism out of the remark.

"We usually had Mama come up to us in Atlanta," Liddy explained. "We had so much more room."

"Makes sense," he said, as he fastened her gas cap back on.

"I'm supposed to be in Paris," she found herself telling him. "When I heard about Mama's fall I was actually at the airport, if you can imagine. I was thinking of opening a bakery in Atlanta so I'll be doing a little research in Paris." *Why was she telling him all this?* She *had* been thinking of opening some kind of little shop when she returned from Paris. She hadn't really put it into words until now though.

"That sounds real interesting," he said.

"How do I pay this Jessie?" She held up her credit card. "I don't have cash, I'm afraid."

"Don't worry about it," he said. "When you come back, you can buy me lunch at the diner and we'll call it even."

"I really appreciate it, Mr. Jones."

"How long you staying?"

"Through the weekend. They'll be moving Mama to the rehab center about then," she said.

"Sounds like you've got a lot going on, what with your Mama and all."

"She'll be coming back with me to Atlanta to live," Liddy said, nearly convincing herself.

"I'm sure she'll like that fine."

"Oh, yes, she loves Atlanta."

"Well, safe travels." He grinned at her and put his hands on his hips as though waiting for her to get in the car and drive off.

"Well, thanks again." Liddy slid into her SUV and pulled out of the station. As she turned, she waved to him and he waved back.

Tucker walked down the block, turning once to look back at where her SUV was still sitting at the traffic light. That light was that moron Mayor's idea. Probably a thank you for some favor Jessie had done for him. Most people in Infinity just treated it as a four-way stop. Otherwise you'd sit there forever. Which is what the woman from Atlanta was doing. Even for a Sunday, Miz Mears' daughter was way overdressed by any estimation, he thought. He couldn't remember the last time he saw a woman in high heels in Infinity. She was wearing that get-up for a trans-Atlantic flight? He shook his head. Full-on hose, heels, makeup, and a tight skirt with matching jacket. People in Infinity didn't dress that much for weddings, let alone a six-hour flight. He turned back toward the church where the evening fellowship was in full swing. Let alone a long car drive to a backwater southern town. All of which confirmed what he thought he already knew: in his experience, people from Atlanta —even damn fine looking ones like Liddy James—tended to have about as much sense as God gave lettuce.

Later that evening after a surprisingly pleasant dinner of sweet potatoes, mustard greens and chicken and dumplings at the little town's only diner, and another brief visit with her mother, Liddy drove back to her motel by way of the downtown shopping district.

She couldn't tell whether the quiet streets were a result of the recession or just the usual state of things on a Sunday. All shops were shuttered, curtains pulled across showcases.

She parked her car in front of a shop with a large CLOSED sign obliterating whatever they might have been selling on display in the large picture window.

Things felt like they were moving faster than she had planned.

She glanced down the vacant main street in the direction of the hospital.

She would have been shaking off the last vestiges of her jet lag about now. She would have spent her first full day in her new life in Paris and now she would be sleeping in her Paris hotel ready to begin the search tomorrow for an apartment. And now none of that would happen.

Two things Liddy knew for certain after just a few hours in Infinity: She was not going to be able to leave her mother even in the rehab center. And her mother was not going to agree to come to Atlanta.

Christmas lights hung from the rafters of the shop right in front of her (it was July) pulsing on and off against the midnight blue of the dusky southern sky.

She punched in the number of her girlfriend Bea but the call went straight to voice-mail. Sighing, she fumbled in her purse for a pack of Benson and Hedges she had bought earlier in the day. She hadn't had a cigarette for over twenty years. Somehow, it seemed like an appropriate thing to do. She lit the cigarette and inhaled deeply, feeling the tobacco pull into her lungs. Instantly, she felt a wave of dizziness and closed her eyes until it passed.

What the hell was she going to do?

Was she going to drag her mother screaming and kicking to Atlanta? Was she going to get on that plane to Paris? Was she going to let her dream die a second time for lack of imagination or gumption or whatever it was that she clearly didn't have?

She puffed angrily on her cigarette. And then coughed. She tossed the lit cigarette out the window and waved the smoke out of the car.

When am I going to finally go the hell forward with what I want?

It was fully dark now and she felt an unusual chill creep into the car with her. It was cold for July, she thought, as she rolled up her window and punched off the AC. She started the car and began to drive down the street toward her motel. As she drove, she noticed that one of the shops looked more than just closed for Sunday. Without thinking, she stopped her car in the middle of the street, got out and walked to the sidewalk in front of the store. It had a deep bay window with tattered country curtains framing the upper windowed portion. Unmindful of the grime on the pane, Liddy leaned against the window and peered in. The inside looked like a bomb had gone off but she imagined it was just the result of neglect and long-time vacancy. It was small. She stepped back and surveyed it from the street, the little "For Rent" placard wedged into a corner of the front door.

It was providence.

Chapter 2

She looked at the blinking cursor, sipped her Sleepytime tea, and gazed out the window of her second floor bedroom as if looking for the answer in the trees. The night had grown cool and she had gotten up earlier to close the window before it was even dark.

So, once I've said I'm forty-five, she thought, *is there really any point in going any further?* She looked back at her laptop. The browser heading read, "Helping you find the love of your life…" She typed into the onscreen box: "I lost my husband of twenty years to cancer a little over two years ago. Since then I have had to sell the house we raised our son in because I couldn't afford the payments, launched said son out into the world, gave up my dream to move to Paris, and recently moved to a tiny town in South Georgia to be near my elderly mother. And I am opening a cupcake shop. Oh, and I bought a horse."

She looked at the paragraph and began hitting the delete/backspace button. Somewhere between the ancient mother and her age (*does forty-five mean they think I'm really sixty?*) she could literally hear e-Harmony registrants signing off *en masse.*

Earlier that afternoon during a visit at the rehab center, her mother had mentioned her belief that Liddy was nuts for buying the horse.

"Why in God's great world," she said as she was being wheeled back to her room after her physical therapy, "would you buy a horse? Are you determined to end up in a wheel chair? You do know you're not young any more, right? How much are you paying to board him? Why, exactly, do you want a horse at your age?"

Liddy couldn't really say why she had done such a crazy thing. It's true she had ridden as a teenager in Atlanta so she wasn't totally clueless about horses but once she had married, neither had she given the idea of riding a second thought. When she had made the, some would say, equally crazy decision to move to Infinity and open up a cupcake shop, getting a horse had popped up at the top of her quickly expanding to-do list, as if she had been wanting to own one her whole life. She just figured she lived in the country now and she could have a horse. In fact, like a lot of decisions she made in her life, this one appeared to be one of those that wouldn't stand up to long and serious scrutiny. She decided not to think about it too closely.

The shop, on the other hand, that she loved to think about. A small storefront sandwiched between an ancient hardware store and a beauty salon, it had a deep window shelf for showcasing full trays of pastries and a small polished wood counter that the landlady said had been there for over a hundred years.

The morning after she first laid eyes on it—a little over a month ago—Liddy signed a year's lease. Ben had finished his summer semester at Georgia and just stayed on in Athens for his classes in the fall. With the Atlanta house gone and Liddy living in a studio apartment, there was no place for him to "come home" to.

Liddy looked around her apartment. Would this ever be the kind of place that held the warmth and love that their beautiful home in Atlanta had? Or was that chapter of her life over?

The apartment was situated over the shop, something that struck her as very quaint and very, well, Parisian. After the estate sale in Atlanta where she had sold all her furniture and dishes and linens—possessions that had taken her twenty years to lovingly acquire and poor Bill nearly that long to pay for—she had driven the U-Haul truck to Infinity with her girlfriend Bea and moved into to her new life. Bea's first words when she saw Liddy's shop-top apartment were: "Well, it sure ain't Paris."

Liddy rubbed her eyes and closed her laptop. She knew she had enough to do to get her life moving again without adding a possible romantic element to the mix but, even in the midst of everything she had to do, she couldn't shake her feeling of aloneness. After twenty years of marriage and companionship, trusting her own decisions did not come easily any longer.

She got up from her desk by the window and closed the curtains. She brushed her long hair and braided it in a single braid down her back, brushed her teeth, slipped a nightgown over her head and climbed into bed. Moving boxes were stacked around the room and likely would for weeks more. Liddy felt she had more important things to do than search for drawer liners or padded hangers. A lamp sat perched cockeyed on a box by her bed.

Too tired to read as she usually did, she snapped off the lamp and slipped deeply into the covers

"I have a horse," she whispered before she fell asleep.

The next morning, Liddy met her mother's real estate agent, Meryl Merritt, for coffee at the sandwich shop down the street from Liddy's shop. A tall, elegant woman, Meryl was one of the first people in Infinity to reach out to Liddy, and although Liddy knew there was a commission involved, she was nonetheless grateful for the friendship. As Meryl approached the corner sandwich shop, she waved to the courthouse directly across the street from Liddy's shop.

"You have a great location, Liddy," she said, reaching out to shake hands. "The courthouse was divided into offices a few years ago and now it's used mostly by attorneys and accountants. You should get lots of traffic, especially at lunch time." Liddy was counting on all of them to eat lots of cupcakes from her store.

After the waitress brought them their coffee and their preliminary business concerning Liddy's mother's house was finished, Liddy watched Meryl visibly relax into the role of a friend. Meryl was beautiful and, as seemed to be typical for most realtors, dressed to the nines with every eyelash coated and her lips stained a faint berry hue against her perfect complexion. Unusual, Liddy thought when she first met her, that a woman born and raised in this part of the state, as Meryl was, would be so obviously not an outdoors person. There was no way that amazing skin had seen more than a month of sunshine in a lifetime.

"A sandwich shop would make more sense," Meryl said, looking around the shop they were in. Liddy could tell Meryl was trying not to be discouraging.

"What about *this* place?" Liddy said. "Infinity doesn't need two sandwich shops."

"But competition is always better," Meryl insisted. "It's just that cupcakes are so…"

"Everybody loves cupcakes."

"Yes, of course," Meryl said and Liddy could see her new friend didn't want to play devil's advocate with her. "Who doesn't love cupcakes?"

The fact was, owning a shop of any kind had been a sort of dream of Liddy's for more years than she could count. The serendipity of opening a shop in Infinity—amidst the carnage of her Paris dream—was so perfect that Liddy had actually convinced herself that this detour in her life's plans was a preferred path.

She stirred sugar into her coffee cup and gazed out of the sandwich shop's window as it overlooked the town square. "After I lived there," Liddy said. "I was convinced that Paris would always be an important part of me."

"Oh, I agree," Meryl said. "I spent a month there after college. You must be dying here in Infinity. At least Atlanta has the High Museum and some galleries."

Liddy sipped her coffee. "The thing I love about Paris," she said, "isn't really about the culture or the things that were available there as in any big city, you know?" she said. "It is something organic, intrinsic to Paris. Hard to explain."

"How long were you there?"

"A year after college and vacations most years after that. I swore I would return and live there again but you know, life happened. Or more specifically, Mama happened. I'm not complaining," she said hurriedly. "I'm happy to be here with her. I think it all worked out as it was supposed to."

"Oh, I know how our plans for life can get derailed," Meryl said, smiling sadly. "But how does the bakery fit into things?"

"Well, I took culinary classes in Atlanta after my year abroad and I developed this passion for baking. All my friends would always tell me how awesome my pastries were. Bill said —and he was absolutely correct—that I didn't have time to run a bakery and raise our son. You would be surprised how involved raising even one child is. Do you have children?"

Meryl shook her head.

"So I tabled the idea of a bakery while I was married to Bill."

"I'm so sorry about your husband. I heard it was brain cancer?"

Liddy nodded and pushed the remnants of her coffee away. "When he died, there was no equity in the house. I couldn't afford the mortgage payments. There was enough insurance money for us to stay in the house long enough for Ben to graduate from high school and for me to spend the year in Paris. That was the plan, anyway. I sold the house last month and, after the realtor's cut, I was lucky to break even."

"So money is tight? Excuse me for asking."

"No, no, that's fine. Yes, it will be tight for awhile but I have my Paris money for the baking equipment, and supplies and for the rent until I start to turn a profit."

"And your son's college?"

"He got a state scholarship and his grandparents are helping out," she said. "I figure I can hold on for six months, maybe a year. And after that, if I haven't made a success of it, well, it just wasn't meant to be."

"And then?"

"Guess I'll have to put the dream to bed for good and go get a real job."

"Not easy to do in this economy."

"Yeah, especially at my age plus with no experience doing anything the last twenty years but raising a child and creating a beautiful home for my family."

Meryl reached over and touched Liddy's hand. "I'm sure the bakery will do well," she said.

Liddy felt a rush of affection for Meryl. "Thanks, Meryl. I appreciate it."

"Infinity is like many small Southern towns," Meryl said. "It can be hard to break in. Are you absolutely positive you want to go with "*Les Petites Gateaux*" for the name? I mean, aside from not being able to say it, I'm not sure people around here are all that fond of the French, you know?"

Liddy looked out onto Main Street. It was midday in the middle of the workweek and there was a good bit of traffic. Looking around the little sandwich shop, she saw that every table was now occupied.

"Can I make a suggestion?" Meryl asked.

"Of course, all help welcome and appreciated!"

"*Le Cupcake Shop.*"

Liddy frowned.

"You can't really bring Paris to Infinity," Meryl said. "Not and succeed the way you need to. Even these yokels," she said with a smile, "understand Frenchifying a phrase as a way of branding it. They may not care for the French, but they all love their French fries and they all know the French make great pastries. Leverage that."

"Understand my demographic audience, you're saying."

"Which is very different from the one you would've had in Atlanta."

Liddy lifted her empty coffee cup in a toast. "To *Le Cupcake Shop* and to the first friend I've made in Infinity."

Meryl touched her own coffee mug to Liddy's and smiled.

Later that afternoon, Liddy stood in her new storefront with broom in hand and looked around. Her Keurig coffee maker sat on the scarred maple counter. She had already had three cups of coffee and was starting to feel a little jittery. The view from her shop window faced the courthouse. She watched people come and go from it. The inside of the old shop was a wreck. She had been sweeping and cleaning for three days and didn't seem to be any closer to turning on the ovens or mixers, let alone opening the doors for business.

A sharp knock on the glass of the front door shook her out of her thoughts and made her drop her the broom. It was that guy who helped her at the gas station. She smiled and moved to open the door, grateful for a reason to take a break.

"Hey, Tucker," she said. "Come to help me clean house?"

His hands full of two venti coffees, Jones stepped into the shop, and looked around. "You look like you got your hands full with this," he said. "I stopped by to see if you could use a coffee but I see you're good."

She reached for the coffee anyway. "First thing I did was plug in my coffee maker," Liddy said. "There's no real place to sit yet but make yourself at home on any wall or counter."

"I can't remember the last time this place was rented," he said, looking around "It's been that long."

"Yeah, well, Danni Lynn—she's my landlady—said it was like a runt puppy. You either loved it or wanted to set a match to it." She frowned. "Now that I think about it, that's kind of creepy."

Tucker laughed. "Well, we know you're a sucker for the fixer-upper anyway."

"I don't know," Liddy said, looking around. "Do you think it's even possible?"

"Oh, sure, it'll clean up."

"Did you hear what I'm going to do with it?"

Tucker's eyebrows went up as he brought his coffee cup to his lips. "Cupcakes?"

"I guess you think that's crazy, too."

"Not my place to think anything," he said.

"Usually doesn't stop people from doing it," she said.

"Well, my opinion shouldn't matter to you."

"So you do think I'm crazy."

"Actually, I really just dropped in to ask you if you'd like to visit our little church here in town some time? I'd be happy to come pick you up."

"Oh, that's sweet of you but I'm not very church-going. Thanks anyway."

"Of course. By the bye I heard you bought old Sugar."

Old Sugar?

"That's right," Liddy said, hearing her voice sound like she was fourteen years old and defending herself to her mother.

"He's an older horse, you know."

"I know that."

Crap. Why hadn't she asked how old he was?

"I heard you paid a thousand for him. Is that true?"

Liddy just looked at him, her mouth open a little.

"That's a lot of money," he continued. "Sugar's a good old horse but he's not worth half that."

Liddy put down the coffee cup and readdressed herself to sweeping the floor.

"Have you ridden him yet?"

She hadn't.

"Of course," she said.

She watched him wander over to the pastry bar where she had her laptop set up. *For a retired redneck or whatever he was, he was awfully nosy*, she found herself thinking with irritation.

"Do you ride Western?" he asked. "A lot of people from the city don't, is all. And I know Sugar won't respond to an English bridle if that's what you're thinking of doing. He neck reins."

"I'm aware of all of that," Liddy said, her face blushing to reveal her lie. "Doesn't take a PhD to learn how to neck rein."

"Good thing, too," Tucker said, grinning. "Seeing's how so many country boys do it."

"Anything else? Maybe you know something about how much my rent is here?" Liddy smiled to take the edge off her sarcasm but she was angry now.

"As it happens I do but I can see you're upset. I'm sorry. It just pisses me off when I see people get cheated."

"Even people from Atlanta? Because I got the idea that ripping off big city fools was major sport down here."

"I wouldn't say *major* sport..." He smiled and then pointed at her laptop. "I couldn't help notice you've got your browser open to an eBay page."

This man was the absolute limit! How far did she have to go with the whole southern politeness crap before she could tell him to mind his own business?

"Yes," she said icily. "I am attempting to purchase a certain kind of oven for my shop as you can probably see on the page there."

"An expensive oven," he said, looking directly at the page and then touching the smart pad to scroll down. "Your cupcakes really need one that big?"

Unbelievable!

"Unfortunately, yes. Well, thanks for the update on my horse that you know so much about because—remind me again how you know so much about him?"

"I used to own him," he said, still looking at her laptop page. "Long time ago. Taught all my nieces and nephews to ride on Sugar."

Geriatric fucking horse. Great.

"Look, Tucker, I don't mean to be rude but I have a shitload of work to do here." In Liddy's experience, swearing in front of these Southern gentlemen usually shut down the visit pretty quickly.

"Absolutely," he said, turning away from the laptop. "I'll let you get to it. Just thought I'd give you a heads up about Sugar."

"Thank you so much."

"And I'll probably see you out there at the barn."

"What do you mean?"

"The barn where you're boarding him. I'm there, too."

Oh, crap.

"Jeez, what a happy coincidence. Then I'm sure I'll see you there. Thanks again for the coffee."

She shut the door after him and smiled one last time as he waved with his free hand through the shop window.

Bumptious twerp.

Liddy sat in her car in the dirt parking lot at the stables and wiped the perspiration from her neck. The air conditioner in her car wasn't working properly and, not surprisingly for August in the South, the temperature was still climbing in late afternoon. She reflected back on her visit that morning with her mother at the rehabilitation center. The nurses were happy with her mother's progress but Liddy had found her mother querulous and sour.

It's almost like it doesn't matter that I'm here, she thought.

As with the purchase of the horse, her mother was very blunt in her belief that opening a bakery in Infinity was a bad idea. "If you're determined to throw your money away," she said as she brushed away the efforts of the nurse's aid to plump her pillow and make her more comfortable, "why not give it to charity where it might do some good? Or, God forbid, use it to live on yourself?"

Explaining to her mother that her intention was that the bakery would generate a living for her simply resulted in a lengthy diatribe of negativity that left Liddy deflated.

She got out of her car and stood next to its front bumper looking out at the grazing horses in the pasture.

And this was the stupidest idea of all.

The last thing she needed with everything she had on her plate was a responsibility the size of a horse. Hadn't she just divested herself—or in the case of her son, got divested—of all her responsibilities? Didn't she have enough to do to get the shop ready for opening without adding a horse that needed daily feeding and exercising? And about a million other necessary, i.e. expensive, items.

Her mother was right about the horse.

Was she right about the bakery too?

"So, you finally showed up to ride your horse."

Liddy hadn't seen him approach. She turned to see Tucker not only standing next to her car but leading a horse.

"You really are quiet," she said, hoping it sounded like she meant sneaky.

"You were lost in your thoughts," he said as he tightened the girth on his saddle. "I may have a soft tread but there's no way Traveler here does."

"Are you coming or going?"

"Just got here. Be happy to wait for you to tack up. I'll show you the trails."

"No, you go on. I have to catch my horse, clean him up and then saddle him. It'll be nightfall before *I'll* be ready to ride."

Tucker laughed.

"Plus, I'm not one hundred percent positive I can pick out which one is him," she said, squinting into the sun in the direction of the pasture.

Tucker swung up into his saddle and kicked his left boot out of the stirrup. He leaned down and held out his hand to her. "Hop up," he said. "I can ID your horse for you and I'm happy to wait while you tack up."

Liddy hesitated, then stuffed her car keys in the pocket of her jeans and took his hand. He swung her easily up and behind him.

"Thanks," she said breathlessly.

"Walk on, Traveler," he said, clicking to his horse as they moved toward the pasture.

An hour later they were walking side by side down a wide trail. Liddy had repented of her earlier near-decision to sell Sugar back to the man who had sold him to her. As she stretched out her spine and let her weight fall into the heels of her paddock boots, she could not remember a time in recent memory when she felt quite so relaxed or…happy.

"It's beautiful here," she said, shielding her eyes and looking down the trail to where it crossed a small creek before continuing on the other side in a tunnel of shadows and shade. "Absolutely beautiful."

"It's my therapy," Tucker said, grinning at her.

"You need therapy?"

"Everybody needs something," he said. "Even if you were retired, daily life brings with it its own set of frustrations and challenges."

"Ahhh, I see you've read last month's *Oprah Magazine*."

He shrugged. "Sometimes the true things are also the corny things," he said.

"I was thinking everybody was right about my getting this horse," she admitted. "I was starting to think I was nuts to do it. Now I think it's the sanest thing I've done yet. Or at least the sanest thing that's been revealed so far."

"Now who's sounding like Oprah? Want to walk the creek bed for a bit? It's a shadier walk in all this heat."

"Sure. Lead on. So, you're retired?"

Tucker moved ahead of her in single file and didn't immediately respond. Liddy let Sugar pick his way into the shallow creek, glad to see he didn't appear to hate the water as a lot of horses did.

"Whoa! Did you see that?" He stopped his horse and twisted in the saddle to look at her. "You see that water moccasin slither up the bank?"

Liddy looked nervously at the creek bank.

"I hate snakes," she said. "I'm pretty sure Sugar hates 'em too."

"Must've been five foot long."

"Maybe we should go back on the trail?"

"Trust me, snakes hate your horse more than you hate them. Just keep your eyes open." He turned and continued down the creek while Liddy turned her concentration to every ripple and movement in the water around her horse's feet.

Later, back at the barn, Tucker noticed a pleasant camaraderie had developed between them that hadn't been there before the ride. After they dismounted, he untacked both horses and she, under his careful instruction, measured out the sweet feed into two buckets.

"I do know how to feed a horse you know," she said, one hand on her hip as he took the feed buckets from her and positioned them on hooks in front of the tethered horses.

"I'm sure you do," he said. "Not really an advanced skillset, positioning a bucket in front of a hungry animal."

"I mean," she said, "I'm not totally clueless out here," she waved to the interior of the tack shed but he got the idea she was also referring to this part of Georgia.

"I know," he said. "Listen, how about coming to dinner next Sunday evening?"

She wiped her hands on a rag and looked up at him with an expectant look.

"I'm having some friends over," he said. "You're new to the area. I think you'd like them. What do you say?"

"I'd love to," she said, rubbing her hands down her hips. "Thanks. What can I bring?"

Tucker noticed, not for the first time this afternoon, that her jeans looked almost painfully tight. He couldn't tell if they were jodhpurs meant to look like jeans or just stretch jeans. He'd spent a good deal of time today trying to figure it out.

"Not a thing. By the way, those trousers you're wearing might not be the best thing to wear for riding," he said. "You chafing?"

Her hands clapped onto her hips.

"Are you really trying to give me advice on what to *wear*?" she asked.

"Not for a minute," he said, his expression belying his words. "It's just that if you're chafing…"

"I'm not *chafing*, Tucker," she said. "For God's sake, these are *riding* pants. They're reinforced at the knee and padded on the inner thigh specifically so they won't rub raw against the saddle."

"My mistake."

"I mean, just because I'm not wearing overalls or whatever it is country women ride in down here doesn't mean I don't know what to wear to a barn for crap's sake!"

"No offense intended," he said and walked back into the tack barn to hang up his bridle. By the time he emerged, she seemed to have cooled off. She was combing her horse's mane and her face looked relaxed.

"So, listen," he said as he picked up a dandy brush to curry his horse while the animal ate. "Interested in grabbing a bite at the diner?" he asked.

She smiled, but she shook her head. "I need a bath," she said, putting her hand to her hair as if her coif was somehow a problem, too. "Rain check?"

"Sure."

By the time Tucker left the barn an hour later and drove away from the stables it was early evening. Liddy had left first. While he wondered about her excuse for not going to the diner with him, he had to admit she looked tired. The color and light had slowly leached from the summer sky and left a cloudless horizon. He felt surprisingly invigorated after a long workday coupled with a late afternoon ride. He smiled to himself. It was true Liddy wasn't like anybody else in Infinity. She was a city-girl in all the ways that could annoy a man, especially a man born and bred in the country. But there was just enough nerve and spontaneity in her to offset the annoyance. In fact, Tucker thought, as he turned Faith Hill way up on his car radio and pointed his truck toward the town's diner, after three hours of trading quips and veiled glances with her, he'd have to say what she had in the way of spunk and optimism, not to mention being sexy as hell, was more than enough to offset the negatives. By the time he pulled into the parking lot of the local diner, he was smiling like he couldn't remember doing in a very long time.

As she navigated the six miles from the stables back to her shop, anticipating the hot bubble bath that awaited her, she accelerated a little, hoping the local highway patrol was having its Sunday supper and not out on the roads. The insides of her thighs were itchy and sore. Her jeans, which were just ordinary blue jeans, had started to chafe thirty minutes into the ride. Liddy couldn't believe how Tucker figured that out. Her stomach tingled at the memory of his easy grin, his brown eyes watching her, missing nothing.

God. Do I like him? Her hand reached out for her purse where she had shoved a pack of cigarettes over six weeks ago. She hadn't bought another pack since she first sat in front of her shop. But the reflex of reaching for her purse to find one now startled her. She realized it was a gesture that she might have made twenty years ago when she still smoked! ...And when something unnerved or excited her.

Weird, she thought, as she pulled into her parking spot behind the shop.

Shaking herself out of the reverie, Liddy moved quickly to lock the car and get inside. One of the things she did not care for about her new living situation was the necessity of parking her car in the alley behind the line of shops. The parking area was now empty and dark. Putting a light out back was on her to-do list.

She grabbed her purse and keeping her finger on the panic button of her car's key fob, hurried toward the back door. Not one for believing strongly in the powers of intuition, Liddy still could not dismiss the feeling creeping up the back of her neck that something was wrong. Hesitant to go off full alert but poised to shake off the feeling as irrational, Liddy jabbed the door key into the lock and pulled the back door open.

Expecting the uneasy feeling to dissipate as soon as she was inside, Liddy was dismayed to realize her nerves were still stretched tautly.

I'm safe, she thought. *So what the hell?*

She pulled the door behind her until she heard it click soundly. Then she immediately drew the deadbolt and turned to move into the back kitchen. That's when she knew something wasn't right.

All the lights were off.

She stood quietly, her back to the door, facing the darkness and listening to her own breath.

There was absolutely no doubt that she had left lights on. And now they were off.

She listened. There was no sound but the heavy clicking of the mechanical clock over the stove in the kitchen and the hum of the air conditioning unit in the window.

She reached behind her without looking and flipped on the light switch.

The kitchen sprang to bright life before her. Two empty bays where the new ovens would fit, the brand new bench counters that had arrived today, still with the plastic wrapping on, the oversized and ancient refrigerator she had bought on Craigslist, the broom she'd been married to for most of the last week propped against the far wall.

She pushed off the wall and let out a long sigh.

Get a grip, girl. The stairs that led to her upstairs apartment were to the left of the refrigerator. She would just double check that the front door was locked before she found herself something to eat in the fridge and then retire upstairs to her bathtub and her laptop of Netflix videos for the night.

She thought of Tucker's dinner invitation and sighed. She would have loved to extend the afternoon but it was one thing to look like Annie Oakley on horseback as you cantered across hill and dale. It was quite another to be eighteen inches from each other across a dinner table with not a shred of make up on, horse manure on your heel, and no breath mint.

That's funny, she thought, with a smile as she walked to the front room of the shop. *I guess I care?*

As she pushed past the swinging half doors that separated the kitchen from the front sales room, she saw the tattered half curtains that hung in the bay window moving when they should not have been. The jagged glass that framed the streetlamp outside glinted diamonds around its edge and drew her eyes to the floor where a carpet of broken glass lay scattered under the large mound of what she would quickly identify as her brand-new and expensive industrial bench mixer smashed to bolts and splinters.

Chapter 3

"It could've been worse," Danni Lynn said, handing Liddy the whiskbroom and returning to her seat in the café chair by the front window. "You can replace a mixer."

"It was really, really expensive, Danni Lynn," Liddy said. "I'm not sure it could've been worse. Of all the things to vandalize in the store, it's the one thing that might keep me from opening."

Danni Lynn squirmed in the small café chair. Clinically obese, with brownish-blonde hair that hung in tangles to her chin line, she squinted at the newly replaced bay window with its sticker still on.

"You're really lucky we were able to get it replaced so quickly," she said. "If it had happened on Sunday, we would have had to wait a full day."

"I don't feel lucky," Liddy said, sweeping the floor with the little broom. She stood back to see if she could see any trace of the broken appliance. One of the tiles in the floor had been cracked where the mixer had hit. The only reason Liddy could figure how the window was broken was that the vandal must have first thought about stealing the mixer and then, perhaps deciding it was too heavy to lug around, lobbed it through the front window.

"And Meryl told you not to call the cops?" Danni-Lynn shook her head like she couldn't believe such bad advice.

"She said it would probably not be a very good PR move for me to call the cops before I've even opened the shop. That kind of advertising, I can do without. And it wasn't technically a break in since I didn't have a lock on the front door."

"Yeah, sorry about that," Danni-Lynn said looking not at all sorry. "I meant to have Leroy get that lock for you all day yesterday. Well, you got it now."

"I just wish I knew why me, you know?" Liddy said. "I mean, is there a problem with vandalism in Infinity that you know of?"

"No, but we do have a little ol' drug problem round here parts. Did you know that?" Danni Lynn asked.

"I heard all small Georgia towns do." Liddy took the whiskbroom back to the counter area and looked at her landlady. "But nothing was stolen. I haven't even opened yet so there's no money in the register."

"Will this delay your grand opening?"

How could she make multiple batches of cupcake batter and different flavors of frostings without an industrial mixer? The one that was destroyed had cost nearly three thousand dollars.

"I don't know," she said.

"I got me a mixer," Danni-Lynn said, "I use it for making the brownies and cakes my Leroy likes? I got it over at Wal-Mart. I think it was only about two hundred dollars."

"To break even," Liddy said, her words dragging her down as she spoke them, "I have to be able to produce and sell about two hundred cupcakes a day. Every day."

"Whoo-wee!" Danni-Lynn said. "I don't think you might could do that with a Wal-Mart mixer. Two hundred. Damn. That's a lot of cupcakes."

Had it all been for nothing? Where would the money come from to replace the mixer—even if she could find a cheaper replacement? It was money that wasn't in the budget. But if she didn't get another mixer she was out of business before she started.

Liddy looked around the front room. Two small café tables sat in the direct sun patch of the bay window. She had placed a series of Parisian watercolors from her own collection on the walls, painted the interior, and even redone the wood floors. It was simple, spare and, Liddy believed, quietly elegant. Except for the birth and first two years of her son's life, Liddy didn't believe she'd ever been so exhausted, so fretful or so proud of herself as she had these past few weeks. She had waited a long time to realize this dream.   *Was it all going to go down the drain because of one smashed mixer?*

"I don't like it."

Liddy handed her mother the cup of water and frowned at her.

"Why don't you like it?" She was wearing a silk blouse in plum with linen slacks and a pair of leather kitten heels. She had a Hermes scarf that Bill had bought her for her fortieth birthday knotted at her throat.

Her mother, tucked into blankets and quilts in her bed, squinted up at her.

"The last thing you need is to get involved with someone. Don't you have enough on your plate?"

Liddy sat down next to her mother's bed. She had helped her navigate a route around the rehab facility nurse's station twice with her walker and they were both feeling a little worn out.

"Is this about the horse again?"

"No, this is not about the horse again." Her mother scowled at her. "But now that you mention it, I still cannot believe you got a horse. Are you actually riding it?"

"Yes, Mama," Liddy said, her glance involuntarily going to the face of the clock over her mother's bed.

"But dating Tucker Jones," her mother said, smoothing out the lumps in the quilt that covered her. "I just don't like it."

"I don't think going to dinner at his place is really a date."

Her mother looked up at her, her eyes sharp as a raven's. "His place? No, I guess you're right. Not a date," she said. "More like a hook-up."

Liddy's mouth fell open for a moment and then the two of them burst out laughing. "How do you even know that word?" Liddy said, laughing.

"My soaps," her mother said, grinning. "But it's true, isn't it?"

"I don't think so, Mama," Liddy said. "I mean, I'm a little old to be seduced, don't you think?"

"A woman is never too old to be sold a bill of goods," her mother replied primly. "Or too old to be talked into something."

"Tucker doesn't strike me as a fast-talking womanizer, though, you know? Besides, I don't see him in a romantic sense."

"Then why are you going to dinner at his place?"

"Wasn't it you telling me I need to make more friends in Infinity? He's got some people for me to meet."

Her mother snorted.

Liddy laughed. "You think I'll get there and it'll just be me and him?"

"I think if you're not interested in him, you sent him a confusing message."

"Seriously?"

"My point is that he thinks tomorrow night's a date."

Liddy frowned.

"And if you were honest, you do, too."

"Well, I don't."

Her mother shrugged. "How's Ben?" she asked, pawing her covers for the remote control and effectively signaling to Liddy that the visit could now begin its official wind-down.

"He's good. Enjoying his classes. He's coming to Infinity for Thanksgiving."

"Are we going to have turkey-flavored cupcakes?"

Her mother clicked on the television set positioned on a bracket on the wall opposite her bed.

"I can make other things besides cupcakes," Liddy said. "As you well know, since you've come to my house for Thanksgiving for the last twenty one years."

"And you're still determined to go ahead with this cupcake shop? If I were you, Liddy, I would take this vandalism as a message."

"A message from God?"

"Do not blaspheme, young lady." Her mother looked away from the television set to frown at her. "No, a message from the town of Infinity that you're not fitting in."

"So you think my getting broken into last night is somehow my fault?"

34

"I'm just saying, if you have to spend more money to do this dream of yours, maybe you should think twice."

"I am thinking twice, Mama. I haven't bought a replacement mixer yet, have I?"

"If you want the people of Infinity to stop breaking into your place—"

"It was only the one person I'm pretty sure, Mama."

"—you need to get yourself to church and show them you are not some stuck-up Atlanta hoity-toity."

"Fine."

"I don't need your sarcasm, Lydia Jane."

"I'd already decided to go. I'm going tomorrow."

"Really?"

"Yeah, the church is a big deal in these small towns, I get that. So I'm going."

"Saints be praised, she finally listened to me."

"Okay, I think that's my cue." Liddy stood up and shouldered her handbag. "I'll drop by again tomorrow, okay?" She leaned over and kissed her mother on the cheek as her mother punched in numbers on the television remote control. "Hope you have a good night, Mama," she said.

Her mother nodded distractedly as she pointed the controller in the direction of the TV set. As Liddy turned to walk to the door, her mother called out: "Mind you start carrying a toothbrush with you from now on," her mother said from the bed, taking her eyes off the television just long enough to give her daughter an impish smile.

Liddy grinned back at her and waved.

Tucker held the door open for the two little old ladies as they inched their way inside the church. The two blushed and flirted—neither of them a day younger than eighty—and delighted in his attention. He showed them to their seats in the church and returned to the narthex to help with the next batch. Because the church was a poor one and what money they got from the community needed to go back to the community in the form of daycare for the kids and lawn work for the chronically unemployed, the little church had never had central air conditioning put in. The two ancient window units were ineffective against the Georgia summers and most everybody just wore fewer clothes and fanned themselves with the bulletins. Except for weddings, Tucker couldn't remember the last time he'd worn his jacket in church. Even funerals, for some reason, had a looser dress code in Infinity.

When he saw her, what he saw first was what he knew everyone else in the church would see first: an out-of-towner who didn't belong. But it was worse than that. Tucker instantly saw what he knew every woman (and likely every man who wasn't dead from the waist down) would notice immediately: Liddy was wearing pantyhose. In August. No lady in Infinity would ever dream of such a thing. Not in August. Not even for a wedding. To make matters worse, she was buttoned up to her chin in some kind of loudly colored matching suit—probably stunning on the streets of Manhattan, Paris or Peachtree Street—but nothing less than ludicrous at the *True Way* Baptist Church of Infinity, Georgia.

What was the matter with her? Did she not even look around and see how people dressed down here? Did she want to stick out like tits on a bull? Tucker shook himself for having these uncharitable thoughts in the Lord's house. He forced his face to remain pleasantly impassive as he greeted her. What was it to him anyway? He acted like the way she dressed was some kind of personally embarrassment to himself. She caught his eye, smiled and tottered over to him. Lord, she was wearing what looked like five-inch heels...

After he seated her, he had the uncomfortable experience of seating every other woman in Infinity who felt the need to whisper about Liddy and how she was dressed and did Tucker know she had opened up some kind of cookie bakery across from the courthouse and wasn't it terrible to see how uncomfortable she looked, sweating like a migrant worker? Lord, she certainly must be hot. Pantyhose *in August!* Have you ever seen the like before? Someone heard she hardly ever visits her poor Mama over at the nursing home and someone else heard from someone absolutely reliable that she's as foul-mouthed as a drunken sailor on leave. She says she's a widow, but with a mouth like that, it's almost certain she's a *dee-vore-say*.

Liddy sat and squirmed in the pew during what had to be the longest sermon ever experienced in the history of churchdom. *Lord, did these people not believe in air conditioning?* She could literally feel her makeup dripping off her face into the handkerchief that, thank God, she had thought to bring. While the service was not the first Baptist meeting she had ever been to, it wasn't far off from being the first. She found herself wondering with increasing agitation, if the *True Way* was just backwater enough to involve snakes in the worship. It hadn't occurred to her before but once she started worrying about it, she found herself becoming increasingly obsessed with the likelihood. Why else would people be dressed so informally for church? she asked herself. She looked over at a pair of inquisitive little old ladies next to her but they quickly looked away. When she did manage to get eye contact with someone, they would smile woodenly and then dive back into their hymnals or appear to refocus on what the pastor was saying.

Even Tucker, after he politely led her to her pew, had disappeared. She had twisted in her seat a few times to try to see where he was sitting but never found him.

Dear Lord, and people go through this agony every week? She mopped up more beige makeup into her handkerchief, wondering if there would be any left on her face by the time she sloshed out of church. She felt the sweat under her clothes too and especially her legs. When the interminable service ended and –thank God! –without a single serpent, she was so miserably hot, all she wanted to do was bolt out of their into the air conditioning of her car. Hurriedly, she bypassed the receiving line where the pastor was shaking hands and nearly ran into the parking lot. Unfortunately, the parking lot was really just a grassy section of lawn that when church wasn't in session was also used as the children's playground. When it rained, most folks dropped the old ladies and babies off at the front door because the parking lot was only fit to wrestle pigs in. Unbeknownst to Liddy, it had started to rain about fifteen minutes into the service. By the time she got half way to where her car was parked in the lot, her shoes were ruined and her favorite Chanel jacket was drenched. And she had yet to say hello to one single Infinitonian—vandal or not.

Later after a quick visit with her mother, Liddy gave herself the afternoon to prepare for her dinner with Tucker. As she eased into a steaming tub of soapy bubbles, she let herself do something which she normally never did: she indulged in reflecting how different her life was now from what it had been for so many years. Living a life with another person prompts slight personality shifts that aren't necessary when one lives alone.

She and Bill and Ben had been such an intimate family for so long. Because there were no siblings to compete with, Ben had grown up confident, assured of his parents' love, and the adored focus of every extended family gathering. Because he was gifted, and because there were no other children, it had been difficult to exclude him from adult conversations. The result was a more equally based unit than most families probably allow. The fact of his maturity—and their encouragement of it—helped make Ben's entrance into the wide world after high school an easy one for him. For Liddy, the anticipated loss of a full third of her nuclear family was one she had found herself dreading for nearly his whole high school experience.

And then came Bill's cancer diagnosis.

Liddy closed her eyes against the remembered horror of that afternoon when he had come back from a routine visit to his doctor to tell her that something appeared to be wrong.

A year later, he was gone.

The little family was, in fact, reduced by a third, as she had known it would be, just not the third she had expected. And so now, here she was, alone for the first time in twenty years, waiting to see what life had in store for her.

Liddy kept her eyes closed, took in a long breath and felt the anxiety seep slowly out of her. The fragrance of the lavender bath milk lilted lightly in her nostrils and an image of the courtyard in front of the Cathedral de Notre-Dame in Paris came into her mind. In the summer, there were always kiosks of people there selling the little bundles and sachets of lavender. Liddy used to buy them every week during her summer there. She had kept many of them as souvenirs when she returned to the States to marry Bill, loving to see them every time she opened up her lingerie drawer. But that was a long time ago, she thought, opening her eyes as she felt the bath water becoming too cool to enjoy. The little bundles of sweet-smelling herbs had long since fallen apart, lost their fragrance, and been tossed away.

The drive to Tucker's house was longer than Liddy expected. Her GPS got confused in Infinity with all the trees and logging roads and so she tended to rely on old-fashioned maps. One more reason, she told herself, why moving to Infinity often felt like moving backwards to another time. She knew he didn't live very near town but, up until the moment where she was actually attempting to locate where he did live, she hadn't given much thought to where he lived. He was such a regular feature in town—and at the barn—that she had gotten the impression, wrong as she now realized, that he was physically closer to her than he was.

When she finally found the turnoff to Tucker's driveway —after having driven past it first—she found herself feeling thankful it was paved. Out here, where she had left street lamps and other helpful landmarks and lighting far behind, it was difficult to tell the country driveways from the drainage ditches. Not a problem to the locals, Libby found herself thinking with some frustration, but a major challenge especially at dusk when you didn't know the area.

As she turned into the long narrow drive, her cell phone began to vibrate in the console. Needing all her concentration not to steer the car off into the shallow culvert that ran along both sides of the drive, she tried to ignore its insistent call to her until she could bring the car to a stop in front of the house. With relief, she put the car into park and grabbed the phone. She didn't recognize the number on the screen.

"Hello?"

"Mom?"

She smiled. *Dear boy.*

"Hi, sweetie," she said. "You okay?" It wasn't exactly unusual to hear from Ben during the school week—or anytime— but she was surprised at the call.

"Oh, yeah," he said. "Everything's good. Just calling to see how you're doing. And Grandma. She doing okay?"

"Yes, yes, she's making great strides," Liddy said, peering out of the front windshield of the car at Tucker's house. It was a ranch but not the typical squat ugly things that one tends to find out in the country. "Well, not literally, of course."

"Good, I'm glad."

"What are you up to? No studying tonight?"

"No. In fact, that's kind of why I wanted to talk to you, Mom."

Liddy directed her attention away from the house and back to her conversation.

"What do you mean?" she asked, hoping she didn't sound as wary as she was starting to feel.

"Well, now, don't freak out," Ben said. "But I'm thinking about taking a kind of break, you know?"

"A break?" Liddy found the peace of the day gone with two little words. "No, I don't know," Liddy said. "A break?"

"Now, Mom, don't freak out…"

"I'm not freaking out, Ben," she said, feeling the tension creeping down from her shoulders into her arms and into the hand that held the phone to her head. "I am just trying to understand what you're saying. You have finished one year of college and what, two months? Are you saying you're dropping out?"

"You know, Mom," he said, "that whole dropping out thing is really language from your generation."

"Ben, do not try to move the conversation around. Are you telling me you want to leave school right now?"

There was a brief silence.

"Well, I've kind of already done it," he said.

"I see. Where are you now? You're not in Athens?"

"No, I'm in Atlanta, staying with Julie."

"Julie."

"I told you about Julie, Mom. We met in school."

"Has this Julie left school, too?"

"I knew you'd freak about this," he said. "Mom, it's okay. What can I tell you to convince you that I know what I'm doing?"

"Maybe age ten years in the next few minutes?" Liddy looked back at Tucker's house. The porch light switched on. He was wondering why she hadn't come to the door yet. "Maybe explain to me how a gifted honors student with a GPA of 4.75 —?"

"That was always more exciting for you than me, Mom," Ben said.

"What?!" Liddy sputtered. "Do you really think…"

"Look, Mom, I didn't mean to upset you," he said. "Can I ask you to think about it and we'll talk again?"

"You mean I still have input into this decision? I thought you'd already done it."

"Okay, Mom? Can we do this later?"

Liddy bit her lip and watched the front door to Tucker's house open. "Fine, alright," she said.

"I'm sorry to upset you, Mom," he said. "Love you."

"I love you, too, sweetie," she said, the weariness settling into her shoulders as she watched Tucker come out onto the porch and stand, silhouetted against the porch light.

She disconnected the phone and waved to him.

He waved back, tentatively it seemed to her, as if to say: *is everything all right?*

She wanted to cry.

Two hours later, the dinner was not going well.

Tucker had invited one other couple (*take that, Mama*) and Liddy pretty much hated her from the get-go.

When she climbed out of the car, pushing her upsetting phone conversation with Ben to the back burner of her mind, she walked up the porch stairs to where Tucker was waiting and tacked her smile firmly in place. She had to grab for the porch bannister when her heels caught in a slat. It occurred to her that she might be a tad overdressed for a casual dinner in the backwoods of small town Georgia. *Why did she wear her Manolos, for crap's sake?*

"Sorry about that," she said. "Ben called from school and he does it so rarely I didn't want to just blow him off."

Tucker grinned. He looked somehow bigger here on his own porch. As if a man's stature was somehow affected by the proximity of his castle.

"Oh, good," he said. "I was afraid you were checking the address against the database of registered sex offenders or something."

Liddy laughed, the tension from her phone call beginning to drain from her shoulders.

"I was pleased to see you at church today," he said.

"Oh, yes, well…" *Don't get used to it*, she wanted to say.

Tucker ushered her into the house to make the introductions. Without looking at all self-conscious, the décor had a southwestern feel to it. Liddy noticed a western saddle in one of the corner leather armchairs where Tucker had obviously been mending or cleaning it. Apache blankets draped over railings and in the main living area the ceiling shot up at least twenty feet.

"Wow, it's big," Liddy said. "Looks like a ranch from the outside but that's deceiving. Really looks like you, Tucker."

"Liddy, this is one of my oldest friends, Jeff Armstrong. Jeff and I were in grade school together."

Liddy shook hands with a heavyset man with a friendly face, open and slightly ruddy.

"And his wife, Carol."

Liddy turned her smile to her and could see immediately that Carol was not interested in being friends. "Hey," Liddy said, keeping her hand by her side.

Carol had sharp features, a long nose, and curly, frizzy blondish brown hair. She frowned at Liddy.

"Drink, Liddy?"

Liddy snapped her attention back to Tucker who was holding a Margareta pitcher.

"Yes, please," she said. The group moved into the living room where they had obviously been sitting before Liddy came in. Liddy hesitated long enough to allow Jeff and Carol to sit first before she chose a seat. She wasn't sure what the daggers in the eyes thing was about with Carol but sitting next to her didn't sound appealing. Tucker handed her a frosted and salted glass.

"Cheers," he said.

"Yeah, absolutely," Liddy said, holding the glass up in a toast and then taking a long healthy sip from it.

"So, Liddy," Jeff said. "I hear you're the town cupcake lady, is that right?"

Liddy grinned and glanced at Tucker who had moved into the kitchen to attend a pot and retrieve his own drink.

"I guess that's right," she said. "I'm not ready to open yet, but soon I hope. How did you hear about it? I haven't done any promotions or advertising, yet."

"Well, in Infinity, the most effective advertising you can hope for is always going to be word of mouth."

"Yeah, I guess that's right," Liddy said, watching as Tucker came into the room and sat down on the couch next to her. "One of the benefits of doing business in a small town."

"We are not that small," Carol said.

"Well, yeah we are," Jeff said to his wife. He laughed, his eyes glancing around the room as if inviting everyone to join in. "I'd say we're the epitome of a small town."

"Why would anyone want to buy cupcakes in Infinity?" Carol pressed, looking straight at Liddy.

Liddy looked at Tucker briefly and then back at Carol.

"I don't know," she said. "Maybe they can use them to caulk the holes in their drywall."

Jeff and Tucker laughed.

Carol frowned. "What?"

"It's a joke, Hon," Jeff said, reaching out to take his wife's hand. Carol moved her hand away.

"This isn't Atlanta, you know," Carol said. "Every woman in this county could win a blue ribbon for her baking. Why in the world would they buy cupcakes from you?"

"Hey, Carol, bring it down a notch, why don't you?" Tucker said. "Maybe I screwed up the ratio of tequila in that last batch. Jeff, check to see she didn't get a virgin edition." He chuckled but Liddy had spent just enough time with him to know he wasn't pleased with Carol's attack on her.

The rest of the evening was more of the same.

With sparklers on top.

When it became clear even to Jeff and Tucker that Carol wasn't going to behave, the two picked up any conversation they could and loudly kept it going between them. Not having to speak, and studiously avoiding any accidental eye contact with the glowering Carol, Liddy found herself drifting back to her conversation with Ben. She would bob her head up from time to time to make some innocuous one-size-fits-all comment to whatever Jeff and Tucker were talking about—horses mostly—and then go back to reworking the phone call over in her head.

Was Ben living with this Julie person?

Had he already officially dropped out?

What was he going to do if not go to school?

"Don't you think, Liddy?"

Carol stood up abruptly from her chair. She nodded her head at Tucker. "I have an early class, tomorrow. It's been lovely, Tucker."

"Jesus, you're a teacher?" Liddy said, eyeing her with a frown. "Not little children, I hope."

Tucker spoke loudly over her last comment. "So glad you could come, Carol—"

"What did she just say?" She turned to her husband. "Did you hear what she just said to me?"

"Now, Carol," Jeff said, standing, too and tossing down his napkin. "Let it go."

"Fine." She gave Liddy one last glower, turned on her heel and collected her purse from the couch in the living room. Jeff gave Tucker an apologetic look.

"Sorry, man—" he said.

"I know you are not apologizing for me, Jeff Armstrong," Carol said as she stood by the front door.

Tucker leaned over to kiss Carol on the cheek. He put his hand briefly on Jeff's shoulder and said a few words that Liddy couldn't hear, and the couple slipped out into the night.

Tucker turned and walked back to the table.

"Okay," Liddy said, tossing her own napkin down. "Did you know she hated me before you invited me over? Or is she like this with everyone?"

"Don't be ridiculous." Tucker sat at his place at the table and poured more wine in each of their glasses. "Carol's great. Really."

"Oh, you don't have to convince me, Tucker," Liddy said, reaching for her glass. "I just spent two hours with her."

He looked at Liddy as if trying to understand something. "I was hoping you two would get along."

"Why? Has she got great catering contacts?"

"No, Liddy, I thought you would be open to, you know, having a girlfriend."

Liddy laughed. "Really?" she said. "This was a blind date? Because not to worry, Tucker. I've got a local pal. My realtor."

"Meryl Merritt."

"Yes and we can go a whole hour over tea without her once spitting in my eye or dragging her talons across my naked, unprotected flank."

"Yeah, okay."

"Something I can't say for your friend Carol there. You really don't know any reason why she didn't like me before she even met me?"

Tucker shook his head. "No idea." He looked at her and cocked his head. "When you got here and I went in the kitchen to get the cheese, you didn't say anything to—"

"Are you asking if I somehow insulted her within thirty seconds of arriving that would explain her behavior tonight?"

Tucker grimaced. "I just can't understand why she went off on you, is all," he said.

Liddy looked away from his cool blue eyes. She hadn't noticed before how long his lashes were. "I probably should get going, too," she said. "Aside from sharing a meal with the assassin, it was really nice. I like Jeff."

"Yeah, Jeff's great."

"Did you think she had a point?" Liddy asked as she got up from the table. "About people around here not needing cupcakes because they're all such good bakers themselves?"

"No, people still like store-bought stuff. I wouldn't worry."

"Well, what about Carol's attitude? Do you think she's the only one in town suspicious and resentful of outsiders?" Liddy was thinking of her visitor two nights before.

Tucker frowned and got up to find her jacket.

"I mean, if it was personal, fine, I'll avoid her," Liddy said. "On the other hand, if she's the first wave of a community-wide we-hate-city-slicker-cupcake-bakers, that'd be good to know."

Tucker handed her her jacket. "I'll check with the city council tomorrow," he said. "See if any anti-cupcake baking group has formally registered."

"Maybe they're not that organized."

"Then you have nothing to worry about."

Liddy glanced at her parked car and the phone call from Ben came flooding back.

Yeah, that's me, she thought. *The one with nothing to worry about.*

She walked out onto to front porch, wondering if Tucker would try to kiss her on the cheek like he did with Carol. For reasons she didn't understand, she deliberately moved out of his reach and stood on the steps leading to the driveway.

"Thanks for the dinner, Tucker," she said. "Are you going to be at the barn tomorrow?"

"You're welcome," he said, leaning against the porch railing and watching her with what looked very much like a bemused grin. "I will. Around four."

Liddy nodded and turned to walk to her car. It suddenly seemed like a long walk with a big, handsome, amused man watching every step she took. From behind. She was more aware and self conscious than ever about how her high heels made her hips swivel when she walked. Was he still watching? She felt a blush creep up her neck and was grateful for the dark.

"Great," she said cheerily, adding a little wave over her shoulder. "See you then."

Chapter 4

The car magnet on the side of her car was definitely askew. Liddy had parked the car across the street in order not to take up precious parking space in front of her shop, but close enough that it might serve as a little offsite promotion. Someone must have brushed up against it, she thought, knowing full well it would take two hands and a solid intention to reposition the magnet on the car door.

She stood behind the polished mahogany counter, a full tray of frosted and decorated cupcakes on a silver tray in front of her with a jaunty little sign in front of them that read: *Help Yourself! Welcome to Le Cupcake.*

She looked around her shop and was satisfied that it was as perfect as she could have dreamed. It literally sparkled, from the shiny refinished wood floors, to the spotlight display window showcasing nearly one hundred cupcakes of every possible imaginative fancy. Liddy had mixed the batter two days before with a rented mixer. She still wasn't sure she would spend the money to go forward. She had designed the cupcakes weeks before that, and baked and frosted every one of them last night. All night.

There was a delightful trace of coffee and vanilla wafting through the shop. Liddy had even dabbed vanilla extract behind her ears as she stood at the counter, her starched white apron tied snugly over her French checkered chef's blouse and trousers. Even her chef's clogs were new as she stood and waited.

There was not one single thing left to do but wait. There was nothing to sweep or polish or wipe or straighten. The shop was perfect.

Liddy's eye caught the languorous flap of one corner of her Grand Opening sign outside over the doorway. One of the edges must have come untied, but not enough to run out and fix. If anything, it gave some animation to the storefront.

She had flooded the region with pink fliers offering free cupcakes. She had put advertisements in the church bulletins and all the local community papers. She had tacked up fliers at her mother's rehabilitation center and at every public facility that would allow her within ten miles of Infinity.

She had been standing in front of her tray of cupcakes for nearly six hours.

And not one person had come into the shop.

Not one, not even Tucker.

She watched as a meager stream of people walked past her shop to go to the hardware store on one side or the beauty salon on the other. At lunchtime, she resisted the urge to take her tray and stand outside her shop, not wanting the up-to-now-somewhat friendly proprietors of the little sandwich shop down on the corner to take offence.

I have made a terrible, terrible mistake, she thought as she stood at her counter and watched the light fade from the day. The professional workers from the courthouse across the street were beginning to leave for the day. She looked down at her cupcakes, now stale from having sat under the ceiling fan all day and remembered how excited she'd been last night frosting and decorating them. How full of hope and anticipation for what this day would bring. Never in a million years would it have occurred to her that the day would pass without a single customer walking through her door.

I have made a terrible mistake.

A couple days after the dinner party at Tucker's, she spoke to Ben again, with no more comforting results than from the first conversation. That had been five days ago and she had begun to feel an urgency to go back to Atlanta and talk to him face to face. She was feeling the beginning pangs of being too removed from his life.

"Just because you went off to college and I'm starting this life down here doesn't mean we're done with each other," she had said to him. But later, when she was alone, she had to admit that that wasn't totally true. Saying it out loud had revealed it.

There had been a feeling when he went off to college—as hard as that was on her in so many ways—that he was now taken care of and she was free to find a life for herself that wasn't defined by his needs. These last few days, when she saw him making what she thought was such a mistake, she realized: "I've signed off on him to go off and do my thing." And in so many ways, as smart as he was, she knew he still needed guidance.

Also, for whatever reason—too much to do before the big opening, mostly—Liddy had not made it out to the barn to go riding. She called Tucker to ask him to throw a flake of hay in Sugar's direction and generally keep an eye out. She thanked him again for the dinner and he graciously responded it was his pleasure.

She was sure she had mentioned to him that the Grand Opening was today.

The bell from the front door interrupted her thoughts. She looked up to see Meryl peering in.

"Hey, girl!" Meryl called. "Do you have a table free?" She smiled broadly and came the rest of the way in. "Hey, how'd it go today?"

"Want a free cupcake?" Liddy asked. "How about fifty?"

"Ooooh, no, really?" Meryl approached the counter to better examine the plates of cupcakes. Liddy was struck again by how lovely she was. She must be considered the town goddess, Liddy thought.

"They're so beautiful. But I don't want to spoil my dinner."

"They're stale now anyway," Liddy said.

"I'm so sorry, Liddy. How many people, exactly—?"

"None. Not one."

"Oh, Liddy, I'm so sorry. But don't get discouraged."

"I don't know, Meryl. If they ain't showing up when I'm giving 'em away, why would they come when I'm asking two bucks a cupcake?"

"Really? Two dollars?"

"You said they would pay two dollars. I can't make a profit if I charge much less than that."

"I did?" Meryl picked up one of the cupcakes and licked the frosting off her fingers. "What do they charge in Atlanta? Because you know you can't charge Atlanta prices in Infinity."

"Two and a quarter?"

"Not much of a difference. Is that coffee still good?"

Liddy turned and dropped in a single serving pod into her coffee maker. "Regular okay? I don't have decaf."

"That's fine. These are so good, Liddy. Even a little dried out, they're fabulous."

"Yeah, that's what everyone says. Maybe I should open up a cupcake shop."

"Don't be discouraged, Liddy. They'll come." She looked at her watch. "You know what? Sorry about the coffee. I just realized I'm late for a meeting at the church."

"I can get you a go cup."

"No, let me just run."

"Want to take some cupcakes with you?"

Meryl stopped and grinned. "You know, I think they'll forgive me for being late if I come bearing cupcakes. Thanks, Liddy."

Liddy pulled down a flat cardboard box and began assembling it.

"Hey, it's better than going to the birds. If I get someone coming in tomorrow, I can't give 'em day-old cupcakes."

"Have you got anything set up for donating your unsold baked goods?"

"You mean like a soup kitchen or something?"

Meryl nodded and helped Liddy place the sticky cupcakes into the box. "Or a homeless shelter. My church has something like that."

"Well, fine. Consider it arranged. Someone from your church comes by, I'll have cupcakes for 'em."

"That'd be great."

"Course, it will be even greater if they come by and I don't have anything to give them because I've sold them all."

"And I'm sure that will happen very soon."

As Liddy watched Meryl with her arms full of the bulky box teeter on her very high heels into the street where her car was parked, she felt a tiny bit better about the otherwise total loss of a day. She picked up a cloth and wiped the counter clean. The weariness of the day had found its way into her hips and legs and when she looked up, she was surprised to see that the light had faded so that it was now nearly dark out.

She turned and collected the coffee cup from the machine and took it into the back room to find the milk. As tired as she was, she still had cupcakes to make for tomorrow and the coffee would help. As she was adding sugar to her cup, she remembered she hadn't locked the front door behind Meryl when she left. At the same moment, she heard the bell of the front door chime for the second time that day.

"I'm sorry," she said, as she walked out front. "I'm afraid we're closed."

She stopped abruptly, staring at the front door, open, but nobody there. Her coffee spilled over her fingers that held the cup, and she hurriedly put it down.

"Is anybody there?" she called, wishing she had thought to grab up a rolling pin in the kitchen.

She edged closer to the open door, imagining any moment that someone would jump out from outside and attack her. Hurriedly, she shut the door and threw the deadbolt.

The wind? Was there wind tonight? Was it not even closed properly after Meryl left?

She turned to find the light switch to turn off the lights when she saw it.

One of her Opening Day fliers wrapped around a rock on the floor. Even from where she was standing, she could see there was writing on it. She bent to pick it up and straightened it out, the dark black felt tip shouting up at her.

Her initial relief that they hadn't thrown it through her new window began to merge with a burgeoning anger at being treated like this.

The anger won out.

Tucker put down the phone and glanced at the muted television show on his hotel flat screen.

When was he going to learn to stop believing a word out of her lying mouth?

He would never have taken this trip down to Jacksonville if he had thought for one minute...The phone call from Carol had been brief. Perhaps he was distracted when she called. Surely, if he had been thinking clearly, it would have realized why she was calling.

"Hi, Tucker. Just heard about your little friend with the bakery? She's delaying the Grand Opening a day."

"It's not today? She didn't mention that to me."

"I heard from Meryl that Miss French Bakery Girl decided first of the week would be better."

"But all the flyers she put out—"

"I know. It's almost like she wants to fail, isn't it?"

Tucker sank onto the side of the bed and began to pull off his tie. The grand opening of *Le Cupcake* had taken place as advertised. Today. Saturday.

And he was a no-show.

Damn her.

When would he ever learn?

Liddy spread out the tablecloth on the splintery picnic table and handed her mother a napkin. The day was beautiful but unseasonably warm for early October. It occurred to her as she glanced up at the cloudless blue sky that if she hadn't gotten this great idea to take her mother on this little outing for a change of scenery and some fresh air, she would be riding her horse right now. This was the second mother-daughter excursion in as many weeks.

Her phone rang and she held her finger up to her mother.

"I gotta take this, Mama," she said. "Hi, this is Liddy, are you the woman from Craigslist? About the mixer? Awesome. Yes, I'll take it." Liddy looked at her watch. "Can I pick it up tonight? Jacksonville is about two hours from me. Okay." Liddy scribbled down directions on the back of an envelope. "See you this evening. Thanks again."

"So you decided to replace the mixer."

"Can't have a bakery without one."

"Even a bakery that doesn't have any customers?"

"That's temporary."

"Where'd you get the money?"

"I always had the money. I just didn't want to have to spend it."

"But you decided to spend it."

"Yes, Mama."

"I see."

"What do you care, Mama? I'm here, aren't I? Here in Infinity? Why do you want me to give up so bad?"

"I don't want you to give up. I want you not to throw your money away. Money that you have very little of. And with you not having a job, money you aren't likely to replenish easily."

"I'm not letting these bastards stop me."

"You are referring to your customers? 'These bastards?' Seems like an odd reason to go into business."

"I'm just saying I've decided to make a go of it, that's all."

"Fine, you've decided. Whatever."

Liddy took in a breath and willed the tension and anxiety to flow out of her. She looked up at the sky and let the breath out slowly.

"Am I boring you?"

Liddy looked back at her mother. She had never seen her look so frail and stunted.

So old.

If anything, she looked worse in the sunlight.

"Just enjoying the beautiful day, Mama," she said, reaching for the thermos of coffee.

"And you think I'm not?" Her mother scowled up at the birds flitting in the tree branches overhead.

"Are you in pain?"

"Because that would explain things?"

Liddy felt her frustration begin to build and she made a conscious attempt to rein it in. She held her tongue and poured a mug of coffee for her mother.

"Black," her mother muttered.

"I know how you like your coffee, Mama."

"How blessed I am."

Hold your tongue, hold your tongue, Liddy said to herself.

Her mother sipped the hot coffee, made a face and reached for one of the cupcakes on a plate in front of her.

"Would it kill you to bring Danish just once?" she said.

Liddy set the thermos down with a thud and burst out laughing. "You always do this to me!" she said, shaking her head and grinning. "Make me so mad and then crack me up."

Her mother didn't look up, but was obviously trying not to smile. "So tell me about the big opening day where no one showed up," she said, poking at the icing on one cupcake with her finger.

"Well, no one unless you count the person who delivered the nasty note but no, that was after hours, so you can't count him."

"A nasty note?" Her mother put the cupcake down and wiped her fingers on the napkin in her lap. "What did it say?"

Liddy leaned over to her purse and pulled out the folded up pink flier.

"You carry it with you?"

"I keep thinking I might take it to the cops or something."

Liddy handed it to her mother.

Her mother unfolded the flier and read the few words scrawled out on it.

"*Go back to HOT-lanta and take your crappy cupcakes too.*"

Her mother looked up from the note. "Seems pretty tame, all things considered," she said.

"Yeah, I thought so too," Liddy said, pouring herself a cup of coffee. "No cussing or dog poo smeared on it or anything."

Her mother frowned and gave her an admonishing look.

"Plus, it would've taken nothing to wrap it around a rock and heave it in through the window, you know? But they opened the door and tossed it in."

"Sounds kinda meek in a way, don't you think?"

"Yeah, well, I guess even the meek have their days," Liddy said.

"You know what I think? I mean, if you're determined to go ahead with this thing, why don't you go to the Infinity Business Bureau and see what they can do for you?"

"Never heard of 'em."

"Well, I'm telling you about them now. They are the ones that organize all the business parades and the floats and get the schools involved in doing field trips at various businesses and like that. Plus, they do town-wide promotions like birthday celebrations and holidays."

"Mama, that's a great idea!" Liddy said. "I'll go meet with them first thing tomorrow."

"After you pick up your new mixer."

"That's right," Liddy said. "I need to take the reins of my own life and make it happen."

The two sat quietly without speaking for a moment and then her mother grimaced slightly. "I asked the nursing staff to decrease my pain medication," her mother said as she handed the note back to Liddy.

Liddy returned the note to her purse. "Because you were concerned about becoming dependent?"

"It's been three months! I'm not sure I remember what real life feels like without being stupefied half the time."

"They wouldn't give it to you if they didn't think you needed it."

"Oh, is that right, Miss Got Her Medical Degree While I Wasn't Looking?" Her mother hunched her shoulders in a gesture that Liddy realized she had seen her do quite a lot lately, a gesture that now seemed to be an attempt to brace against the pain. "And people never get addicted to their painkillers. That is a well-documented fact."

"But you're hurting, Mama," Liddy said gently. "I can see that."

"It's temporary," she said. "I just need to ride it out."

Liddy reached over and took her mother's hand. "At least are they giving you something else to help you through it?"

Her mother frowned at her. "More drugs? What would be the point of—"?

"No, I mean like back massages and hot baths and like that."

Her mother looked at her for a moment and then looked away.

"Mama?"

"As it happens," her mother said, still not looking at her. "I find these little picnics of yours to be…" she cleared her throat and looked up into the tree branches, "…extremely soothing. Even if you only ever bring cupcakes. You know, old people like variety! We need stimulation."

Liddy leaned over and hugged her mother. When she did, she could feel the older woman release the tension in her shoulders, as if she could transfer some of the pain and the stress to her daughter. Liddy blinked back tears, realizing she had never felt more needed.

Later that night, after Liddy had arrived back from Jacksonville with her used industrial bench mixer, she thought of her mother's brave fight to reduce her pain medication.

I *didn't come to Infinity to wait for her to die*, Liddy found herself thinking as she flipped on the big mixer and watched the batter blend up and over on itself in the wide silver bowl. *She's got a lot of life left in her.*

Liddy glanced up at the clock. Ten o'clock. She would store the batter in the bowl in the fridge and then be up by three to ladle it into the cupcake pans. While they were baking, she would examine the storefront to make sure it was spotless.

Liddy poured in a premeasured dose of vanilla into the batter as it mixed. A lot of bakeries didn't feel the need to indulge in this extra expense, she knew. They argued that people couldn't tell the subtle difference. That might be true, she thought, recapping the bottle. But at this point, until finances became really bad, she figured she needed every advantage she could find.

When the landline rang, she knew before she answered it that it would be him.

"I am so sorry not to have made your opening," he said.

"That's okay," she said.

"No, it isn't," he said. "I somehow got it in my head that it was tomorrow, not yesterday."

"Opening day on a Monday?"

"I know it doesn't make sense," he said. "And I'm just as sorry as can be."

"Don't worry about it, Tucker," she said. "It wouldn't have made any difference."

"Nobody came?"

"Not a soul.

"Sorry, Liddy. I really am."

"Don't be, but like most bakers, I'm up to my ass in yeast and sprinkles at the moment so if you don't mind…"

"Of course." He paused. "Will you be out to the barn tomorrow?"

Liddy tucked the phone against her neck and poured the batter into the plastic jug on the counter and placed it in the refrigerator.

"Yeah, I'll be there," she said. "Sugar shouldn't have to suffer."

"That's the attitude…"

"Glad you approve. See you there around five-thirty." Just the thought of it made her tired but Liddy was a long way from admitting to anyone—least of all him—that buying Sugar had been a mistake.

"Goodnight, Liddy."

She washed the silver bowl, dried it and put it back in its place attached to the heavy commercial mixer. Since she only had the one mixer, she would have to use it again tomorrow morning to prepare the different frostings while the cupcakes baked. She looked at the clock again. She hoped she would be able to sleep. Four hours wasn't much for an average night's sleep and she would need every minute of it if she wasn't going to be dead on her feet in the shop tomorrow. Or at the barn.

She turned out the light and went upstairs to bed.

The next day, after three solid hours of no customers, Liddy put the *Be Back Soon* sign on the front door and locked up the bakery. The offices for the Infinity Better Business

Association were located in one of the suites across the street in the courthouse. Liddy stepped out of her shop and looked both ways before crossing the street. What she saw was a steady stream of foot traffic on both sides of her shop, to the hair salon, the hardware store and down the block to the corner sandwich shop. A steady stream that appeared to be consciously, deliberately, avoiding her shop front.

She found the Better Business Association offices on the first floor of the courthouse and approached the receptionist with her brightest smile.

"Good morning," she said. She was wearing her favorite Chanel suit. The piping down the sleeves always made her feel a little like a drum majorette and she thought the feel of a uniform might be helpful in dealing with a possible bureaucrat. She also had in her hands a dozen cupcakes, baked and boxed up that morning.

The receptionist, a heavyset young woman with a pleasant face, returned her smile.

"Good morning," she said.

"I'd like to register my business with the Association," Liddy said. "Is there an application or an interview process for that?"

The girl pulled open a desk drawer. "Nope, not really. Just need your name and what kind of business you run." She drew out a form with a list of hand-written names on it and pushed it across the desk to Liddy. "What is your business?" she asked.

Liddy put the box of cupcakes down on the desk and took a pen out of her shoulder bag. She ran a finger down the list to the end and began to write her name.

"I've got the cupcake shop across the street," she said. She pointed at it with her pen without looking. "Do you need my email address?" she asked. "I notice nobody else put theirs down."

"The cupcake shop?" The girl said it like it was synonymous with *the town brothel.*

Noticing the difference in her tone, Liddy looked up from the sheet. The girl's cheerful face had changed so drastically that, for a moment, Liddy didn't think she looked like the same person.

"I'm pretty sure we can't be no help to you in that," the girl said, taking the sheet back before Liddy could finish filling in her name.

Liddy was surprised. "Why not?" she asked.

"'Cause you probably ain't going to be around long enough to make it worth the trouble," the girl said, staring straight at Liddy as if ready to go a couple of rounds with her.

"How do you know that?" Liddy said, still holding her pen as if she might yet get to write on the sheet. "That's not very supportive of a new business."

"And you can take this—" The girl used her pencil to push away the box of cupcakes as if they were radioactive, "—with you. There's nobody here needs any free samples."

Liddy took the box of cupcakes and stared with her mouth open at the girl. She took a step back to ascertain by the sign behind the receptionist's head that this was, indeed the Infinity Better Business Association, but before she could speak, the girl turned to face her computer.

"Close the door behind you," she said and jabbed a button on her computer that brought up a screen of a game of Solitaire in process.

Liddy turned and walked out of the office and felt her face and neck redden with embarrassment.

What the hell was that all about? Should she come back later when the crazy receptionist was gone? Should she call and report her to her superiors? Should she just forget the hell all about all of it?

Liddy hesitated in the hallway of the courthouse and watched a few people come and go, most of them were in summer suits: southern lawyers in seer sucker or short sleeves, their jackets dispensed with altogether. She walked to the directory board and then punched the elevator button to take her to the second floor where she spent the next hour knocking on office doors, chatting with secretaries and receptionists and handing out all but one of her cupcakes. Everyone was civil and, if not actually friendly, Liddy reminded herself that these were lawyers' offices. No one threw her out and most of them deigned to accept the free cupcakes. She had little business cards offering volume discounts attached to the bottom of each cupcake paper. When she had given away all but one of her free cupcakes, she decided the morning hadn't been a total loss, and so left the courthouse just before noon, walking with her head up past the offices of the Infinity Better Business Association.

"Mind if I join you?"

Liddy looked up into the smiling face of a very attractive woman who was standing next to the park bench Liddy was sitting on. Liddy had left the courthouse fifteen minutes earlier and parked herself on the bench, stunned and unhappy at her unproductive but revealing morning. From this position, she could see the front of her shop. And while it was true there was a sign on the door saying the store wasn't open, Liddy could see that no one passed close enough to read it anyway.

"What? Oh, please!" Liddy scooted over. "I was just lost in my thoughts. Didn't even see you standing there."

"Oh, I know how that is." The woman sat down next to Liddy and held a brown paper lunch bag in her lap. She had thick wavy brown hair to her shoulders and beautiful green eyes. "My name's Jenna Dale. I work as a legal secretary in the courthouse."

"Liddy James. It's a beautiful building," Liddy said. She turned back to look at the double story old brick building as if seeing it for the first time.

"Yes, it is," Jenna said. "It's got an interesting history, too. Well, all of Infinity does. You're not from around here, are you?"

Liddy laughed. "How could you tell?"

Jenna laughed too.

"I own the bakery across the street there," Liddy said, gesturing with her cupcake box and then as if just remembering she had it she offered her last cupcake to Jenna.

"Oh, it looks fabulous," Jenna said. "I shouldn't though. I'm trying to watch my weight."

"I think everybody in town is. Although you wouldn't know it to look at them." Stunned that the words had come out of her mouth, Liddy turned and gave Jenna a stricken look. "I am so sorry," she said. "I can't believe I just said that."

But Jenna was already laughing. "It's true!" she said. "We are a very typical southern town in that respect. From our diner and fried chicken to our church suppers with everybody's pies and cakes that you just can't say 'no' too. It's a miracle we aren't all obese."

"So you're from Infinity?" Liddy asked.

Jenna shook her head as she peeled the wax paper off her sandwich. "I'm from Baxley," she said. "The big city up the road." She grinned. "But I married a man who came from Infinity and although we didn't live here, we ended up coming here a lot because of his kin."

"So you and your husband live here now."

"Well, I do but I'm divorced now so Kenny lives somewhere else. Kinda ironic how that all sorted itself out, me ending up in Infinity and him not. His folks are gone now, too."

Jenna offered Liddy half of her sandwich which Liddy accepted. It occurred to her that she'd been getting most of her calories from cupcakes for the last few days and she was grateful to add some veggies to her diet.

"See, Infinity is over a hundred and twenty years old. There's a lot of stories about how it got its name, as you can imagine. Most having to do with it being forever and a day away from any place else, or how being here makes all the days longer." Jenna bit into a peach. "So what's your story?" she asked. "Unless you're born here, nobody deliberately chooses to live in Infinity."

"I'm here because of my mother," Liddy said. "I was born in Jacksonville, but my parents moved to Atlanta when I was two. I've lived up there my whole life. My whole married life, too. I'm widowed." Jenna murmured her condolences. "When Daddy died about twenty years ago, my Mama met Jerry who had a hardware store here in Infinity. They married and she's been living here ever since. When Jerry died, I guess it's been five years now, Mama just stayed. She said Infinity was home."

"So your mother came down from Atlanta too?"

Liddy nodded. "Twenty years ago. I wonder…"

"What?"

Liddy looked at her new friend and smiled. "I've been complaining a whole lot to my Mama about not fitting in, you know? And she must've had the very same situation when she first came down. But she hasn't mentioned it."

"Small towns are notoriously difficult to accept outsiders. Not that you're an outsider."

"It's okay, Jenna," Liddy said. "I think that's exactly what I am. So that's my life story. And I'm here now because my Mama fell and needed me close for awhile. How about you? No interest in going back to Baxley or maybe a bigger city?"

Jenna shook her head. "I'm a country mouse," she said. "Small towns suit me fine."

"Ever been to the big cities much?"

Jenna shrugged. "Been to Vegas and New York on vacation," she said. "It was fun."

"But not for you."

Liddy watched the woman clean the juice from her peach from her fingers with a paper napkin. She was dressed, in Liddy's opinion, in a shapeless brown dress. She was barelegged and wore simple black flats. Her beautiful hair was drawn back in a plastic hair clasp. Liddy found herself wondering if the woman had ever found occasion to flip through a Vogue magazine. She looked down at her own clothing. She had put her highest heels away until she could get back to the city, but she still wore kitten heels. It was too hot for pantyhose so she wore knee-high nylons under her cotton slacks. Her cotton sleeveless sweater was belted at the waist.

"Not for me," the woman said, putting her trash inside her paper bag.

"Must be next to impossible to meet anybody in Infinity, though, I'd imagine," Liddy found herself saying.

Jenna stopped wadding up her trash and gave Liddy a shy smile.

"Funny you should mention that," she said. "I think I've caught someone's eye I've had my cap set for a very long time."

"Somebody at your work?" Liddy asked.

"No, I see him around town. You're right, though, it's hard to meet anyone. I've done E-harmony a few times."

"Really?"

"Yes, we do get Internet connections down here, Liddy!" Jenna laughed and Liddy joined in. "Listen, I've got to get back to work but any time you want to girl-talk, this is my bench noon days Monday through Friday. I'll be here."

"Sounds good. I'll probably take you up on that. And save your calories sometime, okay? I mean it. My cupcakes are worth it. On the house."

"Can't say no to that. Bye now." Jenna walked across the lawn to the front of the courthouse, pausing only long enough to toss her lunch trash in the receptacle by the door and to give Liddy one last wave.

"You're showing up later and later."

Tucker sat on a bale of hay in the barn, his back leaning up against the tack room. Both horses were bridled and saddled in the outer paddock.

Liddy approached Tucker, her car keys still in her hands as she registered the fact that Sugar was groomed and tacked for her.

She knew she was late, and her mind was full of all the tasks she still had to do before she would be able to lay her head down tonight. Not so deep down, she knew trying to fit a horse into her new life was madness. But she'd be damned if she'd admit it just yet.

"It's getting darker earlier," she said. "Thanks for tacking up Sugar."

"Figured it was either that or we'd be trotting around the dressage ring in the dark again."

"Okay, again, sorry," Liddy said tersely, moving to where her horse was standing in the paddock and trying not to sound irritated.

They led their horses through the east gate that bordered the main pasture and mounted up. Liddy buttoned up her jacket because the wind had picked up. It had felt sunny and calm when she left the shop thirty minutes earlier—another day of no customers—but the weather had changed.

"Where do you want to go?" Tucker asked. Liddy noticed how long his legs were as they molded around his big horse.

"I don't care," she said. "How about along the Satilla Creek?"

"Great," he said and took the lead. His horse Traveler didn't like to follow.

They followed the tractor trail as it traced the perimeter of the main pasture until it broke through to the woods beyond. This was Liddy's favorite trail. On the way out, she had the green wide open pasture on her left and the close protection of the tree line on her right. This time of year, the trees were varying shades of burgundy and gold. She teased Tucker that they were wearing the colors of his alma mater, Florida State.

The further they walked their horses into the woods on the far side of the pasture, the more Liddy could feel the tension and stress of her day fall away. When they were deep into the woods, the well-trod path was wide and smooth and the horses, by now warmed up, were happy to canter for a mile or more. The rocking horse cadence of the gait serving to calm and exhilarate Liddy all at once. When they finally shifted back down to a walk, Liddy knew she had a smile on her face. She couldn't help it.

"You always smile after that stretch of the road," Tucker said, looking at her over his shoulder.

"And you always look behind and comment on it," Liddy said with a grin.

"How about we bring it up a notch," he said. "Are you up for it?"

"Like how?" But her voice was eager.

Tucker pointed down the path. "It gets wider and continues for another quarter mile," he said.

She knew that. They'd been there a dozen times before.

"But it's all uphill," he said.

"You're suggesting we gallop?"

"You get so transported by a simple lope," he said, smiling mischievously at her. "I'm pretty curious to see what a full-out run will do to you."

Liddy gathered her reins in both hands. "Bring it," she said.

Tucker turned back to face the path. Liddy could see him collect himself and tighten his legs around Traveler's side. Within a minute, Traveler had gone from a walk to a trot and right into a gallop, eliminating the canter in between. Without even being asked, Sugar copied the horse in front of him.

Liddy could feel the incline and found herself glad for it. It was forcing Sugar to work a little bit harder, but the results, for Liddy, felt the same.

She was flying.

Sugar pounded up the pathway after Traveler as horses have done for millennium. Sugar rode hell-bent to outrace the imaginary predator, or to catch his pasture mate. Liddy bent over Sugar's mane and lifted her hips out of the saddle, balancing on him only with her heels in the stirrups and her now quivering knees against the saddle. The tree branches flew by on either side of them in a green swirl of leaves. The feel of the ground and the sound of Sugar's hooves heaved up into her stomach in a steady, thundering staccato until there was no thought in her head but the experience of the moment.

When she felt Sugar slowing, she was able to notice that there was something else in the world besides the two of them. She saw Tucker's back moving up and down in a jerky posting trot that heralded the end of the gallop. She was glad for it—she thought her heart would burst—and sorry for it all at the same time.

When Sugar pulled up behind Tucker who was waiting at the end of the path, Liddy bent her face into her shoulder and sneezed violently twice. She looked up at Tucker who laughed.

"I'm not sure what I expected," he said, grinning at her. "But I would never have guessed sneezing."

"That was incredible," Liddy said. "My knees feel like they turned to jelly. I'm serious. It was amazing."

"Next time you watch a Western," Tucker said, leaning down to check his girth, "and they've got somebody doing a full gallop, just remember what they must be feeling."

"Because you never get tired of it?"

"Can you imagine ever getting tired of it?"

Liddy rode up beside him now that the path was wide enough to fit two abreast.

"It was amazing," she repeated, reaching down to pat Sugar on the neck. When she looked up at Tucker, she could tell that he too had enjoyed the run. His face was flushed and his eyes sparkled as if he was ready to go again.

"I'm happy to walk back, though," Liddy said. "I've had my thrill for the day. And I think Sugar could use the rest."

Tucker nodded. "Surprised he kept up so well."

They fell into a comfortable pace side by side at a walk which allowed them to talk without shouting. Liddy couldn't remember when she had felt more relaxed.

"How're things going on the bakery front?" Tucker asked absently.

"Pretty good," she said.

"Really?"

"Well, I haven't gotten any customers yet."

"So what's 'good' about it?"

"My attitude, basically," she said. "I had a set back last week where I lost my most expensive piece of bakery equipment."

"How?"

"Long story. Anyway, I had to decide if I was going to eat my losses or spend more money and try again."

"Don't tell me. You decided to spend the money."

Liddy looked at him. "Something on your mind?"

"None of my business."

"Exactly right."

"It's just that you have to see how ill-conceived this whole cupcake bakery notion is."

"Really, I don't," she said icily.

"Why didn't you mention to me that you were at this... crossroads with the bakery?"

"So you could advise me?"

Tucker twisted in his saddle to see what her mood was.

"You are above taking constructive advice from a friend?" he said.

"As long as the friend doesn't try to shove the constructive advice down my throat."

"What part of failure is attractive to you?"

Liddy couldn't believe she was hearing him correctly. She reined her horse to a stop and Tucker did too.

"I respect the fact that you wouldn't do things this way..." she said.

"I would not."

"And so I need you to respect the fact that I am doing things a different way."

"A way that's bound to fail."

"It must be incredible to have all the answers." Liddy felt her face flush with anger. "And to be able to predict the future. You must be very entertaining at parties with those super powers."

"You don't have to be super human to see that opening a cupcake shop in a town of 2,300 people is crazy."

"So now I'm crazy?" Liddy was seconds away from spurring her horse down the path and leaving Tucker sputtering in his own self-righteous, arrogant juices.

Tucker looked in the direction they had come from and then turned his collar up against his neck.

"We might be in for a little bit of weather," he said. "If we don't want to get caught in it, we might have to pick up the pace a little."

As soon as the words were out of his mouth, the light in the little patch of clearing seemed to diminish, and the sound of rain hitting the overhead tree canopy barely preceded the abrupt downpour where they stood. Startled by the suddenness of the rain, Sugar shied violently as if being attacked. Tucker grabbed for his bridle but he was on the wrong side of him. Liddy tumbled to the wet forest floor as Sugar wheeled away and bolted into the woods.

"Shit!" Tucker put his hand on Traveler's neck to calm him. The horse's eyes were white with terror. "Liddy, are you—"

"I'm fine, I'm fine," she said with a rasp, not at all sure she was. It had happened so fast she had not had time to tense up but neither had she been able to put her arms out to help stop the fall. She had landed on her butt and her hip into the strong loamy smell of wet earth and fallen leaves. On top of that, her wrist felt like it had bent hard the wrong way.

"If you're sure," Tucker said, still on Traveler who was moving nervously in an agitated circle, "I'm going after Sugar."

She waved him off, not sure she had enough breath to speak, afraid trying to would only make her sound more hurt than she was. Tucker went from a standstill to a controlled gallop in the direction Sugar had disappeared. One minute Tucker was there, panting, the sounds of squeaking leather and Traveler snorting filling the woodland air, the next, Liddy lay in the mud and the rain, with the encroaching darkness closing relentlessly in on her.

She sat up and steadied her breathing. The only sound she could hear was the rain pounding down on her. She moved her legs under her and grasped a nearby sapling to help pull herself up. When she put her hand out to touch the tree, pain shot up her arm and made her gasp. She pulled her hand back to her chest and looked around the darkened shadows of her surroundings.

How were they ever going to get back in the dark? They must be miles away from the barn.

Her hand began to throb painfully. Between the rain and the darkened woods visibility had shrunk to a few feet in front of her. She looked down the path where Tucker had gone hoping to see him appear. She saw the gray downpour of the rain, and a large shadowy shape of an animal moving across the path.

Oh my, lord...Were there bears here? It's the woods. Of course, this is where bears live.

Liddy struggled to her feet, every part of her body complaining now. Her hip, where she'd fallen, hurt even more than her hand. Her wet clothes clung to her and she was shivering so hard from the cold that she had to lean against a tree to stay upright.

She stared down the path, willing Tucker to return.

A flash of lightning illuminated the path for one moment. Liddy decided the woods appeared less terrifying when things just stayed dark.

What if he's fallen? she suddenly thought.

Galloping into the woods in the dark and in the rain on a terrified horse is a great way to end up impaled on one of the many jagged tree stumps in the woods.

Liddy started to walk in the direction he had ridden. Maybe he needed her. Maybe he was lying broken and hurt just around the bend. Liddy was limping but the thought of Tucker injured quickened her steps.

How could this have happened? she thought, miserably. *One minute everything was just heaven, and the next—oh, Mama will never let me hear the end of this.*

Liddy stopped to rest and let the various pains in her aching body subside before moving forward again. She moved around a gentle bend in the path, craning her neck to see if she could hear or see Tucker coming from around the other side.

What she saw made her gasp and draw back. A large dark structure stood directly next to the bridle path.

It might have been used as a barn at one time but there was no recognizable road or track leading to it now to suggest it had been used as anything for many years. Now it was a hulking black monster that loomed out of nowhere, forbidding and unwelcoming. It had a long, single window in the upper level between the matching slopes of its roofline. There was a pair of floor to ceiling windows on its broad side, both with most of their panes broken out.

There was an air about it beyond abandonment and disuse that Liddy couldn't place. An air of something sinister. She found herself staring at it, immobilized.

That was when she heard the sound of horse hooves coming toward her. She turned away from the house and focused on the path that was swallowed up by darkness a scant twenty feet from where she stood. She held her breath, feeling the icy rain inch its way down her collar and into her eyes. When she used her good hand to wipe the rain from her face, Tucker had materialized, trotting down the path toward her, riding one horse and leading the other.

Liddy didn't think she'd ever been so glad to see anyone in her life.

She walked into the middle of the path and watched him swing down from his horse. He reached her in two strides.

"You are hurt," he said.

"No, I'm...I'm..." Liddy was shaking so badly, she couldn't get the words out.

He put his arms around her and it was all she could do not to just fold up into them. She was shocked at how good it felt to be held by him.

She glanced at Sugar who looked as docile and bored as if he'd never gone screaming into the woods with the devil on his tail not fifteen minutes before.

"You found him," she said, realizing she was whispering, and also realizing she didn't want to say or do anything that would prompt him to remove his arms from around her.

Tucker bent his face to her hair for a moment almost as if to reassure himself that she was okay and Liddy's knees nearly gave way.

Traveler snorted loudly and pawed the ground.

Tucker pulled back and looked into her eyes. "You're walking so that's not it. What did you hurt?"

She wouldn't bother lying to him. For some reason, she didn't feel like being all invulnerable and strong with him at the moment. For some reason, she wanted him to take over.

"My hand, is all," she said, moving her hand where she held it against her chest. "I think I sprained it or something."

He touched her hand but it was too dark to examine it properly. "You can ride?" he asked.

Liddy had no idea if she was up for that. "Is that the best way, you think?" she said uncertainly.

"If we want to get home tonight, yes," he said moving over to where Sugar stood. He quickly checked the girth and pulled down the stirrup. "I'll give you a leg up."

Liddy hesitated, clutching her hand tightly against her. "How about steering him?" she said. "I'm not sure I can..."

"You just need to stay upright in the saddle," Tucker said. "I'll lead him. You know you have to, Liddy." He grinned at her. "It's not just an old saying. There's merit to it."

"I know, I know," Liddy said, now feeling some healthy irritation coming into her. "I'm chafing every place there is to chafe and it's so cold. And what is that place anyway? It's major creepy."

Tucker looked over at the barn. "It's just a barn, Liddy," he said. "Quit stalling." He held out a hand to her.

The rain had slowed to a barely perceptible drizzle. Liddy walked over to Sugar. As much as she wanted to get a hot bath, preferably with a little rum and Coke on the side, how she forced herself to walk over to her horse was the dread of disappointing Tucker.

"If I yell as I get on him, just ignore me," she said.

"I intend to," he said.

She faced Sugar's left side with her hurt hand protected against her chest and gripped the pommel with the other. She bent her knee and Tucker took it and hoisted her effortlessly up on top of the horse.

"Good job," he said. "No screams at all."

"More importantly and a lot more surprising," Liddy said, "no cussing either."

She turned her head away from the looming structure of the ghost barn and focused on Tucker's back. He held Sugar's reins in his hands and remounted Traveler.

As they moved down the road in single file, he shouted back over the sound of the rain. "Having fun?" he said.

Liddy laughed, happy to be off the wet ground and moving in the direction of warmth and dry clothes. But the funny thing, she realized with amazement when he turned away, was that in spite of their fight, her wet clothes and her throbbing hand, she was having fun.

She really was.

Finding Infinity

Chapter 5

Three days after her mishap on the trail, Liddy stood in her kitchen and applied tiny star confections to the fondant topping of a hundred cupcakes. The work took little to no effort and so she was free to hear every word of Haley's moronic and incessant phone conversation from the front of the store. Hired to simply stand and greet customers—any that might show up—the girl succeeded in eating most of the display items and breaking more dishes than Liddy could afford to replace.

Liddy's sprained wrist was bound with vet wrap and still making every chore a clumsy laborious one. That was the reason she had agreed to let Tucker's niece temporarily work in the shop.

It had sounded like such a good idea at the time.

Originally, she had hoped that Haley could lug the heavy jugs of batter and shift the cupcake pans into the oven and give her a rest by overseeing and tending the front sales room. After the first two clean ups, it became clear that if Liddy wanted to have any ingredients left with which to create saleable inventory, she needed to remove the girl from all edible items. And then there was the attitude.

Tucker and Liddy had both hoped that Haley's presence in the shop might encourage others, at least the girl's friends in town, to venture in. But so far, with the exception of one extremely unlikable and unpleasant teenage boy who seemed to be Haley's "special" friend, this had not happened.

Liddy straightened up to ease the kinks out of her back. She had gotten an early morning phone call from a nurse at her mother's rehabilitation center insisting that Liddy's mother would do better with a revised pain medication therapy. The nurse sounded kind and well meaning and told Liddy that her mother was extremely uncomfortable. Liddy promised she would talk to her mother.

She put the piping bag down on the counter and flexed the fingers on her injured hand. In the back of her mind it occurred to her that she had heard the front door bell sound quite a while ago but not again to signal anyone's departure. Come to think of it, she hadn't heard Haley on the phone in several minutes either. Liddy glanced up at the clock. Could there be a customer who'd been in the store for thirty minutes? She wiped her hands on the towel hanging at her waist and slipped out of her apron.

The afternoon sun poured into the large display window, illuminating the dust motes in the air. The pock-marked and thin boy was standing at the counter, his head near Haley's as they whispered to each other.

"Haley?"

Both heads jerked away. The boy swiveled on his heels and marched straight to the door and out without saying a word.

Haley turned to Liddy with a look of open disgust. "We weren't doing anything," she said.

That was when Liddy noticed the girl was standing with her back to the cash register. The open cash register.

Liddy looked at the open drawer and then back to Haley. "Did...did someone buy something?" she said, not really knowing what to say.

Haley pushed the drawer shut behind her. "Yeah, somebody bought something," she said, with obvious disdain and blatant disregard for what Liddy would have considered a very precarious moment for her.

"So if I were to count the money in that drawer," Even before Liddy finished the sentence she knew she was going into an area that was a no-fly zone, or at lease a fly-at-your-own risk zone. "will I find more money in it than when I started this morning?"

Haley looked at her, completely unperturbed.

"Maybe."

"Okay, get out." Liddy's hands were shaking and she wasn't sure when they had started.

"What?"

"I said, get out. Get out of my store."

"You can't do that." The girl, stood unmoving, her chubby hips jammed up against the counter as if ready to resist a physical assault by Liddy to remove her. "You owe me my pay."

"Your pay?"

Liddy was positive Tucker had said he would give the girl something for her time. Was she asking her for money?

"I didn't work here for nothing, you know," the girl said. "Uncle Tucker said you'd pay me ten dollars an hour."

"Well, that's a lie." Liddy's hands were shaking so badly now, she was gripping the front of her cardigan to keep from revealing the fact. "And now you can get out. Unless you want me to count the register drawer right this minute?"

Haley leaned in close to Liddy and said into her face: "Bitch."

Liddy refused to flinch or take a step backward.

Haley moved out from behind the counter, never taking her eyes off of Liddy. She collected her purse from under the counter and, as she moved around the counter to the door, put her hand out and tipped the tray of fifty perfectly frosted and decorated cupcakes onto the shop floor.

Liddy drove slowly to her mother's rehabilitation center. It was warm for November but the late afternoon sun felt good on her face. The car magnet had been stolen days ago and this afternoon she found a bright pink flyer stuffed under her windshield wiper that she now glanced at where it lay on the passenger's seat of her car. The headline read: *Don't let the French steal jobs in Infinity!* The picture was a cartoon drawing depicting her bakery with a French flag flying from it and a huge slash across it. At the bottom of the flyer were the words: *Brought to you by the Infinity Better Business Association.*

On the way, her phone had rung several times—all of them Tucker—and she had ignored it. The three ibuprofen and the hurried cup of tea she had downed before getting in the car were starting to help. It had taken twice as long to clean the front room and kitchen as it would have if she hadn't had her bad hand. Now if she just had something to help the maelstrom of discomfort going on in her head.

Ten days open and not one customer?

Liddy slipped into the side door of the rehab center. She carried a bag of fast food burgers and fries in her arms and nodded to the elderly black CNA standing in the hallway. The old woman was dressed in pink scrubs and smiled at her and nodded back. It always occurred to Liddy when she saw this woman that she, herself, should be living in the nursing home, not working there. Her mother told her one of the "ladies" had worked at the center for nearly forty years. Liddy wondered if this was the lady her mother was referring to.

"Well, even I heard about the shoot-out at the Cupcake Café today," her mother said as she ate a French fry from the bag Liddy had brought with her.

"You're kidding?"

"Well, nobody gossips more than nurses or nurses' aides," her mother said. "Did you get any catsup?"

Liddy rifled through her jacket pockets and handed her mother two catsup packets.

"Did the gossip make me the bad guy?"

"Of course." Her mother licked her fingers.

Liddy was relieved to see her mother looking so good. While she was still hunching her shoulders in what looked like an effort to brace against pain, Liddy thought there was a little improvement.

"And you don't have any idea why a nurse called me to say you were in agony and needed your pain meds again?"

"She did?" Her mother looked away for a minute as if thinking. Then: "Did it ever occur to you that they just want us all to be drugged out lumps?"

Liddy frowned. "Why would they want that?"

"We are easier to deal with as dead weight. Where's the salt?"

"You're not supposed to have salt."

"I'm sure I did not just hear you tell your injured elderly mother—"

"Okay, okay." Liddy dug into her pocket for the salt.

"Could you please put it on for me? Honestly, Liddy! Did I not do this for you when you were little? For years? Is it too much to ask to have you tear the salt packets open for me now that I'm old and dying?"

Liddy sprinkled the salt over her mother's French fries. "You know, Mama? You might have a point there about them wanting you to just be dead weight."

Her mother cackled. "Oh, you are a bad, bad daughter," she said, grinning and wagging a French fry at Liddy.

The two of them munched on fries for a moment.

"How's your wrist?"

Liddy held it up. "It's fine. I can use it for most things."

"So you don't need the girl any more."

"Mama, she stole cash out of the drawer."

"Can you prove it?"

"There was a hundred dollars less in there than when I started that morning."

"So she did it but you can't prove it."

"Well, I wasn't going to have her arrested. I'm not even sure I'm going to tell Tucker."

"You can bet the girl has told her uncle her version of why she left. I'd be careful telling lies to Tucker Jones, if I were you."

Liddy frowned. "Why do you say that?"

"You do know he used to be a homicide detective in Atlanta, don't you?"

Liddy stared at her.

"Oh, I see, you don't know. What do you two talk about if you don't even know that about him?"

"He's an ex-cop?"

"There's some question as to how 'ex' he is."

"What does that mean?"

Her mother shook her head. "Just more gossip," she said. "Look, Liddy, do you mind if we pick this up another time? I'm getting tired."

Liddy could see her mother looked exhausted.

Were the nurses right after all?

"And the pain, Mama?"

Her mother closed her eyes and leaned back into her pillows. "Oh, it's doing just fine," she whispered.

Liddy leaned over and kissed her mother's cheek. "See you tomorrow, Mama."

Her mother didn't answer but looked to be already drifting off to sleep.

Liddy collected the fast food bag and her purse and quietly let herself out of the room. She looked down the hall at the nursing station and decided to have a word.

Later as she pulled into the back parking area of her store, she saw Tucker's truck parked next to her spot. She had swung by the barn after her visit with her mother to check on Sugar and was half expecting to see Tucker out there. The barn manager said he'd been out earlier and had put Sugar, who had lost a shoe, in the paddock for the farrier.

As she parked her car, he emerged from his truck and walked over to her. He waited until she had pulled a grocery bag out of the back, which he promptly took from her.

"So what happened?" he said.

"Oh, good, thanks," Liddy said, smiling. "And you?"

Tucker let out a long sigh and followed her through the back door of her shop. She flipped on the lights, realizing for a moment how nice it was for Tucker to be there and not to have to worry about anything ugly waiting for her in the dark. It suddenly occurred to her that she had been coming in every night since the night of her invasion with a lingering fear.

Hell of a way to live, she thought to herself.

"Drink?" she asked him as she took the grocery bag and set it on the kitchen counter.

"Okay."

Very conscious of him watching her, she pulled a wine bottle off an overhead shelf in the pantry and placed it on the counter. She took a corkscrew from a drawer and handed it to him. She was aware of feeling self-conscious with him. Because her hand had been bothering her, she hadn't dressed to see Mama. She was wearing slacks, driving mocs and a form-fitting cotton sweater that revealed every curve. With her recent diet of too many cupcakes, she also knew her curves were a little more generous than usual. As she became hyper aware of her body and the fact that he was clearly watching her, all of a sudden all she could think of was the moment on the trail when he'd held her in his arms after her fall.

"It just didn't work out," she said, her voice a little unsteady. She placed two wine glasses in front of him.

He uncorked the bottle with a pop, then filled both glasses.

"What did she do?" he asked.

"Let's go upstairs where we can sit down," she said. She grabbed her glass and the wine bottle and led the way up the narrow staircase.

The little alcove off of Liddy's bedroom that served as her sitting room had only a small couch and a coffee table. As soon as Liddy entered the low-ceiling room, she felt like she was seeing it for the first time. For the last twenty years she had lived in a three thousand square foot, five-bedroom McMansion in the suburbs of Atlanta. This sitting area was smaller than her walk-in closet, smaller by half than the pantry off the laundry room.

Tucker settled himself on the couch and looked up at her expectantly. "You were about to tell me what Haley did to make you fire her."

Liddy sat down next to him on the couch. There was nowhere else.

"She stole a hundred dollars out of the register," she said, surprised to hear the words coming out of her mouth. She took a healthy sip of her wine and then closed her eyes and leaned back into the couch. She decided it felt great to have told him. When she opened her eyes, he was staring at her with his mouth open.

"She…she stole money?" he said.

Okay, so maybe telling him wasn't such a great idea.

"I didn't actually see her do it," she said, sitting up straight again. "But she was with her boyfriend and the drawer was open and when I came in he ran and later, when I counted it…you know."

"You were short."

Tucker drank his wine. "Son of a bitch," he said.

"So she isn't usually a handful?" she said.

He looked at her.

"I mean, you look so surprised," she said. "And I gotta tell you, Tucker. She had kind of an attitude from Day One."

"She's been going through a bad patch these last several months," he said. "She lives with her mother, my sister Daisy, who's definitely not going to win any awards for mother of the year. I've been thinking recently about helping Haley make some changes. But I'm still surprised she could do this. A boy was with her, you say?"

Liddy nodded. "I wasn't formally introduced or anything," she said. "I got the impression he was her boyfriend. Scuzzy looking kid."

"Liddy, I am sorry—"

"Don't be. You meant well. And my wrist is good now. I don't need any more help. Let's put it behind us."

"I'll repay the money she took."

"I hate to have you do that," Liddy said. But money was tight and that hundred dollars would buy a lot more flour and sugar.

"I insist."

"Okay. That's cool. Thank you."

They sipped their wine in silence for a while.

"You been out to the barn lately?" he asked.

"Just came from there as a matter of fact."

When he looked surprised, she said hurriedly: "Not to ride. Just to check on Sugar. Thanks for putting him up for me for the farrier."

The room began to feel very small to Liddy. She was extremely aware of Tucker's closeness to her. His knee was millimeters away from actually touching hers. She began to feel warm.

"Is it hot up here?" she said, fanning herself. "I never sit in here. Be great if there was a window or something."

"I'm good."

"You must think I'm crazy to come here and live like this," she waved a hand around the small room. "So different from my other life."

"Everybody thinks you're crazy," Tucker said matter-of-factly. "I thought you knew that."

"Yeah, I know, but sometimes I get a glimmer of an understanding of why they think that. You know?"

Tucker grinned at her, the first time, she realized, that he'd relaxed enough to do it since he arrived.

"When I look at this place through your eyes," she said, "I guess it starts to seem clear why people think I'm crazy. I start to think I'm crazy."

Tucker sipped his wine and his knee touched hers. Instantly, Liddy felt a small electric shock on contact and she moved her leg away.

"I may have some good news on that front," he said. He pulled a piece of paper out of his front shirt pocket and handed it to her. "It's a church fete over in Blackshear. They're interested in having someone make about five hundred cupcakes to celebrate their town's hundredth birthday."

Liddy looked at the piece of paper with the contact information on it and then back at Tucker. "Is it a donation, do you know?" she asked. "Or a catering job?"

"They want to pay you for the cupcakes."

"Tucker, that's great!" she said, nearly spilling her wine in her haste to put her glass down and look more closely at the piece of paper. "If they like what I do—and trust me they will, my cupcakes are to die for—that might create some word of mouth, you know? This could be just what I need to get things started. Thank you so much! This is totally what I needed to hear right now."

She leaned back into the couch, clutching the piece of paper to her chest.

"Glad I could help," he said. "Especially after my niece burgled the till."

"Really, Tucker," she said, sitting up and picking up the wine bottle to refresh their glasses. "This is the best thing that's happened to me all week. Thank you."

They touched wineglasses and drank. Liddy hadn't realized how close he was to her until he leaned over and kissed her on the mouth. It was a full, warm kiss tasting of wine and spearmint that made her stomach do an exquisite flip-flop with excitement.

She dropped her wine glass.

"Oh, crap!" she said, jumping up. "I can't believe I did that."

"I'll take that as a compliment," Tucker said, standing up to reach the roll of paper towels on the top of the small bookcase in the room. She snatched the paper towels from him and began to mop up the mess on the bare hardwood floor. She picked up the pieces of the wine glass and set them on the coffee table, her hands shaking when she did so. She hoped he wouldn't see. As if dropping a wineglass wasn't evidence enough of how much he unnerved her.

"I guess I didn't know that you were going to do that," she said breathlessly, concentrating on cleaning the floor and not looking at him.

"I'm not sure I did either."

She looked up at him and tried to read his thoughts. But his thoughts were clearly focused on trying to interpret her thoughts.

Why did he fluster her so?

He stood up. "Shall I go fetch another wineglass from downstairs?" he said.

She stood up, clutching a bunch of used paper towels, and looked around the room as if checking for another likely place to start scrubbing.

"You know? Do you mind if we don't?" she said, not looking at him. "I'm really beat. And this is such great news about the catering job. I cannot thank you enough."

"Sure. No problem," he said. He pulled out his wallet and extracted a couple of fifties and handed them to her. "I'll take care of Haley," he said. "Thanks for not pressing charges. She's just confused."

"Oh, no, of course not," Liddy said, scrunching up the money with the sodden paper towels and feeling like she had just kicked a puppy.

"Walk me to the kitchen," he said as he moved to the door. "So you can lock the door behind me."

"Oh, yeah, good," Liddy said, still not looking at him. She followed him down the stairs, watching him stoop to avoid the low ceiling. When she got to the door behind him, she noticed her bag of groceries was still sitting on the counter.

He opened the door and flicked on the outdoor parking lot light. It occurred to Liddy that, as a cop, or whatever he was, he would be very familiar with security measures.

He turned and looked at her. "I hope this isn't going to screw things up," he said.

"What? No," she said, holding onto the door and realizing she wanted nothing more than to shut it and be on the other side of it, away from him. "Not at all. I mean, not if we don't let it screw things up."

"You coming out to the barn tomorrow?"

"I am," she said. "Or, I think I am. I'll let you know, okay?"

Dear God, he wouldn't try to kiss her at the door, would he?

As if he could read her mind, Tucker touched the tip of an imaginary hat and walked to his car.

"Lock the door," he said over his shoulder.

She was way ahead of him.

Finding Infinity

Chapter 6

It was madness coming to the barn this early—before the first batch of cupcakes was even shoved into the oven—but any later, Liddy knew she ran the risk of running into Tucker. She brought Sugar in from the pasture and tied him to a hook in outside the tack room.

She didn't need a boyfriend. That much she had figured out in her brief time in Infinity. What she needed was not to alienate one of the only friends she had in town by sleeping with him. She ran her hand down Sugar's flank and lifted another hoof and cleared the packed mud from around his frog.

Should she have acted differently? Should she have rebuffed him? Should she have let the stupid kiss go on as long as it did?

She sighed and eased Sugar's foot to the ground. It was so quiet, she could hear only the hard munching of Sugar enjoying his breakfast, and the scurrying sound of tiny mouse feet behind her in the wide aisle that led to the stalls.

She looked at her horse with satisfaction. She may not know if she was coming or going in love or business. But at least she wasn't the worst horse-owner on the planet. It wasn't much, but even a little boost to her self-worth helped.

It's not that I don't like him, she thought. *I don't have time for everything in my life right now without adding more to it.*

When he was finished eating, she hesitated about tacking him up. Her confidence had taken a hit after her fall and she realized she wasn't as comfortable with him if Tucker wasn't there. Once she realized her hesitation, she marched purposely to the tack room and pulled her saddle and bridle down from their hooks.

What's the point of owning a damn horse if you're afraid to ride him?

"Hi, you riding today?"

Liddy turned to see a young, attractive African-American girl leading a very pregnant mare toward the tack shed.

Liddy waved to her and grinned. "Not sure," she said. "Your mare is beautiful. When's she due?"

The girl appeared to be in her early twenties. She was wearing half chaps with sneakers and a dirty t-shirt that looked like she'd been up awhile. She tied her horse up next to Sugar and patted her fondly on the neck.

"Any time now. It's our first."

"Both of you?"

The girl nodded and expertly ran her hands down her mare's legs one by one.

"Yep. I paid three thousand to get her covered by a decent stallion and now that she's in foal, I'm almost positive I'm not gonna wanna sell him."

"You know it's a colt?"

"That's what the sonogram says." The girl grinned.

"What would you do with him?"

"Train him," she said. She leaned over and extended her hand to shake. "Jessica Dorsey," she said.

"Liddy James, pleased to meet you. What kind of training?"

"Dressage."

"Oh, wow. I thought they only did barrel racing around here."

The girl, Jessica, laughed and slapped her hand to her blue-jeaned leg.

"You work in town?" Liddy had noticed lots of African-Americans in Infinity but never before at the barn.

"I work here at the barn," Jessica said. "As of last week. I came in with my girl, here, Ophelia, from Tampa where I was working at. Got great references, got a great mare in foal to a great mover."

"Good for you."

"Don't get me wrong," she said, straightening up and patting the horse on the neck. "I love this horse better'n I love most family. Way better."

Liddy laughed. "I can see that." Liddy wondered if Jessica was being made to feel welcome in Infinity or if she too was feeling like an outsider.

"I don't suppose you can ride her right now."

"Nah. Ophelia's working on more important things right now," she said, patting the mare's swollen belly. "Can't get in the way of that."

"Well, when you're back in the saddle again, I'd love to go out hacking with you."

The girl turned and gave her surprised but happy look. "I'd like that," she said.

A few minutes after Liddy tacked Sugar up and led him to the mounting block, and Jessica put her mare in her stall before starting her workday, Liddy realized she felt a little better.

Amazing, the power of the affect of a horse on a person, she thought, as she directed him with her legs toward the far gate that led to her favorite path by the river. She opened and closed the gate behind her without dismounting and walked slowly down the trail that she and Tucker always took. The crispness of the fall air and the beauty of the leaf fall combined with the gentle sway of her hips in rhythm with Sugar brought a sense of peace and balance to Liddy that she could not have imagined feeling just an hour earlier. Never even bringing him into a trot, she let the movement of the slow gait and the beauty around her work their magic. At one point, she stopped on the trail, realizing she had come to exactly the spot where she'd fallen and Tucker had held her in his arms. She paused Sugar and let the memory of that moment flow over her like a warm, lingering feeling of pure pleasure.

What do I want? Do I have any idea? Shaking herself out of her reverie, she caught a glimpse of the creepy house further down the trail and decided it was a good spot to turn back. It didn't look nearly as foreboding at this time of the morning, but it still didn't look very welcoming either. Before she turned Sugar's head in the opposite direction, she thought she saw a shadow or movement in one of the windows. Assuming it must be a squirrel or the shadow of a hawk overhead, she squeezed Sugar's sides with her legs to urge him to pick up the speed of his walk. Just before the trail ended, she let him enter the boarding pasture to visit one of the molasses lick blocks set out for cows. While he slurped and maneuvered the dispensing ball wheel with his tongue, she closed her eyes and brought in a long breath of air into her lungs. When she let it out, she could almost feel the tension and unhappiness of her week leave, too.

It's true, she thought, as she scratched Sugar behind the ear with her crop. The outside of a horse is good for the inside of a woman. She tucked her crop away between the saddle and saddle pad, not even sure why she had brought it.

As she turned Sugar's head back to the barn, a sure sign he would begin to pull and get strong with her, Liddy closed her legs around him and sat firmly upright.

"We're going to move forward, Sugar ol' buddy," she said out loud, knowing she was speaking more for herself than to Sugar. "But at my speed."

The horse stretched his head sharply forward, jerking the reins out of her hands, but it was only a gesture and his feet didn't mirror the insubordination. Liddy recollected the reins and they moved back down the path they had taken at a walk.

Wouldn't Tucker be so proud of her?

The words formed in her head before she even knew they were there.

Tucker tossed the cellphone down onto the bed. He actually found himself debating about whether he should call her. He wasn't used to feeling on the back foot. Of all the things he had to sort out with this new project, sorting out how he felt about Liddy was a complication he had not anticipated, nor did he need. Probably best to let her be for a while; let her come to him.

"You okay, man?"

Tucker looked up at the man he was sharing the motel room with. He didn't bother responding. The man, an undercover DEA agent named Greg Barnwell, wore filthy clothes and had deliberately not bathed in several days. His eyes were red-rimmed and he glanced about the room continuously.

"We handle this right," Barnwell said, licking cracked lips with what Tucker thought looked like the tongue of a lizard, "nobody gets hurt, the bad guys go to jail. Everybody's happy."

Tucker collapsed on the motel room bed and pulled his Stetson down across his face.

"You gonna try to sleep first?"

But Tucker had already tuned him out. His thoughts, organized and alert behind the cool façade, the shaded visage, were focused on one person right now, and one person only.

He found himself praying she wasn't stupid enough to fall into his trap.

She was hours behind schedule.

The cupcakes were baking but would need twenty minutes after that to cool enough to be frosted. Convinced that because she wasn't ready, this would be the day customers came to her shop, Liddy was fretting over refashioning the display in the front window. She was using stale cupcakes from earlier in the week. They couldn't be sold to be eaten, but they were fine as props.

She looked at the papier-mâché Eiffel Tower she had found on Craigslist for twenty dollars. Meryl had hinted that it made the shop look "too foreign" for the locals' tastes but Liddy was hesitant to capitulate on her Parisian dream. *It was a French cupcake shop, for crying out loud*, she thought. *What do they want? American flags?* Meryl had suggested that that might be a good idea.

From the window, she could see movement outside as the downtown office workers parked their cars and shuffled up the walkway to the courthouse. One woman dropped her briefcase and when she stooped to pick it up, she caught Liddy's eye. The woman gave her an abashed smile and then proceeded on her way.

Great, Liddy thought. The first time someone looks my way without snarling, and I don't have any cupcakes ready. She heard the timer go off in the kitchen and she quickly disentangled herself from the streamers and crepe paper in the display window. She hadn't taken the closed sign out of the door just yet but had already made several pots of coffee. If nothing else, she wanted the shop to smell inviting if someone did come in.

Hurriedly, she pulled the baked cupcakes out of the oven, burning her thumb in the process, and set them on a cooling rack, then she slid in the next batch. The counter mixer was full of chocolate frosting. Liddy set the timer for the oven and returned to the front room to open up the shop. Even if she had to tell someone the cupcakes weren't ready, she could be welcoming and offer them a cup of coffee.

Five hours later, she had fifty perfectly frosted and decorated cupcakes sitting on a plate on the counter. And not one customer had appeared.

Liddy even found herself looking for the woman who had smiled at her in the morning. When she watched all the office workers stream out of the courthouse across the street at lunchtime, she looked for anyone who might glance in the direction of the shop. Most of them went to the corner sandwich shop, some went to their cars, the others opened sack lunches and sat on benches in the park around the courthouse.

What is the deal? she thought with frustration. *They don't look like they're all in some organized effort to drive me out of Infinity. How is it that not one person feels like a damn cupcake?*

Around three o'clock, Liddy put on a fresh starched apron, applied some tinted lip-gloss to an immovable smile and stood outside her shop with a plate of ten cupcakes. Every fifteen minutes or so, when her arms got tired, she went in, put the tray down and had a sip of iced tea on one of the little café tables in the front of the shop. Then she went back outside and stood.

Maybe I should wear a French maid's outfit. Maybe I should wear a Can-Can girl's outfit. Maybe I should wear a gigantic cupcake costume. Maybe I should just give the hell up.

Fifteen minutes before closing, it happened. Liddy was daydreaming so that when the woman stopped in front of her, Liddy nearly asked her if she needed directions to somewhere It was the woman from this morning.

"I'm so glad you're still open!" the woman said. "I've been fantasizing about these cupcakes all afternoon! Ooooh, are these samples?"

"Yes," Liddy said, smiling with real delight. "Please help yourself."

The woman took a large bite out of one of cupcakes that Liddy had designed to look like a retro Hostess cupcake. "Oh, my God, they're even better than I'd imagined," she said. "I couldn't take a lunch break today, or I would have come then. Do you have more?"

"More?"

"I'm going to a church function tonight and I was supposed to bake cookies." The woman popped the last of the cupcake in her mouth and licked her fingers. She started to move past Liddy into the shop. "I'll need about two dozen to be safe," she said. "God, I can't believe you're here! A real French bakery in Infinity!"

Later that evening, Liddy happily related her good news to Meryl on the phone. "And she wants me to cater an employee goodbye party at her office at the end of the week. Plus, two of her friends came in this morning and one of 'em wants me to bake cupcakes for her daughter's fifth grade class."

Meryl adjusted her bangs in the mirror as she sat at her desk with Liddy on the speakerphone. "So much for the story about all Infinity women baking their own cookies," she said.

"And then Tucker gave me a lead about this place in Blackshear that's looking for a caterer for some major celebration function they're doing. I've been so busy I haven't even had a chance to follow up on that."

"*Tucker* gave you the lead?"

Meryl picked up the phone, disengaging the speakerphone.

"Yeah, a couple nights ago. As it is, I have enough business that I'm going to need to call Jessie to make a mid-week run of eggs and butter. I'm hoping he can deliver them this evening while I'm visiting my Mama. I really think things are going to turn around now.

"That's great, Liddy," Meryl said. "So, are you seeing Tucker?"

"What? Oh, no, not really. I mean, I think he may be interested but I don't want to lose him as a friend, you know?"

"What makes you think he may be interested?"

"Well, he kissed me two nights ago. Totally out of the blue. Really surprised me."

"Goodness, I'll bet it did. But you don't like him in that way?"

"Honestly, Meryl, I haven't let myself think about it. I just know I have so much on my plate right now that adding a romantic element to it just doesn't feel right, you know?"

"Of course. Probably very wise of you. Listen, Liddy, I've got another call coming in. Can I call you later?"

"No worries. I'm going over to see my mother tonight. I'll talk to you later in the week."

"Sounds good."

Meryl hung up the phone and stared out of her office window. The movement of her head caught her eye in the mirror and she looked back at herself. She looked good, she knew. Not twenty-five anymore, but good. She touched her blonde hair as it framed her heart-shaped face. Her lips looked pursed and thin. Her eyes hardened.

Liddy closed up shop early for the day. She had promised her mother she would pick up a few paperback books from the drugstore. She also intended to hit the diner on the edge of town for some chicken fingers. Her conversation with the nurses at the rehabilitation center had been friendly but firm: respect her mother's wishes to reduce her dependency on her pain medication, please do all you can to help her by offering ice chips, massages and more warm baths, and allow her to monitor her own diet, even if that means French fries and fried chicken. The nurse in charge had been polite and seemed almost noncommittal about the requests, sending off a definite attitude of *it's your funeral,* but Liddy's mother reported the staff had, for the most part, complied.

It had been two days and Tucker hadn't called. While it was true she had been trying to avoid him, she was surprised he seemed to be avoiding her too.

See? I was right. The kiss spoiled everything.

After she'd bought their dinner at the diner, Liddy drove to the rehabilitation center, and went over all the things she needed to do the next day for all of the new orders. She rang her egg and butter supplier, a man Meryl had put her in touch with when she first got to Infinity and upon whom she already had come to rely.

"Jessie?" she spoke into her cellphone using the hands-free feature.

"This here's Jessie."

"Jessie, this is Liddy James. I need an emergency delivery of ten dozen eggs and another five pounds of sweet butter." She knew she sounded unfriendly and officious and she hated that. Usually, she made a point of sweet-talking any and all of her suppliers, asking how they were doing, how the wife was doing, how the arthritis was doing, but she was agitated today and, unfortunately, she knew it was coming through over the phone in her voice.

"When you need 'em?"

"Is today impossible?"

"I can deliver 'em this evening. You be to home?"

"Can you just leave them in back? I have to be out this evening."

"Thems perishables, Miz James. I don't like to leave—"

"I know, Jessie, I know," she interrupted, another unforgivable breech in the language of the small town businesswoman. "I won't leave them there long, I promise. I just can't guarantee I'll be there when you come by. There's a bunch of wooden crates in back so you don't have to put them right on the ground if you're worried about...varmints."

"Waaaal, it's warm for this time a year but I reckon it'd be cool enough."

"Thanks, Jessie."

Liddy disconnected.

God! It was physically draining to have to negotiate and work around all the required Southern sensibilities just to get some damn eggs delivered to your house. She needed them there when she got home tonight so she could bake and decorate all the cupcakes for the children's school party. One of the mothers would be by to pick them up around eight a.m. That gave her plenty of time to make the cupcakes for Lisa —the woman who'd dropped her briefcase—for her employee party at ten.

She marched into her mother's room, her high heels clicking against the linoleum her arms full of two large paper bags of fried chicken, muffins and fried okra from the diner. As soon as she entered her mother's room, she saw it.

Something was wrong with her mother.

Liddy sat by her bedside, her stomach lurching, the diner food forgotten at her feet. Her mother stared at her like she didn't know her. One of the nurses aides stood by her chair.

"We were gonna call you," she said. "Only we figured you'd be here today and see for yourself."

"What did the doctor say?"

Liddy stared at her mother, her vacant, slightly angry eyes, staring back at her. "Can she hear us? Is she in some kind of trance?"

"We don't rightly know—"

"What did the doctor say?"

"He don't come on Thursdays. He comin' tomorrow."

"You didn't think a change this big warranted a call to him? Or me?"

Liddy was angry and upset and she knew she was taking it out on the poor woman.

"We can't tell no doctor when to come," the woman said. Liddy assumed she'd probably been fussed at on a pretty regular basis by family members and it no longer upset her. "They come when they come. You know doctors."

"What about the nurse on duty?" Liddy stood up and then turned to look at her mother again. *Have I lost you? Have I lost you already?*

"She don't know no more 'bout it than I do," the woman said, leaning over to plump her mother's pillow. "It happen like this sometime."

"I don't understand. Breaking a leg can lead to dementia?" Liddy shook her head in frustration. "She doesn't even know me."

"She don't know none of us."

"You didn't give her any meds, did you?"

"No, ma'am, it's in her chart not to."

"I'm going to talk to the nurse. Will you stay with her?"

Liddy hurried down the hall to the nursing center. It was the dinner hour and almost all the staff were either with patients or at dinner themselves. An African-American woman in yellow scrubs looked up from her computer screen.

"Help you?"

"I'm Mary Ann Mears' daughter?" Liddy said. "The woman in Two Fifteen?"

"Yes, of course, we all know Miz Mears. We been waiting to talk with you about her change in her condition."

"I was just here yesterday and my mother was fine then," Liddy said, feeling her anxiety crank higher and higher. As she spoke to the woman, she realized she had never felt more vulnerable or in need of help. "And now she doesn't know me." Just saying the words out loud made her want to cry.

"Doctor won't be here until tomorrow," the woman said. "You gonna wanna talk to him."

Liddy felt the anger and the fear rise up into her chest. Her first reaction was to lash out. She quelled the impulse with effort. "Is there any way, do you think, that I might talk with him before tomorrow?"

"He don't come in on Thursdays. If you're here tomorrow morning, he can meet with you after he done examined your mama."

"Okay, thanks." Liddy forced herself to smile. The nurse was trying to be helpful; Liddy could see that. Obviously she couldn't change what couldn't be changed.

Liddy turned and walked back to her mother's room, tears blurring every step of the way. There was nothing more to do. Her mother eyed her hostilely when she entered the room, so she placed the paperback novels on her bedside table, picked up the take-out bag and handed it to the nurse's aide. She picked up her handbag and pulled out a twenty-dollar bill and handed that to the woman, too.

"You're Ebony?"

The woman nodded, clearly surprised that Liddy knew her name.

"My Mama has spoken of you," Liddy said. "I would be so very grateful if you could keep an eye on her for me?" Her voice was hoarse with emotion.

"I always does," she said kindly and Liddy had to fight the urge to lean over and hug her.

She turned to give her mother, who had clearly forgotten she was in the room, one last look and left.

Outside, the evening had gotten cool and she pulled her barn jacket tighter around her. The visit had only taken thirty minutes instead of the hour or more that she'd expected. She looked for her car in the parking lot and wondered for a moment if she should run out to the barn to see if the farrier had gotten around to replacing Sugar's shoe. Just the thought of it made her tired. She decided to call the barn manager, instead, and make it home in time to collect her eggs from Jessie's delivery and have a long, quiet soak in a hot tub.

As soon as she used her keyless entry to unlock the driver's side door, she saw him. She hadn't parked under any of the parking lot lights and now she was sorry she hadn't thought of it. He had been crouching on the far side of her car. Now he moved silently out of the shadows to stand between her and the car.

Chapter 7

It was the shifty-looking kid who had hung out with Haley at the bakery. In the growing shadows of the early evening, he looked taller and considerably more threatening than he had in the sunny bakery.

Liddy faced him, her thumb on the panic button of her key fob. "Can I help you?"

The boy staggered closer to her and Liddy moved back a step. He looked like he'd been drinking, although Liddy couldn't smell alcohol.

"Gotta question for ya," he said. His voice was slurred and his eyes darted madly in every direction as if trying to focus on her.

Liddy held her tongue. If she didn't threaten him, maybe he would keep moving after he said what he'd come to say.

"The whole town hates ya," he said with a sneer.

"That's not a question," Liddy said.

Damn! Don't antagonize him!

"Not a...not a..." He looked at her and put a hand behind him on her car to steady himself. "Oh, yeah? How about this?" he said with some energy, clearly feeling attacked by Liddy's comment. "How about if you end up dead or your bakery all burnt to a crisp, huh?"

Liddy's stomach lurched.

"How's that for a question, huh? Is that a good enough question for you?"

Liddy took a long breath and waited. *Let him say his peace and then just get in the car and get out of here.*

"You being dead? Huh?"

Liddy held the electronic key fob up and pointed it at him. Although she wasn't sure she was really ready to hit the button, the boy reacted as if she'd pointed a Taser gun at him. Perhaps, in his addled state, he thought she had. He flinched away from her aim and stumbled back around the car, keeping his eye on her.

"You heard me," he said, when her car was between them. "For firing Haley, you bitch!"

When she judged she had enough time to get in the car without worry about being rushed from him, Liddy jerked open her car door and jumped in. She locked the doors and started the car. In her rear view window, she could see the boy trotting away in an uncertain line, putting his hand out to push off surrounding cars to help direct his exit from the parking lot.

She filled the wine glass all the way to the rim. It didn't matter if she spilled a little from where she lay in the tub. At the moment, she wasn't sure anything really mattered.

The digital clock on the bathroom shelf read two a.m. Liddy had returned home, dragged the three boxes of eggs and butter from the back door into the kitchen, and made the five dozen cupcakes for the school party. She left the butter out on the counter overnight so it would be soft for making the frosting in the morning and made a new batch of batter for her other catering order later in the morning and stored that in the refrigerator. She was so tired, she could weep. In fact, when she first slipped into her bath she did cry, so emotionally and physically worn out that she didn't even believe a full night's sleep could restore her. She looked back at the clock. And a full night's sleep wasn't going to be possible anyway.

In the flurry of activity after she got home, mixing and pouring, measuring and cleaning up later, she had missed a call from Ben. The message he left was cryptic and she could sense there was something more than what he was saying. She returned his call three times, each call going straight to voice mail, before giving up for the night,

Was it just six hours ago she had thought everything looked so great?

She thought of her mother and reached for her wine. It was a terrible thing to love someone who looked at you through the eyes of a stranger. She prayed it was temporary.

If she doesn't even know I'm here for her, she found herself thinking, *is there still a reason for me to be here?*

The bathwater now tepid, Liddy pushed her empty wine glass back from the counter's edge and climbed out of the tub. She dried off quickly and pulled on her cotton nightie. The nights were still so pleasant that she didn't need much more. Thanksgiving was in two weeks. Her stomach clenched uncomfortably at the memory of so many Thanksgivings up in Atlanta. Her huge dining room with the china set for twelve, the silver relish dishes and crystal stemware. The warmth of friends and family laughing and reminiscing together.

I guess I'm determined to just make this the worst night of my life, she thought as she brushed her teeth and climbed into bed.

Ben was supposed to come to Infinity for Thanksgiving. Liddy suddenly stopped positioning her pillow. Was that what the odd message was from him? She wondered. Was he going to tell her he wasn't coming?

And Mama. At present, she doesn't even remember what Thanksgiving is, Liddy thought miserably. Let alone the family members whom she usually shares it with.

She turned off the light and turned to face the moon which was just visible through her small bedroom window over the bed.

Hard to believe that's the same moon waxing and waning over St-Germaine de Pres, she found herself thinking. And with that, she turned her face into her pillow and quietly cried herself to sleep.

Tucker slammed the car door and mounted the rickety steps to the trailer. He was struggling to control his frustration and anger. The clearer part of his brain told him this could wait until morning. But the coiled anger that had sat so long beneath his cool exterior had had enough of waiting.

He rapped sharply on the door.

"Daisy!" he barked, glancing to the side of the trailer as he heard a small dog bark. "Get your ass out here!"

The impatience bristled off him. If she didn't open the door in the next few seconds, he thought he might break it down.

The little dog barked again shrilly. He could hear his sister releasing the deadbolt on the trailer door. Within seconds, she filled the doorframe. Her hair hung disheveled in her face.

"Tucker?"

Tucker pushed past her, shocked—as he was every time he saw his sister—that she was as heavy as she was.

"Where's Haley?" he asked as he stood in the little kitchen.

"Haley?" Daisy rubbed her face as if she still wasn't awake yet. "What time is it?"

"It's one a.m. Do you know where she is?"

She sighed heavily and went to the kitchen counter and picked up a cigarette packet.

"Don't light that," Tucker growled. "Your daughter is in my truck. Did you even know she was out?"

The woman tossed the cigarette pack back down on the counter. "What'd she do?" she asked tiredly.

"She was caught in a sting, trying to buy Sudafed from the CVS in Tifton."

"Is that a crime?"

Tucker actually thought he might smack her, something he had never done in the whole forty years he'd known her.

"Don't fuck with me, Daisy," he said. "Do you want her to go to prison? Do you even care?"

"Tucker, I've told you, I cannot handle that girl." Daisy reached for her cigarettes again and this time Tucker said nothing. "It's not my fault she is the way she is. If her daddy—"

Tucker put his hand up as if to stop the flow of invective he had heard too many times before about the runaway husband and the reason for every unhappiness and bit of bad luck.

Daisy lit her cigarette and tossed the pack back down on the counter. "Fine," she said. "Whatever. Are you dropping her off or is this, like a courtesy call on your way with her to Arrendale State?"

"Haley is not a bad kid, Daisy," Tucker said in exasperation.

"What the hell is all the noise about?" A man in his underwear emerged from the back of the trailer. "Daisy?"

Tucker looked from the man to his sister.

"I'm thirty eight years old, Tucker," she said, hotly. "And you are not my father."

Tucker turned and walked out of the trailer.

Daisy stood in the doorway and watched him get in his car. "Are you taking her?" she asked. "Is she under arrest?"

Tucker backed the car out of the parking spot, working every ounce of his self-restraint not to carve an angry tire trench in the spotty yard of dirt and weeds in front of the trailer, and drove away.

Liddy sat in the alcove office off the rehab/nursing home nursing station waiting for her mother's physician to meet with her. She had brought in three dozen cupcakes for the staff as a thank you for everything they had done and were doing for her mother. It hadn't been that much more work to add them to her morning's work, but the nurses and aides acted as if she'd given them all coupons to Outback Steak House. She made a note to herself to bring them more treats from her bakery. It occurred to her that they were sort of like family to her mother. They saw her every day, in the middle of the night even. If she needed to be cleaned or fed, joked with or walked outside in the sunshine on a fine day, these were her companions.

The doctor burst into the room and her thoughts in a flurry of apologies and settled himself in chair across from her. Her eyes were red from the crying and the lack of sleep so Liddy made a mental note to comment about how bad her allergies were this time of year.

"I'm very glad to meet you Miz Mears," the doctor said, looking at his clipboard, not at Liddy. Liddy didn't bother correcting him.

"What can you tell me about what's happened to my mother?" Liddy asked. She was determined to be unthreatening or demanding—two things she was sure her mother would insist would be counterproductive to her achieving what she wanted: helpful information about her mother's status.

"Well, she's certainly not herself, is she?" The doctor looked up at Liddy and smiled perfunctorily.

Oh, crap. He was going to treat her like she was an idiot. It might be a little harder to pull off the unthreatening demeanor.

"Can you tell me *why*?" Liddy asked patiently, finding herself squeezing her fists together and digging her nails into the palms of her hands.

"Well, of course, often there is no obvious reason for situations like this," the doctor said, holding the clipboard on his lap and smiling at Liddy as if he were delivering very good news indeed.

"Like a hit on the head," Liddy said.

"Exactly!" The physician looked at Liddy as if delighted to discover she wasn't as stupid as he'd logically assumed. "There was no bump on the head which could explain this."

"So, in absence of a bump on the head…" Liddy prompted.

"We think it could be a vitamin deficiency."

Liddy found herself wondering if there was a team of doctors trying to figure out her mother's condition.

"A vitamin deficiency?" she repeated.

"Or an infection of some kind."

"When will we know which it is? And what steps do we take to treat it?"

"As soon as we have more answers. We did a blood panel today."

"So basically you don't know why she's lost her mind overnight."

"That's pretty strong language, Miz Mears. I wouldn't say your mother has 'lost her mind.' Not at all."

"How would you describe how she is?"

"It's still pending."

"Pending?"

"Pending the outcome of the blood work."

"And then you'll know?"

"Very, very possibly."

"Or not.

"Have I answered all your questions, Miz Mears?" The doctor stood up and smiled broadly as if he had absolutely no doubt without waiting for her reply that he had done exactly that.

After the man left, Liddy went and spoke with the elderly black woman who seemed to be closest to her mother and to whom she had spoken with last night.

"She no different, Miz Liddy," the woman said to her before Liddy could even ask her. The fact that she used her name reminded Liddy that her mother spoke of her, considered this woman a confidant, a friend. The two of them walked down to her mother's room and Liddy watched as Miss Ruby tucked her mother's sheets around her and held her head to help her drink from the straw in the glass by her bed.

"Does she know you, at least?" Liddy asked.

Ruby shook her head. "No'm," she said. "And she's cranky. More'n usual."

"Do you have any theories?" Liddy sank into the chair next to the bed and looked up into the simple, friendly face of her mother's caretaker.

"'Bout what happened, you mean? No'm, Miz Liddy. One minute she's her same ol' ornery self, next minute like this. I surely do not know what happened in the in-between."

"The doctors don't know either," Liddy said.

"No'm."

"You figured that?" Liddy searched the woman's face for answers.

"I figure they wrong about as much as they right," Ruby said. "If I seen nothing in my years here, I seen that."

Liddy watched her mother's face, impassive and unexpressive, for a few moments and then stood to leave. She pulled out her wallet and extricated a fifty-dollar bill.

"That ain't necessary, Miz Liddy," Ruby said. "I takes good care of her. It's my job. You don't need to pay me extra."

"I know, Ruby," Liddy said, tucking the fifty in the woman's smock pocket. "Please just take it for my sake." She leaned down and gave her mother's hand a squeeze and then left the room.

When she got back to her shop, she was exhausted. She had been up at four in the morning to frost and decorate the school cupcakes and tuck them into the little cellophane-windowed cardboard box that cost more than the ingredients in the cupcakes did. When one of the moms picked them up, oohing and aahing over how beautiful they were, Liddy handed her a stack of business cards and a couple of fliers and asked her to give them to her friends.

Then Liddy focused on the cupcakes for Mary Nell's employee party. She felt like she was performing an audition. If the cupcakes were beyond awesome—both in taste and in appearance—she knew she could count on repeat business. While the third batch of cupcakes baked and the ones before that cooled on wires, she went over her finances one more time. Even with the new orders, she was very close to having to take drastic measures to pay for next month's living expenses. Everything was more expensive than she'd planned. She forced herself not to think of what was going on at the rehab center. She put thoughts of her mother away in a vault in her mind and, for now, closed and locked the door. She was chewing on the end of her mechanical pencil when she heard the front door bell. She looked up and smiled when she saw it was Meryl.

"You must be on your way to someplace special," Liddy said, turning on the Keurig and sliding a china cup in place on the warming tray. Meryl wore a simple pale blue pantsuit but her heels gave her easily an extra two inches of stature. Liddy admired her friend's presentation. Even her walk said "class."

Meryl smiled and shook her head as she glided to the front counter.

"Nothing special," she said. "MM-mm, it smells like heaven on a plate in here."

"Which reminds me," Liddy said, hurrying to the back kitchen to pull the last batch of cupcakes out of the oven and park them on a cooling rack.

"How're things going?" Meryl asked.

"Well, I got that extra business I was telling you about." Liddy handed Meryl the cup of coffee. "Black, right?"

Meryl nodded and sipped her coffee.

"It's Blackshear's Centennial celebration party the week before Christmas. I'm just hoping it's enough."

"Really?" Meryl frowned.

"Well, I haven't made a cent since I opened. Unless you count the forty dollars I made this morning." Liddy poured herself a cup of coffee. "And honestly, I'm about out of money."

"Oh, that's terrible, Liddy." Meryl put her cup down, a look of studied sympathy on her face.

"Liddy poured cream in her cup. "I do have a backup plan," she said.

"Not borrowing money from your realtor, I hope?"

Liddy grinned. "Don't worry," she said. "That's way down the list. No, I have some jewelry I can sell if I have to. I was going to ask you if you knew a place in town that might handle that for me."

Meryl pulled out a lipstick from her purse. "You mean like a pawn shop?"

"Yes, I guess so," Liddy said.

"There isn't a pawn shop in Infinity," Meryl said. "But maybe in Tifton? Is the jewelry your mother's?"

The mention of her mother instantly saddened Liddy but she forced herself to smile. "No, it's mine from Bill, my husband," she said. "It's family stuff, really old and I think worth a good deal. I hate to sell it. I wanted to pass it on to Ben but I can't see that happening now."

"Where are you keeping it?" Meryl applied her lipstick and returned the tube to her purse. She looked around the shop as if expecting to see a jewelry display.

"Upstairs. Do you think it's safe there?"

"Oh, I'm sure it is." Meryl reached over and patted Liddy's hand. "I know you've got a full day," she said. "I'd better let you get to it."

"Oh, Meryl!" Liddy said suddenly. "I knew there was something I wanted to ask you. I think I have a plumbing leak somewhere."

"Really?" Meryl gathered up her purse. "Did you tell Danni-Lynn?"

"I did," Liddy said. "She said to tell you. She said you handle her maintenance through your various handymen. Can you get a plumber to take a look at it?"

"Of course," Meryl walked to the door and put her hand on the handle. "First thing this afternoon, okay?" She smiled and was gone.

Liddy glanced out the shop window for a few minutes, wondering if this was the day a few customers might come in on their own. It was just as well. Except for the cupcakes she was making for the two parties, she had created none yet today for the shop. Musing that that probably meant, in all likelihood, that she would get a crowd of people in today, she finished her coffee and went into the kitchen to frost the cooled cupcakes.

She hadn't taken two steps into the kitchen when she saw the rat.

Tucker set the trap in the crawl space and backed out to find Liddy standing in the kitchen waiting for him.

"I cannot tell you how grateful I am," she said. "I'm so sorry but I just didn't know who else to call."

"Liddy, it's fine," he said, dusting the cobwebs and dirt from his jeans. "I'm happy to help."

"I mean, I could have shut the shop and run next door to the hardware store, but Mary Nell was coming for her cupcakes —"

"Liddy, really. Not a problem."

"At least let me buy you lunch?"

Tucker's eyebrows shot up. He looked around the kitchen. "I didn't know you made real food here."

Liddy cleared her throat and let the comment pass. "I was suggesting the corner lunch place. It's past lunchtime for them and they'll be glad for the business."

"And you can leave your shop?"

Liddy picked up her sweater and her purse. "I may have to throw a few patrons out but they will, I'm sure, return another time."

"No patrons?"

"Ergo, no problem. Shall we walk?"

Liddy opened up the menu and ordered the chicken salad on toast with a sweet tea. Tucker ordered the same.

"I know it's going to happen now," she said. "After today, those women will tell their friends who'll tell their friends…"

"That's great," he said. "You've worked hard and you deserve it. How's your mama?"

She sighed. "Not good," she said. "She's got, like, some kind of Alzheimer's or something."

"That came on fast."

The waitress came with their teas.

Liddy nodded and sipped her tea. "I went on Web-MD," she said. "If it is an infection, like the doctor suggested, I'm hopeful antibiotics will clear it up and she'll go back to normal. It's horrible, Tucker," she said earnestly. "Horrible, being with someone—loving someone—who doesn't remember you. I just pray she goes back to normal."

He covered her hand with his. As soon as he touched her, Liddy felt the electricity pinging off her skin. She waited a beat and then slid her hand out from under his. She had felt very self-conscious asking him to help her earlier but the sight of that grizzly rodent standing up on its hind legs in her spotless kitchen staring at her had sent her running to the phone without a thought to how embarrassing it all was. He'd come in a heartbeat and for that she was extremely grateful.

"Still don't want to talk about the kiss?" he said, moving his hand back to his side of the table.

"I'm just…I just don't want it to change things between us," Liddy said, feeling breathless and unsure of herself. "That's the sort of thing that can really screw up a friendship."

"It can," he said, picking up a straw and peeling back the paper from it. "Sometimes what you get in exchange can be worth it."

"But of course you don't know that going in, do you?"

"Would take all the fun out of it if you did."

"Can I ask you, Tucker? Have you ever been married?"

That stopped him. She could see his confidant grin slipped a bit but he answered directly.

"I have."

"You're divorced?"

"That's right."

"So you know how bad it can all go. I'm just saying, I know what I have with you as a friend and I consider it valuable. Very valuable."

The waitress set down their sandwiches with the bill which Liddy tucked under her plate. It was well after the lunchtime rush, and Tucker and Liddy had the little sandwich shop largely to themselves. While the proprietors—a middle aged Hispanic couple—had always been polite and efficient with Liddy the few times she had popped in for a sandwich, they were positively gushing with pleasure to have Tucker in their shop. The waitress, who had to be seventy if she was a day, gave Tucker's arm an affectionate squeeze before she walked away.

"You come here a lot?" Liddy asked.

Tucker shook his head. "Not really," he said. "I helped Eduardo out with something a little while back."

"So they're grateful," Liddy said, biting into her sandwich.

Tucker gave her a look that was meant to be admonishing. "They're decent people," he said. "Good people. And they needed a break at the right time. That's all."

"Sounds very mysterious," Liddy said. Her phone buzzed and she saw in the caller ID screen that it was Meryl.

"Hey, Meryl," she said into the phone, holding up a finger to Tucker to let him know she had to take this call. "Still haven't seen that plumber."

"Oh, sorry about that, darling," Meryl said. "I'm having my cousin do it. He's just started his business and needs the work."

"Okay," Liddy said, watching the frown on Tucker's face.

"So not this afternoon?"

"He's in Willacoochee," Meryl said cheerfully. "He'll be over on Monday."

"Monday? Jeez, Meryl. That's after the weekend. The leak is growing since I talked to you. I think we need somebody in there before then—"

Liddy heard voices on the other end and lost Meryl's voice for a moment. "Meryl?"

"Sorry, darling," Meryl said. "Listen, I have to run. Can we sort this out later?"

"Well, okay, but there's another thing I wanted to—"

Liddy looked at the phone and saw that Meryl had disconnected.

"Everything okay?" Tucker asked, concentrating on his sandwich with more attention than one would have believed it merited.

Liddy put the phone back in her purse. "I guess so," she said. But something didn't feel right all of a sudden. "What were we talking about?"

"The kiss?"

"I'm almost positive we were not talking about that."

"I'll be blunt with you, Liddy," Tucker said, pushing his sandwich plate aside. "I like you a lot."

"Well, I like you, too, Tucker. Gosh, I feel like I'm in high school." The nervousness came back in a sudden roar and she found she'd lost her appetite.

"Only in high school, I might've asked your *daddy* if I could court you."

"Court me?"

"You're not familiar with the expression?" Tucker leaned across the table and nailed her with his gaze. It was all she could do not to squirm.

"I am, of course," she said, picking up her sandwich and putting it back down. She took a deep breath and forced herself not to look at him. "It's a direction," she said, "I would prefer not to go down with you." She glanced up at him and saw the hurt in his eyes covered quickly when he leaned back in his chair and sipped his iced tea.

"Not that I don't think it wouldn't be a whole lot of fun," she said. Suddenly, she had a vision of her mother, dazed and unresponsive, and her heart hardened against the opportunity for any more pain in her life. "But I don't believe the fun would be worth the risk of losing what we have. Which is very valuable to me."

He didn't speak for a moment and Liddy managed to choke down one bite of her sandwich before glancing at his reaction.

"Can't be any clearer than that," he said gruffly.

It wasn't until she was alone in her kitchen, washing the final dish from the long day of work and baking that she found herself reliving the meal with Tucker and wondering if she'd been too hasty? If turning him away was really the right way to go, why didn't it *feel* right? Dismissing her uneasiness as having more to do with her fears about her mother, Liddy finished straightening up the kitchen and went to bed in anticipation of an early morning of baking.

It was sometime in the middle of the night, that the phone calls started. The first one was from the mother of one of the little girls at the school who had eaten Liddy's cupcakes at the party. The little girl had started throwing up immediately after school. They were in the emergency room in Tifton and the mother thought Liddy might want to know that the health department would be contacted as soon as their offices opened Friday morning. The other phone calls came sporadically throughout the night until Liddy stopped answering them. Jenna called a little after three a.m. to say her seven year old was being taken by ambulance to the hospital in Tifton with what sounded like severe food poisoning. She had brought the leftover cupcakes from the office party home to him as a special treat.

Chapter 8

Food poisoning.

Ten cases of it, all under the age of twelve. Some of the adults at Jenna's party admitted to "getting the runs" after eating the cupcakes, but it was only the children who'd ended up sick enough to be hospitalized. By the time morning came, all the children were back home, except one who was expected to be released later that day.

Liddy sat in the front of her shop while the county health department officials did a thorough examination of her kitchen.

They found no other violations apart from what they believed was the likely culprit of the food poisoning—brown eggshells in the garbage disposal. Liddy watched them bag up the garbage from her disposal like she was on an episode of CSI.

"You think it was the eggs?" She asked them. "I just got them yesterday. They couldn't be more fresh."

They'd asked her to write down the name of her egg supplier but spoke very little to her. Before they left, they affixed a large sign on the front door that said the shop was closed by order of the county health department.

And the kitchen sink was leaking worse than ever.

Liddy looked out her shop window, dully watching the passersby.

Would anyone ever give her another chance?

At one point, she thought she saw one of the Moms, Lisa, across the street pushing a stroller. She turned to look at Liddy's shop but when Liddy waved, she only walked on down the city sidewalk.

Jenna straightened her skirt hem and smoothed her sweater down over her waist. She hadn't lived in Infinity so short a time (nearly her whole life) that she didn't know how men around these parts thought. They might Google and Angry Birds with the best of them (although somehow she could not envision Tucker playing video games), but not so deep down, they were good ol' boys who wanted their women feminine, church-going and aiming to please their man. She smiled as she stood on Tucker's porch, her purse tucked primly under her arm, her hands full of the still-warm casserole she had pulled out of the oven not an hour before.

When he answered the door, his grin made her heart leap into her throat.

Down, girl, she admonished herself as she smiled back at him. *So far, it's just dinner.*

"Hey, beautiful," Tucker said, opening the door to her. "Let me take that. It smells great." He leaned over and kissed her on the cheek as he took the casserole. "And so do you."

"Thank you, sir," Jenna said, keeping her voice pleasant and unruffled.

My God, he was tall.

Jenna walked in behind Tucker into his living room. "Hey, there, Haley," she said to the sour-looking teen slumped on the couch watching television. The girl looked up at her and then, without answering, back at her show.

"Hop up there, Haley," Tucker said, his words friendly, his tone not at all, Jenna noticed. "Take Ms. Dale's coat, then switch the TV off."

Jenna noticed the petulance with which Haley obeyed her uncle. She turned off the set and dropped the remote on the couch before approaching Jenna. On the way, she must've had a silent exchange with Tucker because by the time she was reaching for Jenna's coat, she had a pained smile on her face.

"I'll take your coat, Ms. Dale," she murmured, not looking at Jenna.

"Thanks, Haley," Jenna said, slipping out of it and handing it to the girl. She'd only seen Haley once before at Tucker's but already she could see that he was performing miracles with her. Was it just three years ago that Haley used to babysit for Drew? Jenna still couldn't reconcile the sunny, giggly pre-teen who used to play with her son with the sullen, heavyset girl taking her coat. "Drew still asks about you," she said, smiling. "I told him you're all grown up now and too busy for babysitting."

"Yeah, that's me," the girl muttered as she trudged down the hall with the coat. The rest of her sentence was muffled by her retreat.

Tucker returned with a glass of wine in his hands. He handed it to her as she walked to the couch. "How is Drew?" he asked.

"Oh, he's fine," she said. "I mean, it was a scare, but the doctor said he wasn't in any real danger."

"And you're sure it was from the cupcakes?"

Jenna seated herself and took a sip of the wine. She had taken a six-week wine course in Tifton last summer and it had dramatically enhanced her enjoyment of wine. This one was delightful, she decided. Light, yet complex. She was still no good and knowing why she liked a wine. But Tucker never missed a beat with pouring great wines. And somehow she was sure he hadn't taken a wine class.

"It was the cupcakes," she said firmly. "We're all waiting to hear back from the health department, but it was definitely the cupcakes. Didn't you hear that half the fifth grade at Pinckney got sick from their party on Friday?"

"I did, but Drew isn't in the fifth grade, right?"

"I had Mary Nell, one of women in my office, use Liddy to cater the goodbye party for our office."

"And you brought leftovers home to him."

"Yeah, sorry to disappoint you, Tucker," she said. "I know she's a friend of yours." She took a ladylike sip of her wine. "Are you two...?"

"Nope," Tucker reached for his own wine. "Just friends."

"Anyway, I tried to help. Sorry it didn't work out."

"I appreciate it, Jenna," he said. "I'm just glad Drew's okay."

"So, is Haley staying with you for awhile?"

"She is." Tucker repositioned himself closer to her on the couch, his arm stretched out behind her. "She was getting herself into some trouble and Daisy just isn't in a position to do what's necessary." He took a long swig of his wine and looked at Jenna. "Hell, I'm not sure I'm in a position to."

"But you're going to try," Jenna said. "That's great."

"I don't know how great it is," he said. "But she's family and I can't help but think her mama and daddy let her down pretty good."

"She was always real good with Drew," Jenna said. "Maybe we can do a picnic or something and bring the kids? Or how about the barn? If you can borrow a couple of horses, I'd bet they'd love that."

Tucker looked at her for a minute as if in thought. "That is one great idea, darlin'," he said. "That is one absolutely wonderful idea. I think Haley'd like that."

"Can you get some gentle horses? Drew hasn't ridden much."

"Liddy has a horse that's practically comatose—although he did unseat her a few weeks back."

Jenna frowned. "Was it the horse or pilot-error?" she asked.

He laughed. "Good question and I'm not sure exactly," he said. "But I'm sure Drew would be safe on Sugar and he's not getting ridden much these days. I'll ask Liddy. What about you? I didn't know you rode."

"Barrel-racing champ at my high school level in my senior year," Jenna said, almost primly. It was amazing how long the pride of that achievement still lived in her.

"You don't say?" Tucker's hand touched the hair that coiled in waves by her neck. "You are just full of surprises, aren't you, Ms. Jenna?" he said, driving a sudden thrill of tingling anticipation through her stomach and hips.

After dinner, they sat out on the front porch swing. Jenna loved the swaying feeling that Tucker regulated with his foot. Even on a porch swing, he always has to be the one to drive, she found herself thinking with amusement. Haley had opted to eat her dinner alone in the kitchen with her iPod and Jenna was glad for the time alone with Tucker. In the four years since her divorce, she had found very few people to date in Infinity. It was her policy to stay away from dating people she worked with, especially in a town the size of Infinity. That didn't leave much in the way of options.

She had seen Tucker at church on several occasions over the years and knew the generally accepted town pronouncement was that he was the eligible bachelor in town. You didn't need to know that he wasn't hurting for money—rumor had it he'd inherited a tidy sum when his daddy died—or that he had a pristine reputation for being helpful to the elderly and the sick and a good neighbor to anyone else. You just had to look at his striking good looks and six-foot three stature—My God, those legs went on forever!—to put him heads and shoulders above the rest of Infinity's men. Besides, most of them were married.

The only thing that could have made Tucker Jones absolutely perfect would have been if he could've been a widower. There was, unfortunately, an ex-Mrs. Tucker in the picture and like most divorce situations—Jenna's included—it was often a murky, complicated one that adversely affected innocent bystanders as well as the primary participants.

"The casserole was delicious," Tucker said for at least the third time, but Jenna was pleased to hear it again.

"I'm glad you liked it," she said. Nothing like giving a little taste of what you could have on a regular basis if you buy the whole package, she thought with a smile.

At that moment, she heard a buzzing sound and realized it was his cell phone. He disengaged himself from where he had his arm around her on the swing and pulled out the phone. He looked at the caller ID and frowned.

"Trouble?" she asked.

He pushed the ignore button and put the phone back in his pocket. "Nope," he said. "The only trouble I've got is doing her homework in there at the kitchen table." He turned his head to look into the living room. "That is, if she didn't sneak out the back door."

Jenna laughed. "It's a good feeling to know all your chicks are in their nests and safe for the night," she said.

He looked down at her and smiled. "Your mother sitting for Drew tonight?" he said.

She nodded, careful to keep her face turned up at him. "Safe and sound," she said.

He leaned down and kissed her.

Liddy sat at the front counter of her shuttered shop and alternately looked out at the night, watching a fluctuating street lamp spaz out a light show against the window pane while she sketched possible cupcake designs to be made with fondant. Most people liked basic cupcakes, she decided. Plain cake, yellow or chocolate, with butter cream frosting. Maybe sprinkles for the more adventuresome. That was all theory, of course, since she'd yet to sell a single cupcake to a single customer in her shop in nearly six weeks of being open.

Catering to companies, however, usually meant they expected something a little more ornate. They seemed to prefer the die-cut fondant pieces of stars and dots, with more elaborate builds. What with all the cooking channels and celebrity chefs, everybody with a cable connection or a dish knows what a cupcake could be if you didn't settle for ordinary. Liddy found she enjoyed designing and making these out-of-the-ordinary cupcakes. It was a hell of a lot more creative than swirl frosting and casting sugar.

She looked away from her designs at her empty front sales room. As helpful as her recent web searches had been for prompting her design ideas, she had yet to find any suggestions on how to promote a rural Georgian cupcake bakery closed for food poisoning.

She glanced at her cellphone on the counter and debated calling him again.

The laboratory report came back on the eggshells which tested positive for Shigella, a family of microscopic bacteria typically found in fecal matter. Common ways of contracting Shigella, the woman on the phone at the Center for Disease Control in Atlanta said is preparing food without washing your hands. The county health department told her that a rinse of diluted bovine fecal matter had been detected on the eggshells found in her garbage disposal.

If anybody was more upset about this than Liddy, it would have to be her egg man, Jessie, who literally howled on the phone when she called him and told him the verdict.

"It ain't my eggs!" He'd yelled to her on the phone. "I don't even got no cows on my farm. I get my milk for the butter from the Payne farm across the way there. There's no way them eggs coulda been contaminated when I dropped them off."

Liddy was inclined to agree with him.

She hung up the phone after thanking the CDC for calling with the information that they keep a record of all sources of infectious diseases, which now included Le Cupcake in Infinity, Georgia.

Now, as she sat on a chair in the kitchen and stared out through the window in the front room, she realized that all she really knew about the whole awful mess could be boiled down to the simple fact that there was a truth and a lie in all of it. The lie would be seen in the widespread perception that would rampage the county that she made cupcakes without washing her hands. And the truth, which couldn't be proved and so was much less likely to be believed, was that somebody had sprayed watered down cow crap on the outside of her egg shipment the night before.

But who?

Finding Infinity

Chapter 9

From where he stood by the pasture gate Tucker watched her push the saddle onto her horse. He had once corrected her positioning of the saddle on Sugar and he could see that she remembered what he told her. Even from this distance he could see her slide the saddle back off the withers and slip her hand between the pad and the horse's back. He watched her slim form stretch out as she stood on tiptoe to adjust the saddle. He could see the outline of her bottom in her tight jeans as she arched her back to tug the saddle into place and imagined himself standing behind her, his hands cupping that bottom... He shook himself out of the moment with a sigh and led Traveler down the dusty walkway toward her, waiting for the moment she would look up and see him.

"Hey, Tucker," she said, pulling one of the stirrups down and waving to him as he approached. "I thought I might see you here today."

"Beautiful morning for a ride," Tucker said, leading his horse to stand next to Sugar. "You just get here?" He knew exactly when she had arrived by the fact that she was still tacking up. In fact, he knew it fifteen minutes earlier when he had arrived, seen her car parked in the lot, Sugar's saddle still on its rest but his halter missing.

"About twenty minutes ago. You?"

Liddy came and stood between the two horses. Her hand rested on the stirrup of her saddle. Tucker couldn't help notice how pretty she looked today. Her long hair was gathered in a low ponytail but the untethered wisps around her face framed it charmingly. He didn't notice any makeup but she looked well rested for a change.

She acted like she wanted to talk.

"As you see," he said, clipping Traveler's lead rope to the bar and bending to root around in his tack tray by the near wall.

"I guess you heard Le Cupcake is temporarily closed," she said, watching him, an unsure smile on her face.

"I heard."

"Which won't make that much difference in my bottom line, since I haven't made any money on it yet." She laughed and he looked at her to see if it was real or nervous affectation. He couldn't tell. He reached for Traveler's front hoof and cleaned it before moving on to the next.

"Are you here to ride today or just checking on Traveler?"

That, he realized, must not have been easy. Up until now, he had made every move in her direction.

"I'm riding," he said, dropping Traveler's food bucket and straightening up. He massaged the small of his back. God, it was hell to get old. "Or at least Haley is. I'm giving her a couple refresher lessons."

"Oh, that's cool," she said brightly. "Haley's into horses?"

"She used to be," he said. "Not so much anymore."

"Ergo the refresher lessons."

"Exactly. Maybe another time?"

"Of course, yes."

Tucker looked over Traveler's shoulder to see Haley disengaging herself from his car. She tossed her headphones in and began to trudge toward him and the tack room.

"Right, well, guess I'll see you around," Liddy said, untying Sugar and pulling his reins over his head to lead him.

"Have a good ride," he said, smiling briefly at her, and then waving to get Haley's attention.

Well, that was weird, she thought as she swung up on Sugar. Not only is he screening his calls from me, he can barely endure my company even out at the barn. She turned Sugar in a tight circle and pointed him in the direction of the far pasture. She wasn't in the mood for exploring today. Now that she had the whole day to herself—in fact, whole days for the foreseeable future—she really didn't know what to do with herself. She still had the problem of figuring out how to meet her one catering job —guess they hadn't heard the news in Blackshear—without a working kitchen. Then there was Ben. He said he was coming for Thanksgiving and Liddy was so grateful that he wasn't backing out that she didn't bother mentioning the fact that not only did she have no place to make the dinner, and no money to make it with, but his grandmother would not be able to recognize either of them even if she could somehow manage the other two issues.

Thanksgiving was less than a week from today.

As she turned, she could see Haley standing next to Traveler with her arm stretched out along the stirrup. Tucker was obviously measuring her to get an approximation of how short to make the stirrups.

Well, it looked like all the effort she thought she'd gone to in order to save the friendship was for nothing. He obviously wasn't interested in being anything now that the romantic possibility was gone. She found herself hoping he was just feeling hurt and would come around eventually.

She applied her legs to Sugar and he moved, reluctantly away from the barn. As she approached the tack room to pass it, rehearsing the disimpassioned wave she was going to give him on her way to the pasture, he called to her.

She stopped Sugar and patted him on the neck.

"I forgot to say," he said, giving Haley a leg up onto Traveler, "if you need the use of a kitchen temporarily for your big catering job, you can use mine."

She was so surprised—and so grateful for the offer—that for a moment she just sat there and looked at him. "Tucker, thank you," she finally said. "That would be awesome. You are forever coming to my rescue, aren't you?"

He didn't answer but said a few quiet words to Haley who gathered the reins and slowly backed Traveler out of the lean-to.

She watched the girl move the big roan across the dirt walkway toward the sandy jumping ring facing the barn.

Liddy turned to Tucker who was following behind Haley on foot. "I mean it, Tucker," she said. "I really appreciate it."

"No problem," he said, wiping his hands on a small cloth and watching Haley enter the jumping ring. "What're you and your mama doing for Thanksgiving?"

She shrugged. "I think the assisted living is having some kind of formal group dinner for the inmates," she said. "Ben's coming, too."

Tucker nodded and then moved away from her to walk toward the jumping ring.

"We can probably do better than that," he said over his shoulder.

"Keep your legs under you," he called to his niece. "They're too far forward."

"I'm trying to," she said, not moving her legs.

Tucker watched Liddy walk up the farm road to the far pasture. She was obviously going to ride the perimeter. There was nothing much else to do in that pasture but walk and enjoy the weather. It hemmed the polo grounds—off limits to all barn boarders to keep it manicured and level—but it was well populated with cows so cantering and galloping were definitely frowned upon. Looks like Liddy wants to take it nice and slow these days, he thought.

"Uncle Tucker, are you sure my girth's tight?"

"Don't even think about going over one of these jumps, Haley," he said. "You can hop the cavaletti if you're bored."

His thoughts traveled back to this morning. Jenna had had to leave early because of her job, which was fine with Tucker. He liked her a lot. She was a solid woman. Attractive, strong and uncomplicated. She was from these parts, too, so she knew the score. She didn't have to have a translation or a language dictionary for all the unspoken messages that made any small southern town function.

Tucker's glance darted back to the direction that Liddy had gone in but she was already out of sight.

Yeah, he found himself thinking. *A whole hell of a lot easier. In every way.*

As Liddy slid into her SUV, filthy from her morning ride and more tired than she could remember ever being for this early in the day, she dug out her cellphone from the center console. She caught her breath when she saw that there were four missed calls from her mother's assisted living center. And one voice mail. She took a brief moment to glance in the rear view mirror and saw the fear in her eyes looking back at her.

She looked at the timing of the calls and could see that they had come in one right after another—about an hour ago—and then the voice mail and then nothing.

That can't be good.

Taking a long shaky breath, she put in her password for the voice mail, put it on speakerphone and set the cellphone down on the seat next to her. She turned and put both hands on the steering wheel, bracing herself against whatever words would come.

"Liddy? Are you ever going to visit your poor sick mother? What the hell do I have to do? Buy a damn cupcake to get some attention from you? If you're looking at your phone and deliberately not picking up—after the years I been picking up after you when you were little—I will know! So, this is your mother, by the way and please call me or better yet, get your butt over here as soon as you get this message. Love. Mama."

Liddy was laughing and shaking and moving the car out of the barn parking lot before the message finished. She played it three more times as she drove straight to the assisted living center.

Arisen from the dead. Back in the land of the living. Home in time for the holidays. Reclaimed and returned. Every happy turn of phrase and thought that described the return of this wonderful, cantankerous woman, her mama! swam through Liddy's head as she watched her mother eat pudding and point to something on the TV program that was on in the dining room. She had hugged her so much upon seeing her—her old self again!— that her mother had to finally push her away. After all, Liddy thought, watching her with joy and relief, she didn't lose me. I lost her.

"So when did you say Ben's coming home?" her mother asked, not taking her eyes off the muted TV show.

"The day before Thanksgiving," Liddy said.

"And you think we got an invite from Tucker Jones for Thanksgiving dinner?"

"That's what it sounded like."

"Well, I surely hope so," her mother said, handing Liddy her empty pudding cup. "They are all excited here about the green Jell-O and marshmallows they're gonna have. It's enough to make a person want to go gaga. Did they put me back on my pain meds while I was gone?"

"No, Mama. No way."

"Really?" Her mother looked away and then back at Liddy. She smiled. "Coz I feel pretty good."

"Not in pain?"

"No more than anybody my age has."

Liddy reached over and held her mother's hand. "Oh, Mama," she said. "I'm so glad. You did it."

"No thanks to the people here," her mother said, rearranging her napkin on he lap. "So tell me what the plan is. You quittin'?"

"The bakery?" Liddy leaned back into her chair, her eye involuntarily going to the movement on the television screen. "I don't know," she said. "Probably. I mean, I have the rent paid for another two months so I can stay there even if the bakery is closed."

"Kind of an expensive place to live if you can't open the bakery."

"Well, nobody ever came in anyway. But yeah, it kills me that this happened because people were starting to come around and I was getting catering gigs."

"And that's all over now?"

"Mama, I'd have to convince people to take a chance on not getting sick with me."

"How much?"

Liddy looked back at her mother before answering. "I figure I'd need about a grand to keep going for a bit and add some promotions to get people in. Why?"

"I have a little money."

"The hell you say."

"You're not nearly as amusing as you think you are, Liddy," her mother said. "I am offering you a loan."

Liddy leaned on the table in front of her mother, effectively blocking the woman's view of the television set. "I thought you didn't believe I should be doing this bakery," she said.

"Well, you're doing it, aren't you?"

Liddy stared at her mother and then looked away. Until this moment, it hadn't occurred to her that she had officially given up but she must have. Because she now found herself so stunned to think that she still had a bakery that might be successful, she couldn't put the words together to react.

"No thanks necessary," her mother said, gently moving Liddy's shoulder out of the way of her view of the television. "You're smiling face is all the thanks I need."

"Mama, thank you," Liddy said, taking her mother's hand again and shaking herself out of her daze. "Thank you, thank you for believing in me." She leaned over and hugged her tightly.

"Oh! Is that what this means?" her mother said, her eyes sparkling in spite of her waspish tone. "Well, if that's how you want to read it."

The next morning, Meryl's cousin finally arrived and fixed the leaky sink pipe. He surprised her by insisting on payment afterwards.

"The landlord pays for improvements and repairs to her property," Liddy said.

"Don't know nothing about that," the man said with more than a hint of truculence. "The plumber gets paid when he fixes shit." She wrote him a check, and made a mental note to get it sorted out with Danni-Lynn later. She tried to see some physical connection with the oaf who fixed her sink and Meryl. Cousins? It was hard to see. Thinking of Meryl gave her an uneasy feeling. Not only had she completely stopped dropping in or calling, the one conversation they'd had, she'd been practically rude. Had Liddy offended her in some way?

Liddy pulled out a calendar and counted the days she had left until Christmas—which should be her biggest retail opportunity of the year. If she did a bang-up job on the

Blackshear Centennial job that she got through Tucker, she just might be able to end the year in the black.

Liddy smiled and poured herself a cup of coffee. And oh yeah, she thought as she watched the people walk by her shop on this bright and crisp November day and remembered her mother's laugh this afternoon, be thankful. Be damn thankful.

The rest of the afternoon, Liddy spent shopping on the Internet for a few holiday items for the shop. She went out to the barn to groom and feed Sugar. On the way back, she pulled into the diner and got fried chicken take-out with slaw and lady peas for the whole nursing floor. She saw Tucker at the diner with Haley and another woman. She guessed, by her age, that she was Haley's mother, Tucker's sister, Daisy. Tucker smiled but didn't beckon her over so she smiled back and hurried out into the dusk with her supper and a faint sadness that felt like she had somehow lost a friend.

When she got home, her feeling of optimism and good humor returned as she carefully locked the door behind her and made a cursory check downstairs to make sure she had had no disturbances while she was gone. It had been awhile since anyone had actually been ugly to her face, but when she was alone and it was so quiet she could hear her own breath, she would often be reminded of the nasty boy and his threats in the assisted living parking lot.

She decided to eat before her bath so the food would still be warm. She stripped off her clothes that she'd worn to the barn and slipped into a pair of yoga pants and a light sweat shirt and parked her take-out in front of the television upstairs. An hour later, feeling relaxed and full, she took a hot shower and went to bed with a glass of wine and more sketches of cupcake ideas for the catering project.

While the money from her mother allowed her to try again, Liddy knew she had to start making money with the project or she will have just thrown all her chances away. This catering job with the town celebrating its one-hundredth birthday could definitely help make that happen. There would be newspaper and television coverage of the event. The town organizers had already mentioned to her that she needed to be available for interviews closer to the event.

Liddy spread out the sketches on her bedcover and counted fifteen original designs she intended to use in the project. It went without saying that the cupcakes had to taste spectacular—and she never had a problem with anyone not loving her cupcakes—but because there was going to be so much media around this event, it was every bit as important that they look like something off of Food Network. One thing these small towns hated, Liddy knew, was being portrayed or mistaken for a small town. Creating centennial confections that raised their visibility and positioned them on the same level as an Atlanta or a Charleston would do miraculous things for her reputation. And right now, a miracle was definitely what was needed.

She had called every family of a child who had gotten ill off of one of her cupcakes. She had promised herself she would apologize for them getting sick—and not explain or defend. All but two were gracious about hearing from her. She had tried to call Jenna a couple of times but had missed her both times and had not heard back from her.

The designs were original without being too self-conscious. Liddy knew the choice of design toppings posed a fine line to walk. Liddy had to please the event organizers, delight the statewide media, and satisfy the townspeople, themselves.

Not a small feat.

And if she couldn't do it, Mama's money or not, she was done. She could sell the jewelry and continue to sink money into the business or she could admit she had one last shot to make magic happen and after that...Liddy gathered up the sketches and put them on her beside table. She took a sip of wine. After that, she would have to go back to Atlanta and find some kind job, any kind of job. Whether her mother would agree to come with her was a battle Liddy knew she didn't have the energy to think about right now.

And the idea of going back to Atlanta—her old life—only without the big house and fat checkbook and endless days to concoct her next creative project, let alone dream about ever seeing Paris again—was enough to make her want to crawl under her duvet and not come out again.

She would make it work.

She had to.

Noticing the bathroom light was still on, Liddy got up to turn it off and brush her teeth when she decided to make one more check downstairs to make sure she'd put everything away. It had been nearly a week since Tucker had set the rat traps and while she had not heard any go off—and she was hoping she could pay one of the contractors to check them for her—she was still nervous about the possibility of finding a live rodent sitting on her kitchen counter.

Her thoughts migrated to thinking of Tucker. He definitely had that whole polite-but-freezing-you-out vibe going on that drove most women crazy. Was that it? Was he playing games with her? She had to admit that every time she thought of him now she got that queasy feeling in the pit of her stomach. He hadn't seemed like the type to play games but she had to admit it definitely felt like she was being manipulated.

She pulled on her slippers and went downstairs. She stopped at the bottom of the stairs and listened, holding her breath, praying she wouldn't hear anything.

The store was quiet.

Sighing, she moved through the kitchen, on the lookout for any silent shadow that looked like he might belong in a rodent cartoon movie about cooking but definitely not in her cupcake shop. She found herself smiling as she walked into the front room. Good thing she came down. The curtains on the display window were still up. She liked to sit at the front counter and look out, so she raised them every morning, even with the shop closed.

As she stepped to the window to tug on the curtain pull, she saw him. He was standing directly outside the window, his hands black with blood, his face turned away from the window.

The scream was out of her mouth before she ever saw his face.

Chapter 10

Dead possums weren't that pleasant to look at even when they were lying placidly on the side of the road. They were much less so nailed to your front door and stinking to high heaven.

Liddy sat in her kitchen and drank a cup of coffee. She had stopped shaking an hour ago but the police were still milling around her shop and outside so she was still awake.

One of the cops was particularly attentive to her. Tall, late forties, no wedding band. At first, when he showed up out of uniform, she assumed he'd been called on his day off. He explained that he was a plainclothes detective.

"So you didn't get a good look at him."

"I didn't see his face at all." She'd told him this before but she wasn't surprised he didn't want to let it go. The carcass nailed to her door was writhing with maggots and pieces of it had already started to fall off.

"You called pretty quick and our guys are out patrolling but so far they haven't seen anyone who didn't have a good excuse for being out. Let me ask you: is this the first time something like that has happened?"

Liddy looked into the kind, accepting brown eyes of the detective and felt a surprising rush of affection toward him, a stranger. Except for her mother, she hadn't told many people of the other instances of vandalism and ugly notes that had accompanied her first months in Infinity. Partly the reason for that was that everyone else she knew had been so against the idea of her opening a bakery in the first place and only feigned to support. She realized that this moment, sitting in her kitchen at two in the morning with Detective Riley Anderson, was the first time since she moved to Infinity that she felt someone was completely on her side with no interest in telling her she was screwing up.

"Tell me everything," he said.

When he spoke those three simple words, Liddy felt his care and concern for her like a warm hand held against her cheek. As she gathered her thoughts to pour out the whole story, she took a long breath and in the brief silence of the room heard the distinct sound of a rat trap hitting pay dirt. She told him about the broken mixer, the ugly notes requesting her immediate retreat back to Atlanta ("Like I'm some kind of invading Union army, you know?"), the food poisoning, even the run-in with Haley's boyfriend in the rehab center's parking lot. As she spoke, she watched him take notes in his little notebook and she wondered if he could make it all stop now. He looked so capable and official. He knew these people! He probably knew the words to make them behave.

"And there's nothing that you can think of woulda prompted any of this?" He looked around her front room. "You just opened up a little cupcake shop and the whole town went bat-shit?"

"Pretty much."

"Well, small Southern towns," he said as if that said it all. "Don't worry, we have the usual local scumbags we can run down. Although, this guy didn't appear to steal anything…"

"Maybe somebody gave him money to do this," Liddy offered.

He looked at her. "You think there's a single person masterminding this little hate campaign?"

Liddy started to answer and then changed her mind. At first, she thought of Carol who looked to be perfectly capable of hiring someone to nail a dead possum to her door. A nagging feeling in the back of her mind made her think there might be others. Maybe others even closer to home.

"Something like this," she said, carefully choosing her words, "is usually being egged on by someone. That's my guess anyway."

"But you don't know who that someone might be."

She shook her head. "I'm hated equally by all," she said, trying to make a joke of it but failing to add a smile to pull it off.

Riley stood up and tucked the notebook in his front shirt pocket. She noticed his eyes were brown. A very understanding and deep brown with flecks of gold in them. She felt better just having him in the shop with her.

"There was a note under the carcass," he said.

She looked at him and frowned. "A "piss off back to Atlanta" kind of note?" she asked.

He shook his head and looked around the room as if trying to assess it for security.

"Unfortunately, no," he said. "More a "stay here and you die" kind of note."

Liddy looked at the detective and felt her fingertips grow cold.

"Oh," she said. "That's not good."

"No."

"The other notes didn't want me dead."

"Do you have those notes?"

She shook her head. "I kept them for awhile but since I wasn't going to report them, it just seemed kind of sick to hang on to them."

"And tell me again why didn't you report them?"

"I...a friend advised me not to," she said lamely.

He walked towards the back kitchen. The police cruisers were parked in the back alley. "Some friend," he said.

After Riley and his crew let themselves out with assurances that they would be in touch later in the week, Liddy took a sleeping pill and went to bed. She'd deal with the dark red smear across her front door in the morning.

Later the next morning, Tucker watched her car pull into the barn parking lot. The news had reached him around midnight that Liddy's shop had been vandalized but not broken into. He had come to the barn almost two hours earlier to muck out Traveler's stall and, hopefully, in the process, get his feelings under control. He watched her climb out of her SUV. As she approached he noticed there was something different about her but he couldn't put his finger on what.

"Heard you had some excitement last night," he said before she could say hello.

"Don't suppose you heard who caused it?" she asked, tossing a bag of carrots down on a bale of hay and reaching past him for Sugar's halter.

"That would be you," he said. As soon as the words were out of his mouth he regretted them. He knew himself well enough to know he was angry, but he usually had better control.

"Me?" She stopped and turned to face him. Now he knew what it was. She wasn't wearing any makeup. He could see she had a dusting of freckles across her nose. She seemed so much more real, more vulnerable without her war paint. He had to consciously restrain himself from touching her.

"You think I caused somebody to nail a dead stinky possum to the front door of my bakery."

He didn't want to fight with her but he couldn't help the feeling of helplessness he had endured when he got the news that a squad had been dispatched to her place last night. And feeling helpless made Tucker angry. He hated feeling like he had no way to protect the ones he cared about, especially when they were too stupid or pig-headed to allow him to.

"I think insisting on going forward with a store that everyone in town has made clear they're offended by—"

"They are offended by a goddamn cupcake shop."

"Please watch your language. They've made it clear they don't want it so why do you insist on going forward with it? What needs to happen next? You getting hurt? This was a death threat, Liddy." He knew he was getting worked up but he couldn't help himself. She was deliberately walking into a dangerous situation and refused to listen to reason in order to avoid it. He gripped the broom handle tightly to avoid reaching for her.

"Look, Tucker," Liddy said, with both fists planted on her hips and squaring off against him in the tack room, "I appreciate the fatherly interest and all. But I don't need your usual scathing judgment on yet another 'poor' decision I'm making with my life. I mean, God, how is it that you think you know better than I do what I'm doing? Do you think I'm really such a fuck-up?" He winced when she used the word—as she knew he would.

"If even in the face of a damn threat against your life," Tucker said, knowing he was raking more vigorously than the dirt floor needed, "you won't listen to reason, I guess there's really nothing I can say." He found himself having to stifle a cough caused by the dust he was unearthing.

"I expect my friends to support my decisions," Liddy said. "Even if they don't agree with them."

"Those aren't friends," he said. "Those are employees."

"You don't want me to succeed."

"This has nothing to do with that."

"Liar."

Tucker looked at her angrily. "I know people in Atlanta throw certain words around like they mean nothing," he said, using every ounce of self-control not to pitch the rake out in the pasture. "But down here—"

People in Atlanta? Are you joking?"

The barn manager, an overweight middle-aged woman with wild hair, stuck her head in the tack room and both of them turned to face her.

"Either of you seen Jessica?" she asked.

Tucker turned away to store the rake and grab the keys to his truck.

Liddy shook her head in response. "Not this morning but I just go here. Everything okay?"

The woman took a dirty rag and wiped at a streak of sweat that was trickling down her cheek.

"No. Her mare threw a dead foal this morning. She's pretty upset. So's the mare, come to that."

Liddy gasped and put her hand to her mouth.

Tucker stopped moving out the door and turned to the woman. "What happened?"

"Not sure," she said. "The vet was there so I imagine there was nothing for it. The girl's been with her horse all morning but now she's missing and I just...oh, never mind, I think I see her." The woman abruptly left the tack room and Tucker could hear her calling for Jessica.

The two stood quietly in the tack room for a moment.

Finally, Tucker broke the silence. "I gotta go," he said and turned on his heel and walked off.

Liddy stood holding Sugar's lead rope in the opening of the lean-to and watched him leave in a cloud of red dust.

An hour later, after she had groomed and fed her horse, she led him to the pasture, feeling for his carrots in the pocket of her jeans. She fed him one, pulled his halter off, and released him into the pasture. "Guess this means Thanksgiving is off," she said as she watched him wander away. She glanced back at the barn and could see that the vet's truck was still there. Poor Jessica.

Overhead, she watched a red tailed hawk fly lazily in the early morning sky. It was already cold and she didn't expect the coming day to warm up any.

As she was backing the car out of the barn parking lot, her phone buzzed and she looked at the text screen. It was Tucker, which she registered as strange. Although he carried a cellphone, Tucker was proudly anti-technology.

"Sorry about this morning. Still on for T-Giving, I hope."

Three days later, Liddy arrived at Tucker's house a little after six in the morning on Thanksgiving Day. Ben had arrived the night before. He was sleeping in with instructions to pick up his grandmother at the assisted living center at ten o'clock.

Now she was elbow deep in flour and baking pans. So long had it been since she'd cooked a meal—she normally got take out at the diner or made sandwiches for herself—that she found herself blissfully transported by the fragrances of sage and sautéed onions. Haley stood with her in the kitchen and Liddy was surprised to discover she could actually be helpful. In addition, there were a few moments when she was almost pleasant. Or possibly that was a trick of the light in the kitchen. Liddy loved Tucker's big country kitchen. While they would all eat in the rarely used dining room off the family room, there was a heavy French country dining table in the kitchen. It looked scarred and scratched from generations of love and use but Tucker had said it wasn't from his family. He'd bought it at an auction five years earlier.

Liddy made the two pumpkin pies and the biscuits. Tucker was in charge of the turkey, just like Bill used to be, and the side vegetables and dressing were coming with various people who would be showing up later. If it weren't for the fact that Liddy didn't have a kitchen at the moment, she would've been one of those people, too.

As she moved around the big kitchen and intersected with Tucker doing the same, there was no hint of the row they'd shared at the barn two days earlier. Upon greeting her at the door this morning, he'd asked about Ben and her mother but gave no indication of remembering their fight.

Probably best that way, she thought, as she slid another tray of formed biscuit dough into Tucker's Jenn-Air double oven. *For somebody so intent on being Mr. Small-Town-Not-Putting-on-Airs,* she thought, *he sure has all the latest cooking equipment.* Her mother had mentioned once that Tucker had inherited some money when his father died a few years back. Liddy looked around. No way he could have all this on whatever a DEA agent--or whatever he is--makes.

At nine thirty, the three of them stopped for a break and took inventory of all that was left to do.

"I think we're in good shape," Tucker said, looking at the pies cooling on a rack. "The bird'll be out in another hour and people will start to show up by then. Haley, honey, pull out those celery stalks, will you? We can stuff 'em while we're sitting here."

Liddy noticed a complete absence of attitude when Haley got up to walk to the refrigerator. It occurred to Liddy while she was working with Haley in the kitchen that she should say something about their earlier contretemps, but decided not to risk spoiling the day. She did find herself wondering, if just for a minute, if maybe the creepy boyfriend might be on the guest list. She looked at Tucker who was squinting at the cup increment marks on a measuring pitcher and she couldn't imagine him putting up with someone like that, even to accommodate his niece, whom he clearly loved.

"Do you need reading glasses?" she asked, teasingly.

He looked at her and gave her a lopsided grin. "I have reading glasses," he said. "I just don't know where I set them down."

"Want me to hunt them down again, Uncle Tucker?" Haley asked, half out of her chair.

"Again?" Liddy laughed and looked at Haley to see if they could share this joke at Tucker's expense. Haley looked at her uncomprehendingly for a split second and then smiled shyly at her.

"Yeah, he has me looking for them on a regular basis," she said, smiling at her uncle.

"Thank you very much for that," Tucker said to Haley, but he was smiling too. He looked at Liddy and there was something in his eyes she couldn't place. Was that the first time Haley had teased him, she wondered?

Tucker clapped his hands together. "Okay," he said. "We need cream cheese and three spreading knives."

"I'll get them," Haley said, getting up again.

For reasons she couldn't absolutely articulate although she knew it had to do somehow with Haley, she and Tucker shared another smile.

Ben and Liddy's mother were the first to arrive. While she had seen him last night when he got in, Liddy found herself surprised and proud all over again to watch her son walk through the door with her mother. He was handsome and you could tell just by looking at him that he was so bright and ready for life. For Liddy, he lit up the room when he entered it. To see him here in Tucker's house, with his arm protectively around her mother —looking so frail and tottering—made her heart swell. Tucker and Ben shook hands, each taking the measure of the other but with broad smiles, each predisposed to liking the other.

Next came the Hispanic couple who ran the corner sandwich shop. They brought their three grown children--two women and a young man all of whom worked in Waycross. Liddy was surprised to see them. Their cooking assignment had obviously been the dressing. Senõra Jimenez apologized in advance if it was too spicy but insisted that Tucker had told her to make it her way.

When Jenna and little Drew came soon after, Liddy was only slightly less astonished than she was when she saw how Tucker greeted them. Jenna received a full-on kiss on the mouth and Drew a head tousling that indicated this was not the first time they had met.

Jenna and Tucker?

Liddy was as stunned as if somebody had tried to bring a giraffe to dinner. It's not that she hadn't thought that Tucker dated. But, as she watched Jenna put her hand on his waist, indicating an intimacy that was much deeper than dinner pals. She hadn't really envisioned Tucker with anyone until this moment. And it occurred to her that she did not like envisioning it right now one bit.

She found a moment to approach Jenna to apologize for the bad cupcakes.

Jenna shook her head and interrupted her apology.

"No need, Liddy," she said. "These things happen. Please don't give it another thought."

"But your son," Liddy said, looking at Drew as he spoke animatedly to her own son sitting on the couch. "He got so sick…"

Jenna put her hand on Liddy's shoulder. "And he's fine now," she said. "As you can see. Bounced right back and maybe not as in love with chocolate as he was before it happened." She grinned. "So you see. Silver lining."

"I just wanted you to know how sorry I was," Liddy said, finding herself examining the woman closely. *So this is who Tucker likes.* Liddy also found herself pleased to note that Tucker had chosen someone, while not exactly his own age, not that far from her own.

"How long have you known Tucker?" Liddy asked her.

"Tucker? Oh, years. We go to the same church."

"I see. That's nice."

Tucker came up at that moment. "Hate to break this up," he said, "but I could use some traffic copping in the kitchen about the timing for everything." He put his hand lightly on Jenna's shoulder.

"Oh, sure," Liddy said, turning to go into the kitchen.

"I meant, Jenna," Tucker said. "The baked stuff is all done, right? Why not take your apron off and relax. Does your mother need a drink?"

"Good idea," Liddy said brightly and, feeling overly sensitive, she went to pour her mother a glass of wine while Tucker and Jenna disappeared into the kitchen looking not unlike an old married couple. Yep, she thought. Just me and the other guests.

Jenna's son Drew, a blond boy of seven, was laughing at something Ben said, but he was also engaging with her mother. He must be mature for his age, Liddy thought, as she went to answer the knock at the door.

Detective Riley Anderson stood on the porch holding two bottles of wine.

"Oh, my God," Liddy said, grinning broadly. "It's you! How do you know Tucker?"

Riley entered the room and shrugged out of his jacket. "We don't really, but we have mutual friends on the force here in town. He was in the other day and made kind of a blanket invite."

"You two know each other?" Tucker frowned as he came up behind her. He had a dishtowel slung over one shoulder.

"Riley was my knight in shining armor the night of ye old possum nailing," Liddy said.

Haley materialized holding a tray of cream cheese stuffed celery and olives. Immediately, Liddy noticed that she was self-consciously smiling at Ben.

"May I offer you...?" she said, more to Ben than anyone.

Ben and Drew both took an *hors d'oeuvre* and Haley set the tray on the coffee table.

"Thanks for letting me crash the party," Riley said. "Hard day to be alone, Thanksgiving Day. Can I do anything?"

"Nope, we've got it covered," Tucker said, still examining Riley in what Liddy thought was beginning to border on rude.

She pointed to the two wine bottles on the coffee table. "Riley brought some wine," she said.

Tucker picked them up without looking at the labels and nodded to Riley. "Very nice," he said. "I'll put them with the others." He looked at Drew and gave him a wink. "Carry on," he said. "Dinner's almost ready." And returned to the kitchen.

Liddy sat down next to her mother and realized she had been clenching her teeth for much of the past two minutes.

"You okay?" Her mother patted her knee.

"Yep," Liddy said in what she instantly knew was a way too chipper tone to be believed. Least of all by her mother.

The rest of the day evolved into one of the more pleasant Thanksgiving Days Liddy had experienced, which was saying a lot, she mused, because it had always been a great day. She watched Ben throughout the day. This was only his second Thanksgiving without his Dad and while he laughed and teased Drew and got poor Haley's hopes up and generally was his usual charming self, she knew he was remembering the one who wasn't there on this important family day. A couple of times, she caught his eye as if to assure him: *I'm remembering him, too. I haven't forgotten.*

It was also the first Thanksgiving in twenty-five years that Liddy hadn't been one hundred percent responsible for hosting the day. She found the role of a guest amazingly relaxing. She didn't need to worry if the turkey was too dry or the dressing too glutinous. And while she didn't miss for one second the cozy interaction between Tucker and Jenna—clearly the host and hostess of this party—she wasn't sure she envied them their responsibility. At least not this time. This time she felt like she had her hands full with worry about her son, her mother and her limping, wounded travesty of a business. She glanced at Riley.

And whatever *this* is, she thought with a small smile.

So Tucker invited Riley to dinner because he'd be alone on Thanksgiving otherwise. Beyond that, they really didn't know each other that well. Just another example of the big hearted Tucker Jones, Liddy thought as she watched him pour another glass of wine for her mother.

After dinner, she shooed Haley away from the dishes. Riley rolled up his sleeves to help her. Senõr and Senõra Jimenez and one of their daughters had left right after dinner but the other two had stayed and were proving to be good entertainment, at least as far as the easily excitable Drew was concerned.

Riley and Liddy listened to his happy, high pitched laughter as they washed and dried pots and dishes in tandem.

"It was really a nice day," Riley said, taking a wet dish from Liddy and vigorously drying it with a dishtowel.

"It was, wasn't it?" she said, feeling the pleasurable, drowsy effects of the heavy meal and two glasses of wine. "Now we just need a couch to curl up on."

"And a football game," he said.

"I think Tucker has one on in the den," she said, handing him another dish.

"I've kind of lost my taste for college ball."

"I wouldn't say that out loud," she said. "College ball is the South's second big religion. Where are you from, Riley? Not from around these parts?"

"Everybody's from around these parts," he said. "Or they wouldn't still be here. I'm from Jesup. Married a girl from Indiana, worked up there for about ten years. Had a kid, moved to Macon, divorced. This job opened up in Infinity. I took it."

"Boy or girl?"

"Boy."

"You able to see him much?"

"The ex still lives in Macon, barely an hour away," he said, stacking his dried dishes on the kitchen table.

"Well, I guess it is if you can put the siren on and ignore the posted speed limit," she teased. "When did it end?"

"Long time ago. Do you know where these dishes go?"

Liddy shook her head and returned to the sink. "Tucker will put them away," she said.

"But anyway," he said, picking up the dishtowel again, "living away from the SEC for ten years kinda got me outta the habit."

"Well, it's still a big deal down here," Liddy said. "It helps people decide what they think of you if you're aligned with one team or another."

"That's perverse."

"Well, that's people."

"This sounds interesting." Tucker entered the kitchen, a glass of wine in one hand. "Why don't you two relax and come back to the living room." As usual with most things out of Tucker's mouth, Liddy noted, it was more of a command than a question.

"We're nearly finished, Tucker," she said. "It's you and Jenna that need to be relaxing. That spread was awesome."

"Yeah, it totally was," Riley said, reaching for another plate from Liddy. "Again, really appreciate you letting me tag along."

"It was group project," Tucker said. "Everybody helped make it great." He pulled up a barstool and perched on it. "So how long you been on the force in Infinity, Riley?"

Liddy nearly dropped the dish she was washing. She turned around, dripping suds on the floor and gave a look of daggers. With all the people he knew in town *and* on the local police force, there was no way Tucker didn't know the answer to that question.

"Two years now," Riley said.

Tucker ignored Liddy's glare. "Pretty happy there?"

"Pretty much."

"Haven't seen you around a whole bunch. You go to church out of town?"

Why was he giving Riley the third degree? Liddy was one comment away from lobbing a gravy boat at Tucker's head.

Fortunately, the doorbell interrupted the possibility of that and Tucker, frowning, got up, stood briefly in the archway between the kitchen and the dining room, and then moved to the front door.

"Last minute dinner guests?" Riley asked, his eyebrows up in a question.

"Don't ask me," Liddy said, wiping her hands on a hand towel. "But I think I'm ready for another glass of wine and to hear what everyone's doing in the other room. You?"

"Sounds good to me."

Before they even got to the living room, they heard the commotion at the front door. Liddy scanned the living room to locate Ben and her mother and then felt any growing anxiety lessen. If neither of those two were involved, she found herself thinking, whatever was going on out front had to be more of a spectator incident than something that affected her. Unless it was the cops come to report her bakery was on fire.

She heard Haley's shrill voice at the front door and the deep rumble of Tucker's trying to calm her. There were more voices, at least one other, that she couldn't immediately place.

Liddy craned her head to see past Riley's shoulder, expecting to see that nasty boyfriend of Haley's on the front porch.

"Who is it? Do you know?" Liddy asked Ben as she and Riley approached the couch.

"Whoever it is," Riley said. "Tucker isn't rolling out the red carpet for him."

"Actually, I think it's Haley's grandmother," Ben said. He shrugged. "She said she was coming to pick her up after dinner only not to say anything because Mr. Jones didn't know."

Liddy frowned. "Tucker's ex?" She looked at her mother. "I didn't know she still lived around these parts."

At that moment, Haley ran past the gathered group in the living room screaming: "I hate you! I hate you!" The sound elsewhere in the house of a bedroom door slamming followed within seconds. Riley got up and peered through the drapes at the porch landing.

Tucker still stood on the front porch talking with whoever it was that had ignited the outburst.

Liddy looked at Jenna who sat on the couch sipping wine. She shrugged at Liddy as if to say: what can you do?

Drew came over to his mother and spoke softly to her. "Mom, why is Haley unhappy?" Jenna stroked his hair.

"Never mind, sweetie," she said. "Haley's just a little overexcited from the day, is all."

Riley walked back to the couch. "He's still out there talking to her," he said. "Let's just say they are not using their indoor voices."

"Who is it?" Liddy asked. "Is it his ex, do you think?"

"I don't know," he said. "Who ever it is, she's a total knock out. And she has a Southern Realtor's plate on her Mercedes."

Liddy's mouth fell open and she stared at him. She turned her dumbfounded gaze onto her mother, who snapped her fingers.

"*That's* what I keep forgetting to tell you," she said. "Our realtor is Tucker's ex. Is there any more wine in the kitchen, do you know?"

Finding Infinity

Chapter 11

Meryl is Tucker's ex-wife?

Liddy stood in the kitchen gulping Chardonnay from a large wine goblet. She didn't know who to be madder at, Meryl or Tucker. When she thought about how her friendship with Meryl had tanked in the last couple of days, she opted for Tucker.

"Why didn't you tell me Meryl was your ex?" she said to him as soon as he walked into the kitchen, looking tired and agitated.

"What?" He looked around the kitchen as if he were surprised to see her there.

"All this time I've been talking about my 'best friend Meryl,' and you never said a word."

"Yeah, okay, Liddy," he said, tiredly. "I should've mentioned it."

"Damn straight you should've."

Riley walked into the kitchen holding a glass of wine and looking from Tucker to Liddy.

"What would it have mattered?" Tucker said, resting his hands on his hips. "You and she were such great buds. I didn't see the point."

"Or maybe you thought I might feel I needed to choose between you." The words were out of her mouth before she even knew the thought was in her head.

Riley looked at her and then at Tucker. "Are you two together?" he asked. "Because I thought..." He turned in the direction of the living room where Jenna sat within earshot.

"We're not together," Tucker and Liddy said in unison.

"Besides, I thought you knew," Tucker said.

"Okay, that's a lie," Liddy said.

"How could you live in this town five minutes and not know?" he said. "Everybody knows everybody's business."

"He's got a point there," Riley said, downing his wine. "You'd've had to work at not knowing."

Liddy looked at Riley as if she hadn't noticed him in the kitchen before now.

"In case it's slipped y'all's minds," she said, reaching for the wine bottle again. "I've been really busy these last few months trying to run a business." She turned to Tucker as if he were responsible. "In a town that hates me."

"I thought that didn't matter to you," Tucker said. Liddy saw him glance at the kitchen clock as if gauging how much longer this particularly trying Thanksgiving Day was going to last.

The gesture infuriated her.

"Is the face-to-face threat of bodily harm that I received in the parking lot of my mama's assisted living an exaggeration?"

She could see she had hit pay dirt. Tucker's eyes widened and he straightened up as if ready to deal with the perpetrators immediately.

"You were personally threatened?" he said.

"Yes, I was threatened," she said, feeling tears edging into her voice, "and by Haley's boyfriend, if you want to know." There. It was worth the cheap shot to see the startled look on Tucker's face. Guess you're not the only one who can keep a secret, she thought with satisfaction as she watched the shocked look in his face turn to anger.

"When?" he said, coldly. "When did he approach you?"

"Someone *threatened* you?" Ben said as he moved into the doorway to the kitchen. In her frenzy to make Tucker Jones eat his words, she hadn't noticed her son come in.

"It's…it's nothing, Ben," she said, trying to smile. "Just small town orneriness." She glanced at Tucker and gave him a meaningful look. *Don't say anything upsetting in front of my boy.*

146

She watched Tucker struggle with his emotions and then visibly shake himself like a hunting dog emerging from a duck pond.

"Your mother's right," he said to Ben. "It's just small-minded people having trouble adjusting to something new. It's nothing serious." He looked at Liddy and narrowed his eyes.

She could hardly torture him with Ben standing right there in the line of fire so Liddy waved her hand in the air as if to indicate it was all nothing.

"Just silliness," she said to Ben. "Like Mr. Jones said. They'll get used to me soon." She turned to Tucker and said, biting off every word: "It has been a major pain in my ass, however, in the meantime." She turned and walked into the living room.

"Come on, Mama," she said. "Let's move this show on down the line."

"And I was having such a nice little chat with Jenna, here," her mother said, gathering her purse and her cane.

"Sorry," she said to Jenna. "We're all pretty ready to call it a day."

"Well, obviously, *you* are," her mother said, pointedly, but Liddy could see her mother was tired and she wouldn't argue about leaving.

Riley and Ben came into the living room and Jenna excused herself to go to the kitchen.

"I cannot tell you how many times I meant to tell you about that real estate lady, Liddy," her mother said. "It's hell to get old," she cackled.

"Doesn't matter, Mama," Liddy said, helping her mother on with her coat. "Ben, you can head on back to the bakery. I'll take your grandmother back." She handed him a set of keys. "Riley?" she turned to him and gave him a hug. "I'm so glad you could be here today."

"It was a great Thanksgiving," he said, meaningfully, looking into her eyes. "I'd like to call you up—apart from the investigation—if you'd be open to that."

"Yes," Liddy said, glancing toward the kitchen where Jenna and Tucker were talking. "I'm wide open to that."

"Are we going or do I have to drive myself home?" her mother said through a yawn.

Tucker and Jenna appeared and walked into the living room. Liddy watched her son shake hands with both of them and thank them for the day. When it was her turn, she found she really didn't have the energy to be mad at Tucker. Something about seeing him standing there in his jeans and plaid shirt and Jenna's arm curved proprietarily around his waist just seemed to take the fire out of her.

Tucker handed her a piece of paper.

"What's this?" she asked.

"Code to the garage door to get in tomorrow," he said. "Don't you have that big catering project you need to use my kitchen for?"

The truth was, in the pleasure and then upheaval of the day, she had temporarily forgotten. She held the paper and looked at it.

"Oh, Tucker—" she began.

"I'll be gone all day," he said. He nodded to the porch where Ben stood talking to Riley. "If you want to bring in your kitchen helpers, feel free. And I can personally offer Haley's services, too."

She realized that the day was definitely finishing up with mixed reviews as a warm feeling washed over her. "You're a lifesaver," she said to him. "Thank you."

She leaned over and gave Jenna a half-hug and nodded to Tucker. "It was a great Thanksgiving day, Tucker," she said.

"It was," he said, his eyes giving away nothing but not looking relaxed or at a peace either.

"But somebody should've told you," she said, pulling on her coat, her hand on the door knob and Riley waiting for her on the porch, "Most people tend to reserve the fireworks for the Fourth." She turned on her heel and walked out the door. "Goodnight, y'all," she said over her shoulder.

The next two weeks flew by in a blur of sprinkles and colored casting sugar. As promised, Haley helped her bake and decorate the two hundred "designer" cupcakes for the town of Blackshear's centennial celebration. She had expected the baking and decorating to take a full twenty hours. It took forty. Ben had spent the weekend either mixing batter with Liddy in Tucker's kitchen or taking her mother to the mall. When Haley realized that the project was going to involve more than just baking and frosting cupcakes, she became Liddy's assistant in every sense of the word. In the end, she even contributed to a design suggestion that Liddy thought showed real creativity and promise. Careful not to step off the pathway of culinary conversation, the two spoke passionately about fondants, sugar buttons and crème centers for hours. Liddy had even gone so far as to mention to Tucker that Haley might be a candidate for culinary college.

Once, when they were waiting for cupcakes to come out of the oven, they played cards at Tucker's kitchen table. Liddy could not see any sign of the scowling teenager who had stolen from the cash register and called her a bitch just a few months earlier. Haley looked relaxed. When Tucker was in the room, she looked downright happy.

"You don't find it boring living here with your uncle?" Liddy asked as she played a trump.

"Not as long as he has cable and Wi-Fi," Haley said.

"How much more school do you have?"

"I'm a junior," Haley said. "I hate school but Uncle Tuck said he didn't love it either."

That probably wasn't true, Liddy thought.

"You've really got a gift for pastry."

"It's easy." Liddy could tell the girl was pleased at the compliment.

"Not for everyone. You're a natural."

Haley gathered up the cards and started shuffling them. Liddy watched her look at the clock to see how much more time the cupcakes would need in the oven.

"I'm sorry about you and me earlier," she said quietly.

Liddy was surprised. She assumed that they would just go forward and pretend it had all never happened.

"That's okay," she said.

Haley looked at her as if debating telling her something. Finally, she put the cards on the table and her hands in her lap.

"I broke up with Dennis," she said. "That guy who was with me at the shop?"

Liddy nodded.

"I don't know why I was with him in the first place. He's such a tool."

"We all make mistakes," Liddy said.

The girl looked up at her and smiled faintly. "Uncle Tuck says best to get them out of the way early so you can get on with going forward."

"Sounds like something your Uncle Tuck would say," Liddy said, smiling.

"You know Dennis was a crack head."

Liddy didn't say anything.

"I used to do stuff with him," she said. "Stuff I'm not proud of." She looked at Liddy. "Stuff if my uncle found out about, I would just die, him knowing."

"I know," Liddy said, reaching out and touching the girl's hand. "His good opinion is worth the work to get."

"I would just die," Haley said, looking out the window, lost in her thoughts for a moment. When the bell for the oven timer went off, they both jumped and then laughed that it had caught them unawares.

As Haley reached for the oven mitts, she looked at Liddy and smiled. "Thanks, Liddy," she said. "I didn't feel good about something sitting between us like it was, you know?"

Liddy got up to help pull cupcake tins out of Tucker's oven. "I'm glad we talked about it, Haley," she said. "And I'm real glad I've got you to help me with all this. You've been a lifesaver."

Haley didn't answer as she set the baked cupcakes on the cooling rack, but Liddy could see by her face that she was pleased.

After two days of virtually living at Tucker's house with Haley and Ben, Liddy drove to Blackshear and delivered her opus confections to the township well before the deadline. In the flurry of everything, Ben took his leave but not before Liddy was able to extract a promise that he would consider going back to school for the summer semester. The girlfriend element seemed to have been taken out of the equation. Afraid he was deliberately avoiding mentioning her, Liddy asked him outright.

"Are you still living with Julie?"

Ben made a face. "It's not like that, Mom," he said.

"So is that a 'no?'"

"I'm not living with her, no," he said. "I'm staying with Joe right now in his dorm." His friend, Joe, was attending Southern Poly Tech in Atlanta.

Liddy had tried all weekend to ensure her frustration didn't come out in her conversations with him. *It wasn't easy.*

"So what do you do all day?" she asked.

"Mom..." He said it as if he were terminally weary of answering this question over and over again.

She held her tongue and waited.

"I'm just not sure what I want to do, okay?" he said, finally.

"I just don't see why you can't ruminate on 'what to do' while you're still enrolled at the University of Georgia."

Okay, that sounded snarky. Even she could hear it.

"Please say you'll consider going back for summer session," she said.

"Fine. Yes," he said, giving her a kiss on the cheek.

The week after she'd delivered the big cupcake job to Blackshear, she sat in the front room of her shop enjoying a cup of coffee with Riley. She hadn't seen or heard from him since Thanksgiving and while he was on duty now, she was very pleased he dropped by.

"So, Ben get off okay?" he asked.

"Yep," she said. "Although why he had to leave so early, I don't know," she said. "It's not like he has a schedule to worry about."

"And no word back yet on the Centennial celebration?"

Liddy smiled at Riley. "You mean, have my cupcakes killed anybody yet that I know of?"

"That's exactly what I mean," he said, grinning. "Haley really got into it, too, didn't she?"

"I wish you could've seen her when she first worked for me," Liddy said. "She's come a long way."

"Ahhh, the Power of Tucker."

Liddy tried to hear sarcasm in Riley's voice but if it was there, it was too subtle to detect.

"He's done miracles with her," she said.

"And what about you finding out your ex-best friend was his ex-wife. That must've been a shock."

She looked at him with curiosity. "She was never my best friend," she said.

"Still weird not to know it. Why didn't she tell you? And the way you went after Tucker after you found out—it was like he'd cheated on you or something."

"Don't be silly."

"Just saying what it sounded like. And there's nothing between you two?"

"Riley, no, there isn't, as I know I've said."

"So there's room for you and me to be something."

He leaned over and touched her hand. She detected the faintest whiff of coffee and peppermint on his breath when he drew near. Before she could answer, her cellphone vibrated against the varnished oak counter. She could see before she touched it that it was Jenna.

"Hey, Jenna," she said into the phone, but smiling at Riley. "What's up?"

She listened quietly as Jenna excitedly told her about three more holiday orders she was calling about for some friends.

It was all starting to happen now, Liddy thought as she scribbled down the details on a pad of paper on the counter. The holiday orders were beginning to roll in. At this rate, although she'd still finish the year in the red, she'd be able to make major inroads to catching up on her losses, maybe even think about paying her mother back for the loan. She disconnected the phone with Jenna and smiled at Riley who was looking at her expectedly.

All of this and a handsome romantic interest to sweeten her holidays even more.

"That was Jenna," she said. "She's got three more holiday orders for me."

"That's terrific, Liddy," Riley said. "Sounds like Jenna's really looking out for you."

"She's the best," Liddy said, underlining the quantities she'd written on her note pad. "And she reminded me that the community center dance is tonight. She and Tucker are going. You interested?"

"I am if you are," he said. "It appears you didn't poison the town of Blackshear. I say, tonight we celebrate."

Impetuously, Liddy leaned over and kissed him on the mouth. "That's the best idea I've heard in a long time," she said.

As soon as she saw them together, Liddy knew immediately that something didn't feel right. Somehow it was worse than at Thanksgiving. The feeling in the pit of her stomach blossomed into full-on nausea when she saw the two of them and how close they appeared to be. She and Riley entered the noisy community center and were quickly waved over to their table by Jenna and Tucker. Jenna was wearing a long sleeve blouse under a paisley jumper of some kind. Her hair had been teased up high and then pulled back to show her cheekbones off to best advantage. The only makeup that Liddy could see was the peach lipstick that went perfectly with Jenna's flawless complexion. When they approached, Tucker stood up, shook hands with Riley and waited until Liddy seated herself.

She looked around at the community hall, done up for the dance and looking not unlike a high school gymnasium on prom night. It looked old-timey to Liddy. But nice.

The drink choice was either strawberry punch or beer. Liddy chose beer along with Tucker and Riley but she noticed more than a few men around them sipping the punch. Must be spiked with moonshine, she thought, wryly.

Jenna leaned over and touched Liddy's hand. "Hear anything from Blackshear?"

Liddy laughed. "Everyone is just so sure I've poisoned another town seat!" she said. "No, no word yet."

"I'm sure you'll hear nothing but raves," Jenna said, slipping her hand back around Tucker's arm as she snuggled next to him at the table.

"I have high hopes," Liddy admitted. "Oh! How was the ride today?" She looked at Tucker. "Was this the afternoon y'all were going to borrow Sugar?"

Tucker nodded. "It was good," he said. "But Sugar's a whole lot stronger than I remembered."

"See?" Liddy said. "It's not me. He's willful."

"Or maybe it is you," Tucker said, an amused glint in his eye. "Because he wasn't this bullheaded until you started riding him."

Liddy gasped as if to feign indignation. "Are you suggesting—"

Riley interrupted the playful exchange: "So who all went out?" he asked.

Jenna ticked off the people on her fingers. "It was me, Tucker, Haley, Drew and a friend of Drew's from his class."

"On two horses?"

"I borrowed a couple more," Tucker said. "And I mostly walked."

"He was very gallant," Jenna said, looking up at him. "Everyone else's fun before his. He's like that in a lot of ways," she said mischievously.

Tucker coughed and shifted in his chair, which forced Jenna to disengage for a moment before reattaching herself.

Liddy watched the two and reached for her beer. So, it's like that, she found herself thinking. She turned and watched the dancers on the floor while Riley and Tucker talked about the possibility that the coming cold front might contain tornadoes.

Good for them. I'm happy for them.

Riley scraped back his chair, stood and offered his hand to Liddy.

"Got enough energy after conquering the world of baked goods and reestablishing your eminence as local small business hero to dance?"

Jenna giggled, reinforcing to Liddy the belief that she was clearly having a wonderful time.

"You don't talk like you're from around here," she said to Riley.

"I've been out of the loop for awhile," Riley said to her with a smile. "But when it comes to the South, it's a dance I remember the steps to all too well." He winked at her and led Liddy to the dance floor.

It was a slow dance for which Liddy was grateful. Moving away from the table and the lemony, male scent of Tucker mixing with the overly sweet floral tones of Jenna was a relief. She should have seen it at Thanksgiving, she knew then that they were a couple. But it was only now that she saw that they were really together in every sense.

"How did Tucker meet Jenna?" Riley asked as they danced.

"At church, I think," Liddy said. "They're pretty well matched in every way."

"You think so?" Riley frowned as he looked over her shoulder at the couple. "I'd say he was too old for her."

"He's only fifty," Liddy said pulling back to get a better look at Riley. "How old are you?"

"Old enough," he said, laughing.

When she didn't respond, he rubbed her arm and frowned.

"You okay?"

"I am," she said. "Just tired and a little overwhelmed, I think," she said, smiling up at him. "I've still got a lot to do this month if I want to pull off the resurrection you seem to think I've already done."

"You'll do it," he said.

"I can't thank you enough for all the support you've been to me, Riley," she said.

"I'm glad," he said as he leaned in and kissed her on the cheek.

As Riley danced her near the table, she saw Jenna lean up and kiss Tucker on the mouth and her stomach clenched.

Did Tucker just go around kissing anybody whose face happened to be near his? Is that all their kiss was?

"What're you thinking?" Riley said.

She looked back at him and shrugged. "Oh, you know," she said. "Butter cream and powdered sugar and nonpareils. The usual."

The song ended and she pulled out of his arms to applaud the little three-man band of two guitars and a drummer that anchored the dance floor. When they returned to the table, Jenna stood up and grabbed Liddy's hand.

"Lipstick break?" she asked. Liddy could see she was a little drunk.

"Sounds good," she said, picking up her purse. She smiled at the two men standing at their table and walked arm in arm with a slightly wobbly Jenna to the ladies room.

"This is great," Riley said to Tucker as he lifted his beer glass. "Really good music, too."

Tucker leaned back in his chair. "Yep, this group has been playing at dances in Infinity since we were all in high school."

"So you're from Infinity?" Riley asked.

Tucker's eyes narrowed. "No," he said. "But I've known these boys that long."

"Liddy said you and Jenna met at church?"

Tucker frowned. "I guess that's right," he said.

"It looks to be serious?"

"Serious enough."

"She seems like a great girl, Jenna. Very sweet."

"She is. You dating Liddy?" Tucker recognized that he liked Riley well enough but something about him was off-putting.

"Not officially. We're working in that direction though."

Maybe that was it.

"That's fine," he said as he nodded to the returning ladies. "Wish you the best with that one."

When they returned from the ladies room, it was all Liddy could do not to shove Jenna into Tucker's waiting arms at the table and stomp out to the parking lot. Jenna had done nothing but gush about how wonderful and loving and accomplished Tucker was to the point that Liddy had to consciously remind herself how much business Jenna had put her way. In fact, as she was applying her lipstick she was in the middle of reminding herself of precisely that when Jenna burbled out the fact that it was Tucker who had encouraged her to go in to Liddy's shop and buy cupcakes from her.

Tucker.

So it wasn't really Jenna who had been her initial patron. It had been Tucker. Who had yet to buy a single cupcake, himself. On top of that, Liddy wasn't sure why she was so mad about it all. As she looked in the restroom mirror and saw the forty-six year old Liddy next to the forty-year-old (tops) Jenna, she felt like all of it was just a hopeless mess. *What am I trying to do?* she wondered. *At my age?*

And yet she really liked Jenna. She was open and friendly and sweet. In fact, she could absolutely see why Tucker liked her. Loved her, probably. With that thought, her spirits began to tank and the noise and music in the place only served to remind her that everyone else was having fun except her.

Back at the table, she was relieved to see that Riley was ready to leave if she was ready to.

After they said their goodbyes and moved to leave the community center, Riley held her arm as if she might slip any minute. She turned to look back and saw that Tucker was watching them leave. Jenna was talking, oblivious to the fact that Tucker's attention was divided.

He doesn't like Riley, Liddy thought, turning and putting her arm around Riley's waist. *And he really does believe he can control the world.*

It was clear that Riley wasn't ready to call it a night.

Liddy poured him a second glass of wine and hoped her accompanying yawn would alert him to the fact that she was ready for him to leave without having to tell him to.

"I still don't know why you won't come out with me to the barn tomorrow," she said, sinking back into the couch holding her own wine. "It'd be fun."

"I'm not really a large animal lover," Riley said, reaching over and moving a curl of hair from her eyes. "I got stepped on once and it cured me."

"We can just feed him if you want," Liddy said. "We don't have to ride."

"Rain check?"

Liddy laughed. "Permanently, right?"

Riley put his wine down and leaned in to kiss her. As soon as he did, Liddy got a flash of memory of the only other time she'd been kissed on this couch. This time she didn't drop her wine glass.

"I've been waiting a long time to properly kiss you," he said in a whisper that was scented with wine and beer.

Liddy kissed him back and it was then that she knew.

She didn't want this. Not like this. Not with him.

"It's late, Riley," she said.

He was a good sport about it, she had to give him that. Although as this may or may not qualify as a first date, he had to have had little to no expectation for intimacy. In Liddy's experience with men, that usually didn't stop them from having expectations. In any case, he exited like a gentleman, reminding her to double check all the locks behind him.

After he left—even with all the lock checking—she realized she felt uneasy, as if someone was in the shop with her. She couldn't shake the feeling and found herself pausing on the stairs to the bedroom to listen for any indication that there might be somebody else in the shop with her. She heard nothing unusual. But the feeling did not go away.

An hour later, she woke to the vibration of her cellphone on the bedside table. When she snatched it up, fearful that it was from the rehab center, she saw it was the number for the barn.

"Hello?" She sat up in bed and tried to see the face on her digital clock. Midnight.

"Liddy? This here's the barn where you board your horse?"

"Yes, is everything okay?" Liddy felt her stomach clench. Obviously everything was not okay.

"Well, no ma'am, not really. We think someone done stole your horse."

Chapter 12

By the time Liddy had pulled on a peasant skirt and a sweatshirt and driven out to the barn, thirty minutes had passed. As she drove into the darkened parking lot of the barn, she noticed Tucker's truck was the only other vehicle in the lot. She saw him standing under the lone searchlight in the tie-up area outside the tack room talking with the barn manager. Two horses stood with him.

Liddy parked and as she walked over to where they were standing, she heard the manager say: "Well, I'll leave you to it then. Need to get my beauty sleep." As Liddy passed her on the way to where Tucker waited for her, the woman said: "He'll update you. Sugar's fine. G'nite."

Liddy could see Sugar was fine, if a little wild-eyed. Funny, she thought as she approached Tucker, she could almost say the same thing about him.

"What happened?" she asked. "Why are you here?"

"I'm here," Tucker said as he unclipped both horses and handed one of the leads to Liddy, "because the barn manager called me in the middle of the night to tell me my horse had been stolen."

Liddy took the lead rope and looked at Traveler.

"Same with me," she said. "So what was the deal? They weren't stolen?"

"No, they got out of the paddock on their own and were wandering the countryside. I found them both trotting down US41 when I was on my way out here."

"Wow, that's lucky," Liddy said as she walked with him to the pasture gate.

"That's one way to look at it," Tucker said as the opened the gate for them.

Liddy unsnapped the lead from Sugar's halter and shooed him away from the gate. "Go on, Sugar," she said. "I don't have any carrots for you tonight."

When Tucker released Traveler, he turned and latched the gate with a loud thud.

"Is there something the matter, Tucker?" She could tell he was mad. She couldn't for the life of her figure out why his anger seemed to be directed at her.

"I had other things to do tonight besides traipsing around the highway leading two damn horses back to the barn," he said. "Things like sleeping."

"Well, you seem to be mad at me," Liddy said, grabbing his sleeve as he marched back to the tack tavern. When he didn't speak, she jerked his sleeve harder. "Wait, you think it's my fault that they got out?"

He pulled his sleeve out of her grasp. "Did you or did you not put your horse up for the farrier?"

"I did! Just as you showed me. I put him in the damn pen thingy with Traveler."

"The paddock. And then latched the gate."

"Of course."

"You remember latching the gate? Because the latch on the paddock is different than the pasture gates."

"I…"

Now that he mentioned it, Liddy wasn't sure. She had a distinct memory of closing the gate but not hearing the resounding click she normally heard when she closed the pasture gate. "It's…different?"

"Dear God, Liddy. Did they not even teach you how to close a damn gate up there?"

"No! No, they did not. Are you happy? I can't even close a gate. If there's a trick to it, a small-town only-people-in-bumfuck-know-how-to-do-it-trick to it, then I guess I didn't properly close the damn gate." Liddy was shaking she was so angry at him, at herself. When she looked at him, she had to look away from those piercing blue eyes bearing down on her. She felt like a naughty schoolgirl being reprimanded by the principal. It made her want to throw a chalkboard eraser at his head.

He stood with his hands on his blue jeaned hips in the very definition of sexy cavalier. He stood like he wanted an answer, like he'd damn well better get one, too. She felt the panel slats of the stall behind her and she realized that she'd been backing up as they fought. She hadn't noticed that he'd stepped forward with every assault, every angry question, and that she'd retreated in a dance of perfect counterbalance.

Knowing she was in the wrong, knowing it had been her fault, even knowing he was off limits all combined to creating a near unquenchable feeling in the pit of her stomach and between her legs. He looked like he wanted to eat her up or turn her over his knee, she couldn't tell which and at this point, she didn't care as long as he touched her.

If she was reading his expression right, she was going to get her wish.

Without removing a fraction of his scowl and without warning his hands were on her and she launched herself into his arms. Their lips met with a hungry desperate need that felt like it had been too long overdue. When he plunged his tongue into her mouth, she thought she would melt into him, so exquisitely did the kiss fill her up. She ran her hands down his long back and to his belt buckle. She didn't even care that she hadn't brushed her teeth or that she looked like a Goodwill bag lady in her skirt and sweatshirt. She had never felt a more powerful need than the ache between her legs that insisted he be in her, now. She groaned against his face as she felt his hand pull her skirt up and then jam between her legs inside her panties. She clenched her thighs around his hand and gasped out loud as his fingers slipped into her.

They toppled to the floor of the stall, her lips kissing his beautiful full lips, his unshaven face, smelling of coffee and peppermint. She arched her back and felt the world whirl away in a rush of color and motion.

"Oh, my God," she whispered, tightening her legs around his strong, long back as if to keep him there forever, pinning them to the floor of the sweet straw, the sounds of the horses nickering in the background. "If you apologize for this," she rasped, "I swear I will take a pitchfork to you." She heard him laugh and felt that laugh—deep and rumbling—into her innermost core. He relaxed the arm that had been keeping him above her and eased himself down to her.

"No way in hell," he said.

Later that morning, Liddy stopped for McMuffins for everyone at the nursing station and two big cups of diner coffee which her mother preferred to "the swill" on tap at the center. She whistled the whole way to the rehab center, the enticing fragrance of coffee and eggs filling her car. After she left the barn this morning, with warm kisses and nuzzling from Tucker making it almost impossible to drive away, she had had no difficulty falling happily asleep for the rest of the night.

Of all the things she had ever been wrong about in her life, thinking she shouldn't date Tucker Jones had been the most wrong. As she showered and brushed out her hair before leaving to visit her mother, she had the unmistakable feeling, deep deep down, that the best part of her life was just about to begin.

She and her mother ate their late breakfast at an outdoor patio table in one of the larger courtyards. It was a warm day for this time of year—Christmas less than two weeks away—but her mother wore a wool cardigan buttoned up to her chin. She finished her egg sandwich and Liddy gave her the rest of hers.

"You're in an awfully good mood," her mother said suspiciously. "One of the nurses aides mentioned she'd heard from a cousin who works at the Happy Holler liquor store on US41 that you and Tucker Jones had a late night rendezvous at the barn."

"Dear God! This town really does know everything that goes on."

"What else is there to do in a small town?"

"We both got calls that our horses had been stolen."

"Well, that's a bit of luck anyway," her mother said absently, looking for a tissue she'd stored up the sleeve of her sweater. "Was he insured?"

"He wasn't stolen, Mama," Liddy said, sipping her coffee and trying not to relive too much of last night's delicious moments for fear she'd start blushing and her mother would know something was up.

"Did I tell you that that woman, Jenna, seemed to think she and Tucker were minutes away from making an announcement?"

Liddy came flying back to reality with a thud. Even though she knew it couldn't be true, it made her stomach hurt to hear the words.

"Is that what she told you at Thanksgiving?"

Her mother nodded. "I told you you should've made a move with him while you were still under sixty."

"I am under sixty, Mama, as you well know and that is *not* what you told me. You told me you didn't like the idea of me dating him."

"I can't believe I would have said that. Tucker Jones is a great catch. Everyone in town knows it."

"Everyone except Meryl Merritt."

"Well, even she must've known it at one time since she did marry him."

"Have you heard anything on the grapevine about that? What her Thanksgiving visit was about? Or why she hasn't returned any of my calls?"

"The grapevine isn't like the Internet, Liddy. The information comes when it comes."

Later, after Liddy walked her mother back to her room and was leaving, she noticed one of the orderlies hunched over a mop and bucket on the far end of the hallway. She hesitated outside her mother's room until she realized she was trying to get a better look at him. Was there something about him? Did she recognize his body or his posture? Riley still hadn't gotten any leads on her possum death-threat guy.

She shook herself out of the feeling that she could somehow know or recognize someone without seeing their face. It still didn't make the weird feeling go away, however, that she was somehow being watched. Smiling at one of the nurses aides as she made her way down the long hall into the sunshine of the afternoon, Liddy deliberately pushed her uneasiness aside and began to mentally plot the designs she would make for her next big catering project, due in just a few days. She found herself whistling as she walked to her car.

And why not? Her business was on the uptick, the holidays were coming, her mother was well and happy. And she and Tucker had entered a phase that promised to be better than anything she could have possibly imagined as "just friends." Life was good.

The next morning was a beautiful Sunday morning. Cold but sunny, and a mere twelve days before Christmas. Liddy switched off her computer and felt very smug about how self-reliant she had obviously become. Her calendar was full of twelve gorgeous cupcake-packed days of parties and gifts and every manner of frosted celebration—all of which *Le Cupcake* would be an integral part of. Yes, the town of Blackshear had loved the cupcakes, and *yes*, after a brief phone interview with her, the media had done a very sweet little story on Liddy and her shop—she had made copies at the local print shop and turned them into testimonial flyers she'd virtually papered the surrounding townships with. She even had a customer in the store yesterday! Granted, it was no one she recognized from Infinity, and they only bought one cupcake, but it was a start.

There was one tiny little glitch. Her oven had stopped working. But her newfound confidence and general happy affect took that little problem easily in stride. Liddy pulled her digital tablet from the kitchen drawer where she kept it, propped it up on a stand near the oven and brought up a how-to videos on it. *Why spend a hundred and sixty dollars an hour for a repairman when the Internet was full of videos showing you step by step how to fix a non-firing oven?*

She watched the video carefully twice then opened her toolbox, opened the oven door and peered inside. She hesitated. The video was telling her she needed to unscrew the floor of the oven to get to the electronic gas lighter thingy, but every instinct in her was telling her she didn't know what she was doing and that this oven was the only way she was going to be able to fill the two new orders that had come in just this morning—let alone a big one due Christmas Eve that could possibly put her and Le

Cupcake in the black. She removed one of the large screws holding the oven floor in place. There were five screws in all. She set them on the narrow shelf over her mixing bench so as not to lose them. Twice in the middle of her attempts to relight the oven pilot light her cellphone rang with a catering job. They were small but in terms of reestablishing that Liddy was once again a viable baking business in the community, they were very big.

It was a Sunday so she thought Tucker might stop by. She had called him a couple of times and was actually surprised that she hadn't heard from him since what had happened between them at the barn. He was probably busy busting drug dealers or whatever it is he did, she thought. She paused for a minute to realize she didn't really know for sure what it was that Tucker did. Talk about mysterious!

As she cleaned off the grit and grime around her electronic lighter—just as the online videos instructed her—she felt a flood of pride in a job well done. It hadn't been easy, none of it. Not helping her mother or getting the bakery up and going or watching Ben's helter skelter launch from the home nest or learning to live those first few months and years without Bill, the man who had been her helpmate and best friend for the past twenty years. But she was making it work.

Just as she was repositioning the bottom plate over the newly cleaned and now working igniter, her cell phone rang. She looked at the screen and smiled.

"Hey, sweetie," she said, placing the screwdriver back in the toolbox and settling in against the wall to talk.

"Hey, Mom," he said. "Everything okay? How's Gran?"

"She's good," she said, but she could tell by his voice there was something he had to tell her.

"How about yourself?" she said, the smile gone from her voice. "Everything okay with you?"

"Yeah, but Mom, I gotta tell you..." She heard him take a long sigh as if trying to fortify himself for the mission ahead.

"I don't think I'm going to be able to make it down for Christmas."

Liddy's stomach plummeted. "Oh?" she said. "What's going on?"

"It's Grandpa and Grandma James," he said. "They've been calling me lately..."

"I remember," she said. "You mentioned at Thanksgiving they were in touch a good bit."

"Yeah, well, they really want to see me at Christmas and I'm not sure I can say no."

Liddy would have thought that the excuse of a widowed mother and a newly injured grandmother would've sufficed nicely but maybe her in-laws didn't care. They could be very prickly. "Do you want me to call them?"

He paused. "Do you think it would be okay?" he asked. All of a sudden she heard the little boy in his voice who would turn to her to make something right, and she felt tears burning in her eyes.

"I'm sure it will, sweetie," she said. "Let me give them a call. Have you seen them at all this year?"

"I saw them, I think, sometime this summer?" Which meant he hadn't seen them since the funeral.

"Can you get over to Dothan to see them for a visit maybe before Christmas?"

"I don't know, Mom," he said. "I'm crazy busy."

Doing what?

"It would help if I could tell them you'll visit them another time, Ben," she said. "In fact, you should visit them sometime. You know your Dad would want you to."

"I know, I know," he said. "Let me know what they say, okay?" he said.

"And you're definitely coming to Infinity for Christmas then?"

"Of course, Mom," he said. "Just fix it so they're not all mad, okay? They are sending me money each month."

"Do they know you're not in school?"

"I don't think so."

"Alright, sweetie," she said, wearily massaging the bridge of her nose. "Let me talk with them. You think about when you can get over there."

"Will do. Thanks, Mom. Love you."

"Love you, too, sweetie."

Liddy stood up and felt something unpleasant catch in her back. She hobbled to a kitchen stool and took a moment to stretch out her back.

There was always something.

An hour later, Liddy still couldn't find three of the five screws she had so carefully placed on the narrow shelf. She had retraced her actions a hundred times—one trip to the bathroom, three phone calls, including the one from Ben—and the very clear memory of placing the screws on that shelf still led to only two screws on the shelf. She looked everywhere on the floor thinking they might have rolled off the shelf and then rolled again. The floor was clear. No screws. She could see that only two of the screws in place left a definite gap, which would allow a faster buildup of grease and residue. It wasn't ideal but it would have to do. As she tightened the second screw in place, she gave it an extra turn of the screwdriver to secure it better when the screw gave an ominous click sound and then spun loosely in its socket. She had stripped the threads.

Liddy looked in horror as the floor plate gapped even more, pinned now by only one screw.

And then the pilot light went out.

Sunday wasn't a good time to call an appliance repairman—especially in the boonies—but Liddy left a message to have someone come out first thing in the morning. She knew she'd succeeded in making it worse and she also knew she didn't have the money to pay the guy when he came. She thought of the two diamond rings and the heavy antique gold bracelet that Bill had given her and she knew it was time.

Later that night, when she padded into the darkened kitchen to make herself a chocolate toddy to help her sleep, she found the missing three screws. She found them seconds after she heated up a pan of milk on the stovetop (at least that part still worked) and scooped a quarter cup of semi-sweetened cocoa into her mixer, adding sugar, cinnamon and a tablespoon of softened butter. In fact, she found them a split second after she hit the "blend" button on her nine hundred dollar industrial mixer and discovered where it was that they had rolled.

The next morning, Liddy called the appliance repair shop again and got only the voice mail. Forcing herself not to panic, she called the local Baptist church—the one that Jenna and Tucker belonged to.

"Hello?" she said breathlessly. She took a breath and forced herself to calm down. "I'm a friend of Tucker Jones? And I have a problem I was hoping you could help me with?"

The woman on the line listened to Liddy's problem and then transferred her to the person in charge of the True Way's Christmas fellowship program, Anna Simpson.

"Can I help you?" The voice on the other end sounded friendly and very chipper.

"Yes, I hope so," Liddy said. She explained what she needed—the church's big industrial mixer for one day. She had already figured out if she could have the use of a mixer for just twelve hours, she could stay up all night making the batter for all the jobs and then just freeze and bake as she needed them. "And in exchange, I would be delighted to provide all the cupcakes for your annual Christmas banquet after services."

The woman laughed on the other end of the line. "The angels must have been listening to me," she said. "I was just telling my husband this morning about your cupcakes. I had the opportunity to sample them at a party I went to this weekend. You have been given the gift of hospitality, Miss James, that is surely true if anything is."

"So I can borrow the mixer?"

"Bless you, of course you can. I'll have one of our boys run it by to your place if you'd like. I'm grateful to be able to help out a friend of Tucker's," she said. "Not to mention, supply the banquet with those delicious cupcakes of yours."

"I cannot thank you enough for this, Miz Simpson. You have literally saved me."

"Oh, Miz James, you know it's not in my power to do that, but I'm surely glad to have been of help to you."

When Liddy hung up, she put another call into the repair shop, left another message, and hoped the build-up of messages from her would serve to alert them to her urgency so she didn't have to come out and actually get hysterical on the phone. She'd been in Infinity long enough to know that saying you're upset and showing you're upset are two different things and the former gets attention a whole lot faster than the latter.

Just the opposite, Liddy thought, with how the rest of the world runs.

She went upstairs to collect the package of jewels she'd carefully wrapped the night before, then came down and grabbed her car keys. While it was a Monday, she was so in the habit of not anticipating customers, that she didn't give a thought to leaving the shop during "open" hours. So she was surprised to find a customer waiting for her in the anteroom as she was about to lock the front door.

It was Tucker.

"Oh, hi," she said. "I was wondering when I'd see you. Crappy timing, though. I was just headed out."

"Great," he said. "I'll go with you."

She locked the front door and pulled the blinds down and turned to face him. He wasn't smiling.

"What's up?" she said, frowning.

"How about if I drive?" he said. "I'm parked out back."

"Tucker, what is it?" she said.

"You'll see."

She saw him glance up the stairs as they walked through the kitchen to the back door.

"After you." Tucker opened the back door for her.

She went out and he pulled the door close behind them, the lock clicking as he did so. She climbed into the front seat of his truck, the jewelry tucked safely in her handbag. She realized she'd never been in his truck before. It smelled of horses and sweet feed and him.

"Been out to the barn lately?" she asked. She meant it teasingly but something about his manner held her back from delivering it with the impish grin she'd intended.

He didn't answer.

"Tucker, is everything okay?"

"Fine," he said. "You got your smartphone on you?"

"You need a GPS?" She dug out her phone.

"Go to wwwATLbakerywhoredotcom."

As soon as he said it, her stomach flipped over. She looked at him.

"Go on," he said, watching the road ahead of him and pulling out onto the main street.

"What am I going to see?" she asked quietly, still only holding her phone.

Tucker glanced at her. "Did you know photos can live on the Internet virtually indefinitely? Even if you take them down, they never really go away."

Liddy punched in the web address and waited for the site to come up. Infinity was near a cell tower and regardless of how backward it was about many other things, it had ready and instant web access.

Liddy groaned as the page materialized on her phone and she felt her face creep a hot and steady scarlet. In some cultures, they might have been considered tasteful nudes. In one photo, her back to the camera, Liddy was looking over her shoulder and while clearly naked, the only thing visible was the round and perfect bottom of youth. It was a beautiful and beguiling portrait of the arrogance of youth. The second photo was a frontal nude shot of Liddy standing, her arm above her head in a stretch, every curve, dimple and freckle laid open to the world.

The third was her in recline. Liddy had been eighteen when she'd posed for the photos and her boyfriend photographer not much older. At the time, the photos had seemed artful and intimate, a celebration of their youth and their love. It's not that Liddy had totally forgotten about them, but in the intervening years—and they had been taken long before the ease of digital storage—it just hadn't occurred to her that they had survived.

Oh, how they had survived.

"I'm not going to ask you how you could pose for those," Tucker said. "But you should know they're now up where everyone can access them."

How did whoever ran this site even find them? She glanced at the web text and saw the line "Sponsored by the Infinity Better Business Organization."

Liddy cleared her throat. "I can't imagine these photos can give very much competition to the real porn that's on the Internet," she said. "Who would care?" She noticed her hands where trembling as she held her phone.

Tucker looked at her. "The people of Infinity would care very much," he said.

Like you, she thought.

"Where are you taking me?" she said primly, tucking the phone away back in her purse. "I have an errand in Baxley."

"I'll take you to Baxley," he said. "This place is right on the way."

They were driving down one of the back roads lined with mobile homes and perfectly manicured lawns. There were even a few pink flamingoes dotting the sloping lawns that led up to dirt-poor shacks.

"Besides," Liddy said, her embarrassment giving way to anger at the way Tucker had ambushed her with this. "The people in Infinity barely know how to work their cable TVs. They won't have access to those photos."

Tucker pulled his truck off the road and put it into park. She looked at him with surprise and then out the window at the very rural, residential road. A goat across the road looked up from its pen.

"Which is why the people who uploaded those photos made sure folks had another way to see them," Tucker said, using his thumb to point up at the billboard on the side of the road.

Liddy's mouth fell open at what she saw. There, for all the world to see, was her eighteen-year-old self, wearing the black rectangles of the dishonored to cover her private parts and grinning like she had no shame. The headline read: "It's not just your real estate values that come down when the immoral come to town."

The name on the board was the Infinity Better Business Association and Meryl Merritt Realty.

Finding Infinity

Chapter 13

"Put your seatbelt on," Tucker said, starting his truck back up.

"Wait a minute." Liddy put her hand out and touched his shoulder. "How is Meryl connected to the Better Business Association?"

He gave her an exasperated look like she must be joking and then pulled the truck back up onto the road. "She's President of the Association," he said.

"She's *President*?" Liddy was stunned. "But she…that means…"

"Where in Baxley do you need to go?" he said.

"So she's the one behind the whole run-the-Atlanta-whore-out-of-town campaign? How can that be? The flyers, the posters…? I don't understand. We were friends." Liddy stared out the window not seeing the passing scenery. "She *hates* me?"

"That's probably an exaggeration," he said, his eyes focusing on the road and the nonexistent traffic.

"Oh, really? Did we not just come from a fucking billboard she's erected in my honor?"

"Do you always have to use that word when we're talking?"

"Are you serious?"

"I don't know what her problem is."

"If you don't, nobody does. So what is it?"

"It's probably just jealousy."

"Jealousy? Is she still in love with you? Is that it?"

"For God's sakes, Liddy, drop it. Where in Baxley?"

"Does she act this way with *Jenna*? Is there another billboard up somewhere about Jenna or is it just me getting the special treatment?"

"I can't imagine Jenna having something like this in her past to worry about."

"Stop the car. Stop the fucking car!"

"I am not stopping the car."

"How dare you say...well, that's why you're together, right? The two of you? She's all perfect and church going and small town and so are you and so it's all just perfect. God forbid she would've had a life before she met you. That would just be too messy."

"Of course she had a life..."

"A boring life! A life of playing by the rules and never cussing and hanging on your every word or some small town boor just like you..."

When Tucker pulled the truck over to the side of the road, it was so violent, Liddy, who wasn't wearing her seatbelt, nearly ended up on the floor.

"Is that what you really think?" His eyes were blazing and his voice, hardened. "Is that what you think of me?"

"I think you want a perfect little wifey type who doesn't have a personality or a past. Yes, that's what I think. And you know what? Get a load of this, Tucker. I'm not ashamed of the girl who posed for those pictures. How's that for a shock?" Liddy was so upset she was crying and didn't even realize it. "I think that girl was...was awesome and young and free and she was beautiful and didn't...didn't..." Liddy was searching for another word, when Tucker flipped off his seatbelt and pulled her toward him. When he kissed her, it was, singularly, the most unexpectedly erotic moment in her life up until then. Without thinking, she wrapped her arms around him and fell into the kiss as deep and exquisite as anything she'd ever felt.

When he finally pulled his face away, his dark brown eyes searched hers for a moment and then his voice, raspy with emotion: "I think the woman she grew into is pretty awesome, too," he said.

"Oh my God," Liddy whispered. "Did Tucker Jones just use the word 'awesome?'" She leaned in and kissed him again. This felt right. This felt so amazingly right.

Tucker pulled away and faced the steering wheel.

"I've got something to tell you," he said.

"Is it worse than nudie pictures on a public billboard?" Liddy tried to smile but Tucker wasn't looking at her. All of a sudden she didn't feel so amazingly right.

Tucker looked at her. "I just don't know how it happened," he said, and suddenly she knew he meant the other night at the barn.

Liddy turned and straightened out her jacket that had gotten twisted when he grabbed her. She picked up her purse from the floor where it had fallen.

"Now it's you that's sorry," she said, hoping with every fiber in her being that he would deny it.

He didn't.

"It was wrong," he said. He started up the truck. "Put your seatbelt on please, Liddy," he said.

They drove without speaking for a moment.

"I need to go to the pawnshop in Baxley," she said, wondering what had happened and what had gone wrong.

Tucker nodded. She could see that he was fighting with himself and she decided, uncharacteristically, to give him the time he needed.

When they pulled up to the pawnshop, she unhooked her seatbelt and waited.

"Jenna and I are engaged," he said.

Liddy nodded and thought for a brief moment like she might throw up. Then she gathered up her purse and opened the car door. "I should only be a few minutes," she said.

There wasn't much to say on the ride back to Infinity so Tucker and Liddy didn't try. She had her money from the jewels and the bakery was safe for another month at least. She had been adamant with the pawnshop owner that she would return within thirty days to reclaim the jewelry and he was not, under any circumstances to sell them. He agreed and gave her the pawn ticket that she tucked in her billfold with the cash.

Everything was just so perfect.

Liddy decided on the silent drive back that she wouldn't even bother opening up the shop the rest of the month. No one ever came anyway and she would have her hands full trying to fill holiday catering orders and getting her broken appliances fixed or replaced.

A call had come through to her from the church she'd asked to borrow the mixer from but she didn't take it. She would call them back as soon as she got back to the bakery. She still needed to run by her Mama's place and make sure the oven repairman could come out in time. Otherwise, she'd need to ask to use the church's ovens, too.

She stole a few furtive glances at Tucker's profile as he stoically drove her back the twenty miles from Baxley to Infinity. He seemed implacable, emotionless. Was this the same man who had grabbed her and planted the kiss of the century on her not an hour earlier? The same man who had held her and made earth-rumbling love to her like he would never let her go? When her phone lit up showing a call from her in-laws coming through, Liddy decided to take it. Anything beat the frigid silence that was frosting the inside of the truck cabin.

"Hey, Kitty," she said into the receiver. "How are you?"

"Fine, Liddy," her mother in law replied crisply without an ounce of warmth in her voice. "And yourself?"

"Pretty good." Liddy was set to launch into a slightly jaundiced description of her status—easily done especially at the moment—in order to better set the stage for needing Ben at Christmas but her mother in law beat her to the draw.

"We recently talked with Ben," her mother in law said, "and were hoping he would spend the holidays with us in Dothan. Has he mentioned it to you?"

"Yes, he has, Kitty," Liddy said, suddenly sorry she decided to take the call and play this drama out in front of Tucker. "I know he feels bad about not getting over to see you and Ted but he—"

"We really must insist to you that he come," Kitty said abruptly. "He is our only grandchild, as you know. Our only link to Bill."

"Yes, of course—" Liddy said.

"I don't think it's too much to ask to share him, dear," she said. "You had him Thanksgiving and Ted was very depressed and it would've cheered him up immeasurably to have had the boy there."

"Kitty, this is a hard time for all of us," Liddy said. "My mother—"

"Yes, is she doing well? Ben said she was on the mend."

"Well, yes she is but—"

"I cannot stress to you, Lydia," Kitty said as if she were arguing with a maid or some recalcitrant service person, "how important it is that Ben respect his grandparents and not just the ones on your side of the family."

"Kitty," Liddy said. "Ben does respect—"

"And while I have you on the phone, I need to bring up an indelicate but necessary subject and that is the matter of the family rings that I believe Bill gave to you?"

Liddy found herself momentarily speechless.

"Dear? Are you there? You know the ones I'm talking about? They were his Aunt Ruth's? They have been in the family for generations."

"And they are still in the family in my care," Liddy heard herself saying, a vision of the package being pushed across the counter to the pawnshop owner.

"I need to ask for the return of those rings," Kitty said. "And the bracelet too. They are a set and should be kept together."

Can this seriously be happening?

"I believe Bill gave those rings to me as a gift," Liddy found herself saying. She noticed that Tucker was frowning and was clearly listening closely to her conversation.

"They are family jewelry that must remain with the family," Kitty said firmly. "I will give them to Ben when he is older and has a wife."

"Or I could," Liddy said.

"That won't be necessary, dear," the woman said, as unfriendly and cold as Liddy had ever heard. "Please have Ben bring them with him when he comes at Christmas."

The phone connection ended. Liddy couldn't believe her ex-mother-in-law had just hung up on her. Liddy sat holding the phone in her lap as Tucker drove up the street her store was on.

He cleared his throat.

"Everything okay?" he asked gruffly.

Liddy stuffed the phone in her purse, glancing at the envelope of cash, and put her hand on the door handle. When he pulled up to her storefront, she could see that the crude banner nailed to the front of her door read: *Whore Go Back to Atlanta.*

She lurched open the car door and got out. "Just awesome," she said, "thanks for asking." And slammed the door.

Jenna and her son sat across from Tucker and his niece at the diner. The two children positively babbled—even Haley—and Jenna was reminded of the giddy tension that a accompanied this time of year for children. Funny, how that excitement diminishes as one grows older, she thought.

"Penny?" she said to Tucker. It didn't take much to make any fiancée insecure, she thought. Tucker Jones was a taciturn man but lately he'd been quieter than usual. Not going through the motions, exactly, but close.

He looked up from his plate and smiled at her. "Nothing really," he said. "Just this case I'm working."

"The one in Jesup?" Tucker didn't talk at all about his work as a DEA undercover agent but what with Haley's brush with the law in his area Jenna felt sure he would soon open up more to her.

He nodded. "Just a couple pieces that don't fit," he said. "I'm rolling them over in my mind a good bit but they don't work. I know they mean something, I just haven't figured out what."

Jenna smiled supportively. She had no idea what he was referring to but the way that Haley's eyes flashed to her uncle in the middle of his sentence made her think that Haley might.

Whatever it was, Jenna thought, cutting into the ham on the diner's Nearly-All-Veggie Plate Special, it was definitely distracting him from the joys of the season, not to mention the pleasures of the newly-engaged. For one reason or another, they hadn't slept together since they decided to get married.

"I guess Liddy's having a hard time lately," she ventured. She watched his face closely at the mention of her name but could discern no reaction. He reached for a corn muffin.

"What's happening with Liddy?" Haley asked, looking from her uncle to Jenna.

"You don't need to know the details," Tucker said.

"It's about the naked billboard, isn't it?"

"What's a naked billboard?" Drew asked, looking up from his GameBoy.

"Thank you, Haley," Tucker said pointedly to his niece.

"Sorry. But is that it?"

"What's a naked billboard?"

"Never mind, dear," Jenna said. "Eat your okra."

"Uncle Tuck?"

"Yes, the town's upset about the billboard, Haley. Running any kind of a retail establishment is very difficult, almost definitely a losing proposition..."

"You sound like Grandma."

Tucker looked up from his plate and glanced briefly at Jenna. "Well, in this case, she's right," he said. "It's very difficult to run a successful restaurant especially in this economy. Miz James knew it wouldn't be easy. And it hasn't been."

"Are you mad at her, Uncle Tuck?"

"What?" Tucker looked up at Haley and then Jenna who also looked to be interested in his reply. "Of course not," he said. "That's ridiculous.

"But you advised her not to open the shop, didn't you?"

"Really, Tucker?" Jenna said, putting down her fork. "You told Liddy not to open her shop?"

Tucker looked from one to the other. "Everyone told her not to open the shop," he said in frustration. "It was always a crazy idea." He looked at Jenna. "Do you think opening a French bakery in a town like Infinity is sane?"

Jenna watched him carefully for a second and then shrugged and went back to her meal. "I guess not. But poor Liddy."

"Yeah, I like her, too."

"Awesome."

"I've never heard you use that word before!" Haley burst out laughing.

"He's being sarcastic," Jenna said. She was smiling but somewhere in the pit of her stomach, she didn't feel too good.

She leaned over and tapped Drew's plate with her fork and he put down his game console and scooped up some okra with his spoon. "Use your fork, Drew," she said. "Is there anything we can do?" she said to Tucker.

He pushed his plate away and signaled for the check to the waitress. "Do?" he said. "You mean like loan her money?"

Haley turned to face Tucker. "Yeah, what can we do?" she said. "She's got some big jobs coming up, right?" She looked at Jenna and Jenna nodded.

"I know of two that came from my contacts alone," Jenna said. She couldn't help looking at Tucker to see his reaction. There was none.

"Can we? Can we help?"

Tucker seemed to be concentrating on pulling bills out of his wallet.

"Tucker?" *Why was he so recalcitrant? Did he not want Liddy to succeed for some reason? What sense did that make?*

"Yeah, sure, great idea," he said. "Very spirit of the season idea." He looked at Jenna. "You want to call her and see how we can help?"

The world shifted back into place again and the bad feeling in the pit of her stomach left as quickly as he spoke the words. There was nothing there, she thought. It was just Tucker mulling over his Jesup problem. It was all good.

Jenna reapplied her lipstick as the waitress took Tucker's money.

"Can you come over tonight?" she asked. "Drew has an early night because of a big science test tomorrow."

"Aw, Mom," her son said. The fact that he didn't follow it up with a detailed argument underscored her belief that he was tired. She smiled winningly at Tucker as they climbed out of the restaurant booth.

He ran a hand through his hair and replaced the baseball cap he'd worn into the Diner.

"Sure," he said, putting an arm around her. "That sounds great."

Liddy saw there were over fifty voice messages, and probably more until she disconnected the voice mail, saying she was filth and urging her to please leave Infinity immediately. An extremely terse message from Anna Simpson of the True Way

Baptist Church said that their mixer was *not* available for her use nor would they need any baked goods from *Le Cupcake*. A positively cheerful message from Jenna said she had yet another possible catering job for Liddy and also some personal good news she'd like to stop by and share with her.

Oh, joy.

In the two days since the billboard had gone up, she had alternately sat in her empty bakery with its broken and unusable equipment, visited her mother in the assisted living facility and taken infrequent walks out at the barn on Sugar, always at a time when Tucker was not known to appear.

Her busiest time of the year and she had to sit in frustration and watch the hours and days fall away as Christmas and her deadlines came ever closer—and do nothing.

She was finally able to book the oven repairman to come, giving her just three days to create four major catering jobs of at least five hundred designer cupcakes.

And she still didn't have a mixer.

As for Tucker, she had to push thoughts of him to the very far recesses of her mind or she would become undone. Not only had he made love to her knowing he was engaged to someone else and with no intention of pursuing her, but once he had seen the Internet photos, he had turned into no better than any of the churchy, Atlanta-hating jerks who had been trying to drive her out since the day she arrived. She had never been more wrong about a person than she had when she thought friendship with Tucker Jones was worth having, even worth sacrificing for. Let alone that she might have actually loved him.

On the Tuesday that the oven repairman was to come, Liddy was sitting in the front of the bakery trying to make her financials come out properly. She still had a little money left from pawning the jewelry but didn't want to spend it all if she could help it. She would need every dime to help her redeem them in time for Ben to take them to his Grandparents. Kitty and Ted had never been thrilled with their son's choice of a bride. Liddy suspected it had to do with the fact that they had someone else in mind for him.

Liddy told Ben he could leave Infinity Christmas Day and drive to Dothan to see them. Like most compromises, it wasn't perfect—as far as anybody was concerned—but it would have to do.

Liddy was pouring herself another cup of coffee when she heard the sharp rap on the door. She had closed the shop as planned. Pulling back the curtain on the front window, she was startled to see Danni Lynn standing on the front stoop, looking very professional and from her pleasant smile maybe even a little friendly.

Liddy hopped up and unlocked the front door. "Well, this is a surprise," Liddy said, smiling.

Danni Lynn did not enter.

"If you've come to fix the sink," Liddy said. "I've had it taken care of."

"I've come to tell you that you've violated your lease agreement," Danni Lynn said crisply. "I'm giving you to the end of the week to remove yourself from the premises."

Liddy just stared at her. "On...on what grounds?" she stuttered.

"My lawyer believes the lewd and lascivious nature of your presence in Infinity will be grounds enough but I wouldn't have believed you'd have the funds to fight me in court." Danni Lynn shrugged. "Win or lose, you lose."

"If you're referring to the billboard," Liddy said hotly, "I'm thinking of suing for defamation of character."

"I repeat," Danni Lynn said, looking round the bakery. "You may well win the case. But it will cost you everything to do so."

"Why are you doing this? I thought we were friends."

"That was until I knew the sort of person you were. The end of the week," Danni Lynn said, turning to leave.

"The end of the week is Christmas Day."

"Better known as Moving Day for you."

Chapter 14

"I can't believe you didn't mention to me that Meryl Merritt came to see you."

"Well, it slipped my mind," her mother said. "That happens with old people. Just you wait."

"And she brought you candy?"

"Very good candy. Pecan brittle. It's the good stuff made over there on the other side of Vidalia with the little—"

"Mama, I'm not interested in where Meryl bought her brittle."

"Although, technically, I suppose it's more praline than brittle."

"You are doing this just to drive me crazy, aren't you?"

"It's not all about you, Liddy. If you would visit more often—"

"I'm here every day! Nearly."

"Which is it? Because every day is one thing and nearly is something else."

"Okay, Mama, you know my life has been going down the toilet lately with my baking equipment on the fritz and that stupid billboard and now Danni Lynn trying to evict me."

"Don't forget your horse, Liddy. I know that takes a good bit of your time, too."

"Yes, I'm sorry, Mama. The horse takes time that I could be spending with you. That's true. But even I need a hobby, a release from all the pressure..."

"Pressure that you invented for yourself, don't forget."

"How in the world would I be able to forget? But give me a break. Meryl has shown herself to not be my friend. In fact, she's the leading contender for the role of the person who's leading the charge against me. She's the President of the damn organization that spends more money on Atlanta-Slut-Go-Home posters than any other civic effort. Bringing you candy is at best an insult to me, and at worse…well, I don't know what she has up her sleeve with this."

"Might've just been candy for an old lady, Liddy." Her mother leaned over and patted Liddy's knee. "I swear, I've never seen you this frazzled. And now you're being evicted? What are you going to do?"

"I have no idea. She's right about one thing. I don't have the money to fight it."

"Why would you want to? You've had, what, a total of one customer since you opened?"

"It was right on the cusp of all that changing."

"You mean when you exposed yourself in all your glorious nakedness to a small Baptist town in the deep south?"

Liddy sighed loudly. "It sounds kind of impossible when you put it like that."

"I'm putting it the way it is, Liddy," her mother said. "You can roll a turd in powdered sugar to make it look all pretty, but it's still a turd."

"Oh, that's lovely, Mama. Really nice."

"I thought you'd like the baking reference. I was saving it."

"I still don't know what I'm supposed to do."

"You could always quit."

"That, I am not going to do," Liddy said. "I'm determined these yokels won't run me out of town or close me down."

"Well, then, it sounds like you do know what you're going to do."

"Yeah, I guess I do. Thanks for the clarity, Mama."

"Sarcasm?"

"Nope. Not one bit." Liddy scooted her chair closer to her mother's. "The missing piece that the oven repair guy needs is coming first thing tomorrow," she said. "Once I find a mixer…"

"Can't you borrow Tucker's kitchen again?"

Liddy shook her head. "Not really, no," she said. "But even if I have to drive to Waycross to put a new industrial mixer on my charge card, I swear I'll be baking cupcakes by this time tomorrow, frosting them the day after that and delivering them the day after that."

"So is this your round-about way of telling me I won't see you Christmas Eve?"

An hour later as she was driving home from the rehab center, Liddy got the call that said the oven piece would be delivered express to her the first business week...*after* the holidays.

Tucker pulled the saddle off Traveler and placed it on the saddle rack in the tack room. He hadn't seen Liddy since he showed her the billboard and he imagined she was working as hard as he was to avoid running into each other. The morning was early—too early to imagine Liddy would roust herself to come out to the barn—but it was perfect for a long ride through the woods, the dew still glistening off every leaf and grass blade. It had begun to chill up some, too, more in keeping for this time of year, and he wore a heavy denim jacket over his pullover sweater.

It wasn't a lie what he told Jenna. The Jesup job was a complete balls-up and had every earmark of turning out as bad as one of these jobs could go. It couldn't be helped. He knew that. As so often happened, there were circumstances that prevented him from operating as he might like to tie up loose ends. But that was the end of any truth telling between him and Jenna.

He brushed Traveler's coat in strong, downward brush strokes. This was the last thing he wanted to happen between the two of them. The best part of their relationship, as far as he was concerned, had been how comfortably honest with her he could be. So when did he start evading her glances, manufacturing smiles he didn't feel, and concocting excuses not to go over to her place?

Oh yeah. That would be right after he'd kissed Liddy James and just before he threw her down in a stall in the middle of the night and "knew" her in every sense, Biblical or otherwise, the way he'd been imagining since the moment he first saw her standing in her high heels and tight skirt at Jessie's gas station last summer.

Damn her!

He cleaned each of Traveler's feet, ran a wide-tooth comb through the horse's mane and tail and poured sweet feed into a bucket which he then hung on the hook in front of Traveler. He tossed the picks and brushes back in his tack box and watched his horse without really seeing him.

Everything about the situation sucked but if he knew one thing, he knew he could not break Jenna's heart. Not when he'd presented himself to her as available and willing. He was not going to add himself to her long list of men-who-let-me-down. It didn't start out that way and it wasn't going to end that way. Besides, regardless of how Liddy got his blood boiling just to look at her, she still was a far cry from the kind of woman he could see himself with. That little bit of a wild streak she'd had from her younger days could still be glimpsed—just look at her stubbornness with this whole bakery idea! Plus, there was the bad language...he tried to imagine her sitting next to him at church services. What if she dropped the hymnal? Would she curse in front of the whole congregation? No, it could never work out between them.

The more Tucker thought about it, the angrier he became, which was a little disconcerting. Because every argument he made was a reasonable one. And none of them made him feel any better about his choice.

No oven. No mixer. It was the morning of the day before Christmas Eve. The day before five hundred artistically decorated cupcakes had been promised to no fewer than four different parties in Waycross and Baxley, Georgia.

Liddy sat in her kitchen watching the dust motes dance across the air in front of the big picture window and had never felt more frustrated and depleted. All that money. All of Mama's money. And most of the money she'd gotten for the jewelry which would now not be redeemed and not returned to her in-laws. Liddy hid her face in her hands but the tears wouldn't come. She'd probably exhausted all tears for years to come in the single night before when she realized what a disaster she had made of everything. When she realized how things were irrevocably turning out.

And then there was Tucker.

So this is what the end of a dream looks like, she thought. She always wondered if it came on in increments or died in installments. Hers was ending in one sickening, stomach-plummeting morning two days before Christmas. At least I'll always be able to remember the day it all went to hell, she thought. Even worse? She hadn't cancelled a single one of her catering jobs. So not only was she not going to get paid for them, but they weren't going to get their holiday treats from any place else either. There were four parties in two towns that she knew of that were going to have totally crap parties thanks to her. And that was because of her selfishness. She looked at her cellphone. Is it too late to call and tell them to find someone else? With a day's notice? No way. She picked up the cellphone. At least they could go clear out the pastry department at the local Piggly-Wiggly, she thought. It's the least she could do.

As she sipped her now-cold coffee, she saw a figure standing on her front step. Curious, but dreading the possibility that it was another irate Infinitonian scribbling yet another We Hate You message to be shoved under her door, Liddy hopped up.

Let the cowards say it to my face! she thought. *Maybe I should rip off my blouse and open the door topless. They can deliver their ugly epithets to my naked boobs. God, I wish I had a cream pie baked and at the ready. Is it assault to smack a village terrorist in the kisser with a cream pie?*

When she jerked open the door, her anticipatory anger faded away. It was Señor Jimenez from the corner lunch counter. Liddy was so surprised to see him, she just stood there for a moment. Even more astonishing was the fact that he carried in his arms a large, ancient, but from the looks of it, entirely serviceable food mixer.

"*Señora* James?" he said, peeking out from around the heavy mixer. "I can come in?"

"Yes, yes, of course," Liddy said. She ushered him in and he put the mixer down on one of the little cafe tables.

"You are needing the mixer, yes?" He smiled happily at her and gestured to the mixer. "Señor Jones say to deliver to you. To loan, yes?"

Dear God, how did Tucker know she needed a mixer? Then she remembered her conversation with the church. His church.

"Yes, *Señor*! Oh, my God, you are a life saver," Liddy said, her mind whirling. *Was there a way to do this? Was it not too late?*

"We are so busy now, I must go, but after we close, you are using our ovens, yes? That is good?"

Would the cultural differences understand a hug of the proportions Liddy had in mind? She would have to chance it. She launched herself into his arms and held on.

"Yes! Yes!" she said into his collar, smelling onions and chili powder and sweat. "Thank you so much! How can I ever thank you for this?"

"*Feliz Navida*," the older man said, seeming happy to extricate himself from her arms. "Merry Christmas, si?"

"*Si! Si*! Such a merry Christmas!"

The man indicated the back room and picked up the mixer in his arms again to set it down in the kitchen workroom before scurrying out the front door. The little bell tinkled and made the most wonderful sound Liddy thought she had ever heard.

An hour later, Liddy had made one bowl of wedding cake batter and one of chocolate. She poured the batter into the cupcake papers that lined five cupcake tins. She glanced at the clock. It was seven o'clock. This was probably madness. She had forty cupcakes ready to go into the oven. They would need to be baked, sorted, then decorated. She only had four hundred and sixty cupcakes to go.

Don't give up, she scolded herself. This is my Christmas miracle but only if I make it happen!

Should she make more batter? Or start on the frosting? Or roll out the fondant for the decorations? She looked at the clock again but it was still seven o'clock. When did *Señor* Jimenez say he would come back with the green light for the ovens? How late did the café stay open anyway? She decided to make another batch of wedding cake batter and then transfer the batter to a bowl to wait for a free cupcake tin. Then she'd make her first batch of butter cream frosting. Maybe, with luck, the first batch of forty would be baked and cooled by then. She looked at the clock again. Seven oh four. No way will they be ready to frost by then. They will need to cool.

She separated fifteen eggs, reserving the yolks in a covered bowl in the fridge and made another bowl of the delectably fluffy cupcake batter. She took a spatula and scraped the contents into a large bowl and was in the process of washing out the mixer bowl when she heard the bell ring on the front door.

Please God let it be him, she thought, wiping her hands on a towel that hung from her apron waist.

"*Senõr?*" she called.

"Nope, it's just me," Tucker said as he strode into the little bakery. His arms were full of cupcake pans, papers, spatula knives and several bottles of vanilla extract. "Where do you want me to put these?"

Liddy hesitated. He hadn't called and they hadn't laid eyes on each other since the trip to Baxley and her subsequent car door slamming.

Seeing him now made her nearly go weak in the knees. He didn't avoid her eyes, she had to give him that.

"Jenna is right behind me," he said. "And a few other folk who seem hell-bent on making sure these cupcakes get made. Miguel is getting the ovens hot. Oh, yeah, I'm supposed to ask you. Is three twenty five right? For the cupcakes?"

Before she could answer, the door opened and Jenna and Haley swept it, also loaded down with baking paraphernalia.

"We're here!" Jenna called out. "I may not do fancy-schmancy swirls but I can ice a cupcake! Where do you want us?"

Liddy clapped her hands together in delight. "Y'all," she said. "You have totally rescued me."

"I know, right?" Haley said, dropping a cupcake pan on the front counter. "Look, Liddy—"

"Miz James," her uncle corrected.

"Miz James. I made a couple designs, just fooling around." Haley pulled out a few pieces of tissue paper with scrolls and flourishes on them. "We don't have to do them but I figure if we have leftover fondant, you know?"

Liddy hugged the girl. "Haley, they look wonderful. Of course, we'll do them. Oh, my God, y'all. I can't believe it. Thank you so much."

Tucker appeared from the kitchen holding two trays of batter-filled cupcake trays. "Can I take these down?" he said.

Jenna reached over and gave Liddy's arm a squeeze. "We couldn't let you go down in flames, Liddy," she said. "It's Christmas."

"Jenna, thank you," Liddy said, her eyes already smarting with the tears she was hoping wouldn't start falling.

"Yes, Tucker, if you would. And three twenty five is perfect." She gave him a smile but he was intent on not tripping as he went out the door with his hands full of drippy cupcake batter.

"Are there more?" Jenna asked. "I'll bring a couple of pans, too."

"How many ovens do the Jimenezes have?"

"Two big industrial sized ones. Probably easily get four pans going at once."

"What can I do, Liddy?" Haley asked, squinting at her hand-written templates.

"I was just about to start making the frosting," Liddy said. "Could you do that for me? And I'll begin rolling out the fondant."

In the next hour, while they waited for the first batch of cupcakes to be cool enough to frost, Liddy and Haley worked closely to organize which cupcakes would get which decorations. Liddy figured at the rate they were working, walking the pans down to the corner café, baking them, cooling them and then frosting them, it would still take the whole night to finish. *Even with the mixer and the ovens,* she realized, *I never would've done it on my own.*

They divided up the chores efficiently. Tucker and Jenna walked the trays down to the café and the Jimenezes popped them in the oven and timed them. While they baked and then cooled, Jenna and Haley frosted them while Liddy made different flavored icings and cut out more decorative shapes for the fondant.

Periodically, there came a time when the cupcakes were baking or cooling and work was stopped. To work so feverishly nonstop, only to have to cease and twiddle their thumbs was frustrating for everyone, but they made the most of the time. Tucker brought in a couple of six packs, Jenna snapped pictures with her cellphone of the four of them frazzled and dappled with flour and sprinkles but laughing.

At one point, when Tucker was telling a story that Haley had obviously heard many times and was protesting with much eye-rolling, Liddy realized that these people were dear to her. That they would come out on Christmas Eve to help her was just about the best present she ever received. As soon as Tucker finished his story, she picked up her beer, toasted the little group and told them so.

"Y'all have saved me," she said, holding her beer bottle up in a toast. "And I love you." She looked at Tucker and pointed the bottle at him. "And don't tell me that we Atlantans throw that word around too much, because I mean it." His expression softened into a wry smile, but his eyes held her captive with their message of want and desire.

"Here, here!" Jenna said, the tiniest bit inebriated. "We love you, too, Liddy."

The timer went off and Liddy jumped up. "Places, everyone!" she called. Tucker drank his beer and watched Liddy as she ran into the kitchen to begin the assembly line of icing and decorating the cooled cakes. He looked over at Jenna and she was watching him.

"You gonna go get the other cupcakes down at the café?" she asked, slurring her words.

Tucker drained his beer and hopped up. "I was just thinking I needed to do that," he said.

It was a little before five in the morning when the last cupcake was frosted, decorated and tucked away into its little presentation box with "*Le Cupcake*" printed on top. Haley had fallen asleep an hour earlier on Liddy's upstairs sofa and Jenna was snoring, sitting up, in the front room of the bakery. Tucker had offered to run her home at least twice—she had become steadily less useful the more she drank—but she refused to leave until the job was done.

Somewhere after midnight, maybe because they were all so tired they were punch drunk, she and Tucker had begun to tease each other like they used to before The Kiss. When she saw him with Jenna, she didn't have to remind herself that he was taken and she certainly couldn't pretend that they weren't a couple. It helped at the same time it hurt.

I screwed that up, she thought, watching him at one point in the evening as he teased Haley by putting sprinkles in her hair. *I could have had him.*

But something was different about him tonight. He was friendlier than he'd been in weeks. It was almost as if he'd somehow come to grips with it all: the rejection, the naked billboard, the lovemaking at the barn, and the psycho ex-wife. When he smiled at her tonight, Liddy thought with bittersweet pleasure, he seemed to really mean it.

"Let Haley sleep here," Liddy said to Tucker. "You guys go on. I'll give her breakfast and we'll deliver the cupcakes in the morning and I'll drop her off at your place afterward."

Tucker nodded, stood up and stretched. "Sounds good," he said.

"Let me get a box for a couple of the rejects," she said. "It's the least I can do." When she turned to leave the room she noticed that morning was beginning to peek in through the front room blinds. She was reaching for a small cupcake box on the higher shelf when the light in the small walk-in pantry dimmed. She turned around and nearly bumped into Tucker who had entered the little room and closed the door behind him. Instantly, Liddy felt a rush of excitement to be alone with him—and so close. Afraid to broadcast her rush of emotions, she made an effort to pick up the mood of their earlier bantering.

"Hey, handsome," she said playfully. "Lose your way to the men's room?"

Without a word, Tucker reached for her with both hands. He gripped her bottom in his hands and pulled her slowly to him. Even in the dark, Liddy could see by his face that he was serious. Feeling his hands on her and the press of his chest against hers,

Liddy moaned with pleasure. With what felt like slow motion, Tucker leaned down and kissed her, his tongue probing deeply into her mouth. Liddy dropped the cupcake box and let the feeling wash over her until her head started to spin and she felt a rush of wetness between her legs. When he pulled back, he looked into her eyes and smiled.

"I've been needing to do that for days," he said.

"To what do I owe..." she cleared her throat but the witticism wouldn't come. She didn't want to banter and joke with him. She wanted him to take her upstairs finish the job he'd started at the barn. Just the thought of him fully naked up against her skin made her knees tremble.

"God, you're so beautiful, Liddy," he said. "So fucking beautiful." His voice was hoarse with desire. "I'm sorry. So sorry for behaving like such an ass about the billboard. Truth is, I can't stop thinking of you."

He spoke lowly and Liddy thought she could hear voices in the front room. Had Jenna left? What they were doing was very dangerous. She stood quietly, her heart pounding in her throat, waiting to get her voice back.

"We shouldn't do this," she said finally. She could hear her voice shake.

"Maybe not," he said. There was nothing shaky about his voice or his words. "But if you want me to stop, you're going to have to tell me to." He kissed her hard and she found herself wrapping her arms around his waist, sinking into the kiss and feeling the world fall away around her. The feeling of his hard length against her stomach and his warm lips on hers gave her a sudden flash of realization that this was what she had been waiting for her whole life.

"Oh, Tucker," she whispered when he finally pulled away. He grinned slowly and touched her chin with his thumb.

"Oh, baby," he said with a devilish smile.

"Why didn't we figure this out earlier?"

"Some of us did," he said. He was still smiling when he said it but there was pain in it, too. He leaned in to kiss her again but this time Liddy did stop him.

"We have to tell her," she said.

He said nothing.

"If you want us to go forward."

"I can't," he said.

Liddy felt a thrill of anger race through her. She pushed him away. "Then what is this?" she said.

"I thought we both agreed it was something we couldn't say no to."

"I guess I thought it meant you wanted to be with me."

"I do." He watched her for a moment and then let her go. "In a perfect world."

Liddy disengaged from his arms and stepped aside, her heart continued to pound, now for a totally different reason than before. "I appreciate all your help today, Tucker," she said.

"Liddy, don't be like that."

"Like what? Like not understanding you marrying someone else?" Liddy felt her face flush. "You really do think I'm a tramp, don't you?"

"That's not what I think."

"I get it. She's all churchy and sweet and I don't blame you for choosing her."

"Liddy, stop it." Tucker took her firmly by her arm. "I don't want to hurt her."

"But it's okay to hurt me?"

"I haven't made you any promises."

Not in words, maybe. But the fight went out of Liddy. "True," she said. "You haven't."

"I'm sorry for whatever this is between us, Liddy. Fact is, I can't seem to stay away from you and when I'm around you I just want...I just want you. I want you all the time and in the worst way. It's like a sickness."

"Sweet talker," Liddy whispered, not looking at him.

"I don't know why you affect me the way you do. Trust me, I've given it a lot of thought. But I made a promise to Jenna. Maybe I shouldn't have, okay, but..."

"Why did you?"

Tucker ran his hand through his thick brown hair in exasperation. Liddy had seen him to do the gesture many times. She realized now that she found the habit endearing but today, right this minute, it was contributing to a very nauseating feeling in the pit of her stomach.

"The truth? You made it clear you weren't interested. I'm not the kind of guy to force the issue if I'm not wanted. Being with Jenna felt like I was moving on. It felt like the healthy thing to do."

Liddy nodded. "It's just that..." Don't say it! Keep your mouth shut! "If you marry Jenna you will be making a mistake that's a whole lot harder to fix than just hurting her now."

He looked at her.

"Any woman with an ounce of self respect would rather get dumped on the way to the altar than marry a guy who's got the hots for someone else." With that, she picked up the dropped cupcake box and pushed past him out the door.

Chapter 15

The next morning, Liddy poured a cup of chicory-flavored coffee with a pinch of vanilla into a Go Cup and handed a practically somnolent Haley an egg and cheese sandwich. Liddy had showered, dressed and made breakfast before waking the girl who slept through all of Liddy's noisy preparations. Deciding against help in loading the car with the cupcake boxes from someone who appeared to be barely awake enough to get herself safely on board, Liddy packed the car herself.

She strapped herself in and looked cheerily at Haley who appeared, at least at this time of the morning, to be regressing to her old snarling self. Liddy chose to ignore it. What she couldn't ignore as she backed the car out of the tight parking lot behind her store was what had happened between her and Tucker.

Just when I thought I was getting a handle on all that, she thought with frustration. Knowing he wanted her, was attracted to her, and yet would not take steps to properly pursue her infuriated and saddened her. At the same time it pleased her. Knowing he was so honorable was not news. Knowing she was on the wrong side of having this honorable man for her own was a bitter pill. But there was still something, amid the sadness and frustration that pleased her about Tucker and his old-fashioned refusal to hurt the woman he had made a commitment to. Truth be told, she couldn't bear to see Jenna hurt either.

The drive to Alma and then on to Baxley to make the drop offs were so quiet, it was almost as if she were alone. At one point, Haley bunched up her jacket and leaned against the window to resume her sleep.

I probably should have just taken her home, Liddy thought, as the girl began to snore. But she wanted to have the cakes delivered—signaling the fact that the impossible was, in fact, done—and the checks in her hand. After the last delivery, which Liddy had arranged purposely to be in Baxley, she drove to the pawnshop.

"What do you mean, you don't have them?" Liddy stared at the pawnshop owner and felt her blood pressure rise. She began scanning the shelves behind him as if the jewelry might, somehow, be in plain sight.

"I'm sorry, ma'am," the little baldheaded man behind the counter shook his head. "I don't normally do nothing like this—"

"I have a ticket. You gave me a ticket to redeem them." Liddy pushed forward the ticket she had already shown the man.

"I know, ma'am." The man picked up the ticket and handed it back to Liddy. "Someone came in not ten minutes after you left and wanted the lot."

"Someone…who? What did she look like?"

The man looked uncomfortable. "I'm not good with people's faces—" he said.

"You have a name, surely? The person gave you her name—"

"She paid in cash. More'n three times what I done give you."

Liddy snatched back her ticket and jammed it into her bag. "I'm reporting you to the Small Business Bureau," she said, so angry she could barely get the words out.

"I know, ma'am," the man said sadly. "Been done before."

"You…you are a liar and…and a miscreant." Liddy thought she might start crying and so hurried out of the shop.

"Don't know about that last one," the old man called to her back, "but I'm sure sorry!"

Liddy slammed the car door, waking Haley, and burst into tears.

Tucker picked up the buzzing cellphone and read the screen. It was Jenna. He had dropped her off at her house this morning. Drew was due to return home from his grandparents around noontime and it would be at least that time before Jenna would awaken.

He hadn't stayed.

After a few hours sleep, Tucker made himself a big breakfast of hash browns, fried eggs and muffins. He didn't want to tell Jenna, who loved to bake him biscuits and muffins but he was just as happy with the frozen kind. He stocked up on those and a few other culinary items whenever he was in Atlanta. He smiled to himself as he loaded the Texas Pete onto his eggs. *Wouldn't do to let Liddy know he didn't exactly hate Atlanta.* He went up several times a year for shows, great restaurants, and a few other items he couldn't get anywhere else.

Liddy.

If he had ever mismanaged any situation in his life—including his marriage to Meryl which had been a mistake from the start—it was his relationship with Liddy James. Why had he given up so quickly? Why didn't he listen to what his behavior was telling him? When he was at the barn, he spent most of his time looking to see if her car was about to drive up. *You don't have to be a crack detective to know that those behaviors mean something*, he thought with disgust.

And now? Now he'd lost even her friendship. How could he be friends with her after what had happened that moonlit night in the stall? How could they ride together and joke around when she knew what he really wanted to do was slip those tight jeans off that perfect ass and get between those long legs?

Tucker pushed his breakfast away. What a mess he'd made of all this. And then there was poor Jenna. He shook his head. Not much of a start, thinking about your beloved as "poor Jenna." Was he really going to go through with this? Was Liddy right? Was the bigger disservice to Jenna giving her a life of being second-best? Would he get over Liddy? Would things settle down once he was married to Jenna? He twisted uncomfortably in his chair, trying to rearrange the tighter fit in his jeans crotch, and groaned.

Was he just fooling himself?

Liddy sat next to her mother in the outdoor courtyard of the Assisted Living facility. She had dropped off a still-sleepy

Haley at Tucker's but didn't have the emotional energy to go in. She told Haley to tell her uncle thanks again for last night and drove straight to her mother's.

"You think it was Meryl that done it?" Her mother sipped from a can of diet cola and turned her face to the sun. It was finally a little chilly for the time of year, but the sun was out today.

"Who else? You think it was just a coincidence that someone bought that jewelry for three times what it was worth?"

"Does seem suspicious."

"She probably told them to call her as soon as I dropped the jewelry off."

Her mother gave her a puzzled look.

"In the days when I thought she was a friend," Liddy explained. "I told her about maybe needing to pawn some jewelry."

"I see."

"Don't start with me, Mama," Liddy said. "You're not such a great judge of character either. You married Daddy, didn't you? You always said it was the worse mistake you ever made."

"Well, it worked out pretty good for you, since you wouldn't be here if I hadn't married him."

"Whatever."

"I know you're in a crabby mood, Liddy, but please do not take it out on me. You see my world?" She waved a hand to encompass the outdoor sitting area of the facility. "Nothing tops this."

Liddy took a long breath and reached over and took her mother's hand.

"I know, Mama," she said. "I'm sorry. After so many years of having your own house and being your own boss, this must really suck."

"It's not wonderful, I have to say," her mother said, sniffing.

"Look. Why don't you come to my place for the holidays?"

Her mother looked at her and Liddy thought she could detect hope and excitement in her voice. "Really?"

"Yeah, definitely. Ben will be in early tomorrow morning. He can sleep on the couch and there's plenty of room for the two of us in my bed. It'll be much homier than here."

Her mother struggled to get out of the chair. "I'll need to pack a few things," she said, the smile all over her face and in her eyes.

Liddy helped her stand and felt a little better, herself.

"You hungry?"

"No, Uncle Tuck, I told you. Liddy fed me."

"Miz James fed you. Did you talk with her this morning?"

Haley turned around on the couch and used the remote control to mute her show. "What?"

Tucker could tell she was trying to be polite with him. "Never mind," he said. "Go ahead and watch your show. I just wanted to know if Miz James and you talked about anything this morning."

"I slept all morning," Haley said, turning back around and pointing the remote at the TV. "Until we got back from the pawn shop. Then she was really upset. She cried."

Tucker came around the couch and sat down. "She cried after coming out of the pawnshop?"

Haley sighed and dramatically dropped the hand holding the remote control. "The pawn shop people sold some jewels she pawned after they told her they wouldn't. She was really bummed. Okay, Uncle Tuck?" She held up the remote. "My show?"

"Yes, yes," Tucker said. He got up and walked into the kitchen. The jewelry she needed to give back to her in-laws. He looked at his cellphone and hesitated. Something wasn't adding up here or, even worse, was adding up all too well.

"I like what you've done with the place."

"You've never been here before, Mama."

"I was referring to the big *Tramp Go Home* sign on the front of your store. Very nice."

"Yeah, well, I pull 'em down, Meryl's people puts 'em back up. Can I get you anything before I go?"

"And why do you have to go to the barn on Christmas Eve, for pity's sake?"

"Well, first because Christmas Eve doesn't really start until this evening when we drink mulled wine and play Christmas songs and call all our loved ones around the country…"

"We don't have any loved ones around the country."

"And second because Sugar doesn't know it's Christmas Eve and I haven't seen him in two days and I need to make sure he's okay. You'll be fine here, Mama. I'm only going to be gone an hour, tops."

Her mother grumbled but Liddy tucked a blanket around her on the couch and put the remote control in her hand. She also made her a hot coffee with a tot of rum in it. She grabbed a couple carrots out of the fridge and yelled up the stairs to her mother: "One hour, Mama!"

Liddy led Sugar in from the pasture. There was nobody at the barn tonight. Originally, she had planned to just throw him a hay flake but lately she'd noticed a little bit of bullying action going on in the pasture and she was afraid he wouldn't get any of the flake if she just threw it in and walked away. It would only take a few minutes more to bring him up and feed him.

She wondered if Tucker had been out today. She couldn't see Traveler but that didn't mean anything. She cleaned Sugar's feet and hung a bucket of feed for him. She brushed his tail and mane while she waited for him to finish eating.

Liddy picked out a snarl in Sugar's mane and pulled some of the longer hairs. *How was she going to tell Kitty the jewelry was gone forever? Did Meryl really take the jewelry? Why would she? But if she didn't, who did?* Sugar snorted and Liddy realized she'd been brushing his mane a little too energetically.

"Sorry, boy," she said, patting him on the neck. "Getting a little carried away. You about done?" She unhooked the bucket and stashed it in the tack room before coming back for him, the carrots carefully hidden in her jacket pocket. The weather had turned downright cold and she hadn't dressed appropriately. She had gotten so used to the unseasonably warm weather that she had only brought a light cotton jacket with her.

"Liddy? Is that you?" Liddy's mother grabbed up the remote and quickly muted *Bayou Billionaires*. She knew she had definitely heard the back door open. She held her breath, waiting. When no one answered, she began to paw the blankets for the cordless phone Liddy had left for her. Before she found it, she could hear the stairs beginning to creak.

Liddy fed Sugar his carrots and pulled off his halter and watched him amble back to his pasture pals over the rise. The color and light had leached out from the afternoon sky and the temperature felt like it was dropping by the minute. As she turned to head back to her car, she checked her watch. It was still early. She would run by the diner and pick up something for their Christmas Eve supper. Her mother would like that.

As she drove back to the bakery from the diner, she deliberately worked to avoid thinking of Tucker. She would see him plenty over the Christmas break. Haley had asked for some baking lessons and Liddy thought that partly had to do with her interest in seeing Ben again. In any case, it meant Liddy would likely bump into Tucker Jones a few times and she honestly did not know how to act. Would he give some thought to what she said about marrying Jenna? Did she want him to? Wasn't half his charm the fact that he was so gallant and old-fashioned? She shook herself. Ridiculous. Of course, she wanted him to choose her over Jenna, if choosing was still an option.

Of course, that would pretty much put the kibosh on my absolute last friend in Infinity.

Suddenly, Liddy noticed that the early evening sky had a more dramatic tinge to it than normal. On the horizon, where downtown was situated, there was a faint but virtual Alpenglow in the distance. Not used to seeing a beautiful sunset in Infinity, Liddy quickly realized it wasn't the sun setting that she was seeing, but a fire. As she squinted to determine where the source of the fire might be, she saw two fire trucks in her rear view window and she pulled over to let them pass.

Wow. Maybe some Christmas trees caught fire? Maybe the one in the courthouse square? She pulled back out onto the road and headed toward her apartment. It wasn't until she was fully in the downtown area, two blocks from her bakery, that the fear crept into her bones and took her breath away.

The fire trucks blocked entrance to her entire block, two police cars were parked on the courthouse yard across from her bakery. She couldn't see any more than that and she couldn't go any further. There was a crowd of people on the courthouse lawn. Some looked like they were just gawking. Some were actually directing people. Liddy stopped her car in the middle of the street and jumped out. She ran down the street, pushing past anyone standing still, until she stood breathlessly, her side aching, on the lawn across the street from her burning bakery.

Chapter 16

The flames of fire shot from the upstairs windows. The display window was smashed and black smoke poured out onto the street. One fire truck was parked on the street in front of Le Cupcake, the ladder raised and a fireman climbing it to the top window.

Liddy sank to her knees. They literally just gave way.

Mama!

She scrambled to her feet and ran to the fire truck before being grabbed by a pair of strong hands.

"No, you don't, ma'am," the fireman said. "You need to stay behind the—"

"My mama's in there!" Liddy knew she was shrieking. *Did they know? Did they know someone was inside?*

"Your...this is your place?" The man frowned at her and then loosened his hold on her. He looked around and called another man over.

"Chief!"

"Did you get everyone out?" Liddy said, her eyes wild with terror. "She's elderly! She was upstairs off the bedroom!"

"Chief, this lady's the owner. She says there's an old lady upstairs."

At that moment, a terrible explosion erupted from the top floor of the bakery. It knocked the climbing fireman off the ladder. The windowsill crumbled and fell to the sidewalk in a shower of timber and wild sparks.

"Get back! Get back!" The Chief and the man holding Liddy ran toward the fallen fireman. The front line of onlookers backed away from the fire. The heat was terrible and Liddy felt her cheeks begin to blister.

She looked wildly around her to see if there was anyone who could help. She heard herself praying out loud.

"Mom! Mom!" She snapped her head in the direction of the voice which carried up and over the hum of the crowd. Ben's voice. There, across the street, over the heads of the curious and the emergency first responders, she saw him frantically waving to her. She started to run toward him but fell. There was burning debris everywhere and so much noise she could barely orient herself. She picked herself up and saw that she'd burned her hand on a large burning ember when she fell. She looked for Ben again and forced herself not to run to him.

When she got closer, she saw he was standing by his car parked at the end of the street. The passenger door was open. There was a figure sitting in the seat.

Dear Lord, let it be Mama. Please let it be Mama.

It was.

When she reached Ben, he crushed her in a bear hug that took the rest of her strength right out of her. She wanted to weep with the sheer joy of having her boy and her mother safe from the worst of this nightmare.

"You came early," she said, the tears streaking down her soot coated face.

"Oh, Mama…" She sank to her knees next to the car and put her arms around her mother. "Are you okay? Did you get burned?"

"Hell, no I'm not okay," her mother said, but her voice was soft and her arms clung to Liddy. "Ben saved my damn life. He saved me, Liddy."

"Mom, you're not going to believe this," Ben said. "When I came in tonight? There was a guy in your apartment. I mean a scuzzy thug type of guy. He set the fire."

"And he hit me!" her mother said. "I played dead so's he wouldn't do no worse to me but then he went and burned down the bakery with me in it!"

Liddy was reeling with what they were telling her. She opened the back door of Ben's car and sank into the car seat.

"How did you get your Gran out?" she asked in awe as she watched another part of her bakery crumble and fall to the sidewalk in front of it. "Has anyone called the cops?"

"Well, I called the fire trucks," Ben said, wiping a swipe of grime from his face. When he did, she could tell that he had a small gash across one cheek. "I think they automatically notify the cops. There's at least two cruisers here but no one's talked to us yet."

"You're hurt, Ben!"

"I don't think it'll need stitches, Mom," Ben said, looking at the blood on his shirtsleeve. "I'll tell you about it once we get Gran settled. Hey, there's Mr. Jones."

Liddy twisted in her seat to see Tucker arrive in his truck. He must have already talked with the cops on his phone because he didn't automatically rush over to them. She watched him approach and she never felt so glad to see someone in her life.

He walked up to Ben and put his hand on his shoulder. "Hey, Ben, y'all alright over here? Miz Mears?" He poked his head in the front seat to talk with Liddy's mother. "You managing okay?"

Liddy's mother nodded her head, her mouth in a firm line as if afraid she might cry if she opened it to speak.

Tucker reached in and patted her hand. "Never mind, Miz Mears. You're safe now." He looked in the backseat at Liddy and raised his eyebrows in question.

"I'm fine," Liddy said, her voice hoarse from the smoke and the fear that still nestled in her chest.

He turned back to her mother. "I'm gonna take Ben away for two quick shakes," he said. "And then y'all go ahead and go to the Seabreeze Motel, alright?" He looked at Liddy and she nodded. "Alright then. It's gonna be fine, Miz Mears. Don't you worry a bit." Then he and Ben walked over to where two policemen were standing by their car. Liddy watched them for a minute and then reached her hand out to touch her mother's shoulder.

Alive. She was alive. Not much else mattered tonight as far as Liddy was concerned.

"Carol, do you have something to say to Tucker?" Jeff stood next to the couch in Tucker's living room, his hands on his hips and stared at his wife. Tucker sat opposite her, the cocktail table between them, the packet of vintage pawnshop jewelry in center place.

"I just did a favor for a friend," Carol said. She wouldn't look at either man.

"A friend, as in my ex-wife?"

"Where did you get the money for these, Carol?" Jeff asked. Tucker could see how angry he was if Carol couldn't.

"It was a loan," she said, wringing her hands now.

"Okay, here's the deal, Carol," Jeff said. "So far, whatever you've done hasn't included lying to my face, okay?" He looked at Tucker and then back at Carol. "Unless you've already passed that milestone awhile back?"

"No! No, Jeff, I'm not lying to you," Carol said. "Meryl gave me the money to get the jewels. She said she saw them in this pawn shop in Baxley and she knew how much I loved vintage jewelry."

Tucker leaned back into the chair. "Meryl is shopping in pawn shops now?"

Carol looked at him and then her husband. Something about the look on her face telegraphed that she knew she'd been caught.

"Not very believable, is it, Carol?" Jeff said. "We got a major problem here and you pawning that jewelry with money that's not ours is only half of it."

"I'm sorry, Jeff. Can we do this at home?" Her voice became thin and pleading. She looked at Tucker. "They're not stolen. I bought them legally."

"Jesus, Carol!" Jeff exploded. "Are you saying you want to walk out of this house with those jewels?"

"Well, I don't *want* to, Jeffy—"

"Don't call me that."

"But I didn't break any laws and I do legally own them and—"

"You mean *Meryl* legally owns them. You bought them with her money and I swear if you say it was a loan I'll start divorce procedures Monday morning."

"Jeff…" Carol looked at her husband with horror. "I can't believe you're on his side against me, your *wife*. He just wants them so he can give them to her because he's sleeping with her."

Tucker stood up. "Don't worry about it, Jeff," he said. "Once Meryl is arrested for conspiracy to commit arson, these'll just be a part of everything that gets claimed."

"What?!" Carol clapped a hand to her gaping mouth. "Arson? No! Meryl would never do that! I mean nobody died from the cupcakes, did they? It was just some tummy trouble. Everyone knows that."

"Wait. It was Meryl that poisoned the cupcakes?" Tucker asked.

"Not *poisoned*," Carol said in near hysteria. "I…she just sprayed the eggs with…with this potion of…of…" she looked at her husband and faltered when she saw the horror on his face. "Jeff, I had nothing to do with that. You have to believe me."

"Because you've been such a paragon of truth up to now?" He looked at her with disgust.

"Five children ended up in the hospital with Shigella which is potentially lethal in children," Tucker said. "To deliberately poison them will look to a jury like a sustained charge of attempted manslaughter."

"Oh, my God! But I know Meryl never meant to hurt any children! She just wanted that horrible Yankee to leave."

"Liddy is from *Atlanta*, you moron," her husband said.

"Meryl said Atlanta has more Yankees now than Chicago," Carol said, but by now she was crying.

"Something's not adding up here," Tucker said, more to himself than anyone in the room. "Meryl's not going to risk her whole career, risk going to prison, for the sake of one irritant. There's got to be more going on."

"She was really jealous of you and that woman," Carol said, tears streaking down her face in a pantomime of abject misery.

"Jealous enough to try to kill her?" Tucker asked, shaking his head. "I don't believe it."

Jeff turned and walked away. Carol watched him leave and then was sobbing uncontrollably into her hands. From where he sat in the living room, Tucker could hear the sound of Jeff slamming his fist through one of the kitchen cabinet doors.

The next morning Liddy, her mother and Ben woke up at the Seabreeze Motel. It hadn't been the most beautiful Christmas morning she'd ever woken up to, but surrounded by her dear mother and son after their narrow escape, it was one of her all time top ones. Even though Liddy and Ben's clothes had been destroyed in the fire, the motel had been able to launder the clothes they'd been wearing. She let Ben sleep a little longer while she drove her Mother to the rehab center for a dress for church.

When Liddy walked into church this time, she was wearing her clean barn clothes, not a spec of makeup and her hair twisted into a loose bun. Her mother, looking elegant in her best dress, moved nimbly up the aisle with her walker, reminding Liddy that she really was getting better.

As usual when she was in public with Ben, Liddy found herself basking in the admiring looks of strangers. The church was packed to the gunnels for this Christmas morning service but people scooted and squeezed over to make room for Liddy and her family. At one point, she caught a glimpse of Tucker but he was surrounded by a large group of friends and relatives. Liddy saw and exchanged a smile and a wave with Haley but she didn't see Jenna in the throng. She assumed she was probably already back at Tucker's whipping up the start of what would be a new tradition of Christmas lunches at "Tucker and Jen's place."

When she sat down, she was surprised at how many people came by to wish her and her family a Merry Christmas. The friendly outpouring of love and affection felt so genuine to Liddy the she found herself shaking hands and grinning like she was running for office. At one point, she felt a firm squeeze on her shoulder and when she turned around, she saw that Jessica, the young girl who's foal had died, was sitting behind her. Liddy turned and gave her a hug and the two made plans to ride the following week.

"Gosh, Mom," Ben said. "This can't be the same town that wanted to run you out on a rail. They, like, love you."

"I'm as surprised as you are, Ben," she said, smiling at the throngs of well wishers as they shuffled past them in the pew.

"Course you are out of business now so maybe that's why they're all lovey-dovey," he teased. "They got their Christmas wish."

His grandmother gave him a light slap on his knee. "Behave yourself, Ben," she said. "This is my town you're talking about."

"Sorry, Gran," Ben said, grinning.

After church, which, all total, took nearly two hours including the time it took for everyone to get through the receiving line, they went to the diner hoping most people went home for Christmas lunch and it wouldn't be too crowded. It was still very crowded but a special effort was made to give them a booth without any waiting at all. They had all been too exhausted the night before for many of the details of the terrible night, so while they waited for their food, Ben explained how it all came to happen. Having decided to come down a day early and surprise his mother, he didn't call but went straight to Gran's assisted living center. When they told him his grandmother was spending the holiday at the bakery, he figured he'd find them both there. He saw that Liddy's car was gone so he used the spare key she'd given him and let himself in—only the door wasn't locked, which he thought was weird. Once inside, he ran smack dab into this low life who was in the kitchen.

"I just couldn't imagine you knew he was there, Mom," Ben said. "So I kinda got all tough with him like 'Hey, what're you doing here?'"

Liddy nodded and leaned over and put her hand on top of her mother's. Her mother was still shaken but otherwise unharmed. Liddy had insisted they all go to the emergency room after they left the scene of the fire. Her mother's knot on the head—not bad enough to break the skin—was deemed nonlife-threatening and Ben's gash took five stitches to close up. The pair had resisted the trip mightily but Liddy was glad for the reassurance later that their injuries were not serious.

"So he like goes crazy on me! I mean, he was a lunatic. He just dropped the thing, whatever it was and just charged me," Ben pointed to his bandage to illustrate and then helped himself to an extra serving of sweet potatoes. "I wrestled with him sor

and then he broke free and ran for it. By then, I could hear Gran upstairs hollering—"

"I most certainly was not hollering."

"So, anyway, I ran upstairs and there she is, like freaking out—"

"I most certainly was not freaking out—"

"Mama, just let him tell the story."

"Fine. Go on, Ben. I admit I may have been a little…"

"Incoherent, Gran," Ben said. "Trust me."

They all laughed. Liddy was so happy to have her little family safe and with no longstanding scars from the incident that they could all laugh at it the next morning.

"Anyway, I'm like all 'Gran, you okay?' and that's when we smell the smoke downstairs. I mean, Mom, you have no idea how fast it turned into a blazing inferno. One minute I'm down there and it's nothing and the next, bam! It's everywhere."

Ben paused to take a long swig of his sweet tea. "So I took two steps down the stairs to see if maybe you'd left a pot on the stove or something and man! the whole room was on fire! So I rush back to Gran to haul her downstairs—"

"Lovely word choice, grandson, thank you."

"—when I notice there's smoke coming from under the door of the bedroom by where Gran's sitting."

"So the lout must've set a fire in there after he conked me on the head," her mother told her. "Please quit hogging the biscuit basket, Liddy dear."

"So I grab Gran and carry her down the stairs."

"I sustained more injury from the rescue than the assault," her mother said, rubbing an elbow. "Not that I'm not grateful, Ben."

"It was so bad, we were dodging flames just getting out and I'm telling you the bastard had just started it." Ben shook his head. "Love to know what took fire so fast. It was totally bizarre."

"I may be able to help you on that score. May I join you?"

Liddy looked up to see Tucker standing by her shoulder. As usual, he was so quiet, she never even saw him come in, let alone approach the table.

"By all means," she said, pointing to a free chair next to Ben. "Sorry we didn't stop to say hello at church this morning. You and Haley were pretty swamped with people."

"No worries," he said, seating himself. "So how are you feeling, Miz Mears?" he asked Liddy's mother. "You look good this morning."

"Why, thank you, Tucker," Liddy's mother said. "It's family style. Please help yourself. Ben, hop up and get Agent Jones a plate."

"Thank you kindly, Miz Mears," Tucker said. "But I have to get back to my own dinner back at the house. We've got a few people over..." Liddy felt disappointment blossom in her chest as she imagined Jenna playing hostess at Tucker's Christmas lunch.

"...but I wanted to let you know what we found out about the fire last night."

Liddy brought her attention back to what Tucker was saying.

"From your description, Ben, we think the guy who broke into the bakery was this guy we've had our eye on, Dennis White," he said. "The lock doesn't show signs of being forced so either you forgot to lock up..." He looked at Liddy.

"No way!" she said.

"...or he had a key somehow. Anyway, after he attacked your mother, he went about setting this accelerant in the kitchen."

"Wait, so he wanted...he intended to..." Liddy looked at Tucker and at her mother and her face flushed with the realization.

"We're treating it as a case of attempted murder," Tucker said solemnly.

"But why would he want to kill Mama?"

Tucker looked at her and she thought his eyes looked angry and maybe a little lost. "It's not logical to assume he went there with the intention of killing your *mother*."

"Whoa, Mom," Ben said. "He was after *you*."

Liddy looked at Tucker but he was looking at his cellphone.

"Anyway," he said, putting the phone down, "We don't know why he lit the place up but we will."

"How'd the fire get going so fast?"

"They said it was started by a binary of what they call two Class B combustibles. At this point, the chemicals used to cause the fire are not available for purchase over the counter. How this lowlife got a hold of them is anybody's guess."

"What makes them so different?"

"Well, first, a class B fuel grows a fire much faster than it would normally burn. And that's clearly what this guy wanted to do—burn the bakery, and Miz Mears in it—as fast as possible. The question is, how did this crackhead get the chemicals? They're restricted."

"And if he had to mix them just right, how did he know to do that?" Ben asked.

Tucker stood up and shook his head. "Unfortunately, this guy is probably half scumbag and half chemist. Most meth addicts can whip up their product in the back of a moving Kia."

"I hear a lot of times they blow themselves up in the process," Ben said.

"Not enough times."

"Why, Tucker! And on Christmas Day."

Tucker grinned. "You're right, Miz Mears. I don't know what got into me. Well, I'm glad to see y'all are doing okay. We'll let you know as soon as we know anything else. I'll be heading back now. Merry Christmas." He tipped a nonexistent hat to Liddy. "Liddy."

"Tucker," she said, nodding, but her cheeks were rosy with a blush she didn't know was coming. *Was it her own thoughts or his telegraphed to her?*

After lunch, her mother asked to be taken back to her room at the assisted living center.

"It's more comfortable than the motel," she told Liddy. "And nobody tries to burn me alive in it. Besides, I want to take a nap."

Ben had promised his other grandparents that he would be there in time for Christmas dinner and so had to leave. He agreed with his mother that nearly being burned alive and five stitches in the head probably wouldn't qualify as an acceptable excuse for missing Christmas with them. She had hoped to give him the jewelry when he went, but that wasn't going to be possible. She hugged him close and made him promise to come back soon. She didn't begrudge him leaving to go to Kitty and Ted's. Their own boy would never come home again. It was little enough that they could spend time with their cherished grandchild.

After Liddy dropped her mother off at the her place, she decided to head into Baxley to pick up some clothes. There was bound to be a drug store open on Christmas Day. The fire, of course, had destroyed everything. As relieved and grateful as she was that her loved ones were safe, she still needed to process what had happened to her.

As she drove to Baxley, she reflected that every item of clothing she owned was gone. Every photo of Bill or of Ben growing up. Every diary or journal. Every cookbook, every DVD, all her electronics, what little jewelry she had left and, of course, the bakery itself. All gone. The equipment, the little café tables, the cheery little curtains that hung in the bay window that she had sewn and hung herself.

Everything, gone.

And while it was true there was insurance, it was only renter's insurance—not enough to start another bakery. And certainly not enough to revive a dead dream.

Suddenly Liddy found herself crying as she drove to Baxley. She felt guilty and ungrateful for shedding tears of self-pity and despair, which just made it worse. Finally, she pulled off the side of the road to compose herself and realized she was parked under the billboard with her nude picture on it. Vandals and the elements had stripped the board of anything recognizable except for her face. Her young, beautiful face, full of anticipation and excitement for the future, stared down at forty-six year old Liddy where she sat in her car on this cloudy, cold Christmas Day.

She put her head down on the steering wheel and cried until she had nothing left in her.

Tucker sat in his living room staring at a football game on television that he was not really seeing. There was something he was missing about all this and Meryl was only a part of it. An earlier phone call to her had left her literally howling in rage and indignation.

"Don't be absurd! Why would I nail a disgusting animal to her door? The wretch hadn't sold a cupcake since the day she opened! All I had to do was sit back and wait!"

"And get Danni-Lynn to begin eviction proceedings?"

"That's just good business, Tucker. I only advise Danni-Lynn. She makes her own decisions."

Tucker could almost see the picture of what had happened to Liddy in Infinity come together right in front of him but then it kept receding. Like the one piece he needed to see the whole story was kept just out of reach.

"You listening to that, Uncle Tucker?"

Haley came and sat down next to him and he reached for the remote control to mute the sound of the game.

"Hey, darlin'," he said. "I wanted to thank you for all your help in making that Christmas dinner about the nicest one I think I ever sat down to. You worked hard and I appreciate it."

"That's okay, Uncle Tuck," the girl said, pulling a strand of her long blonde hair behind her ear. "I enjoyed doing it."

"I'm glad."

"I just wanted to say something, today being Christmas and all."

"Sure, Hon, shoot."

"I just wanted to say that I know Dennis is who they're looking for in Miz James bakery fire and even though you didn't say nothing about him and me knowing each other as well as we used to, I just want to say I appreciate you not looking at me like you might could look at him."

Tucker opened his arms and Haley fell into them.

"I love you, Uncle Tuck," she said. "I know Dennis has done some bad stuff but everyone acts like it's got nothing to do with me and that just kind of blows me away, you know?"

"I love you too, darlin'," Tucker said. "And the reason everyone acts like that is because it has nothing to do with you. That's why they call it a second chance."

Liddy pulled up to the barn and parked her car. Not surprisingly, there were no other cars there. After she had bought a pair of sweats, a packet of underwear and a couple of t-shirts at the Walgreens in Baxley—nothing else was open on Christmas Day—Liddy decided it was still early enough to check on Sugar.

Why should *people* be the only ones to have Christmas dinner?

Her cry on the trip to Baxley had helped but it hadn't changed the facts. Her bakery was gone, her money was gone and she had no back up plan. Leaving Infinity was the only thing she knew, for sure, she would do. And that meant she either needed to convince her mother to come with her, or leave her.

As she tacked up Sugar—it had been way too long since she'd ridden him—she realized that he would be one of the things she would have to leave behind in Infinity.

"I don't care what Tucker says," she said, as she led him to the mounting block. "You've been a great horse for me." She mounted up, adjusted her riding helmet and set out down her favorite trail. *The one Tucker and I used to always take,* she thought sadly.

Would this be her last trail ride? Would she ever ride with Tucker again or were things destined to be awkward between them right up to the moment she left town for good? She shook herself out of the mood and willed the power of the horse to work its magic on her.

"Come on, Sugar," she said, pressing her heels to his sides. "Let's pep things up a bit." The bouncy action of the trot soon gave way to Sugar's smooth canter, and Liddy felt the clear dirt path beneath her with every solid, soothing hit of his hooves. The cadence and the rhythm did even more to relax her. It was late afternoon—her favorite time of day at the barn—with the shadows still long and the sky not too bright.

Invigorated and mentally refreshed from her canter, she slowed Sugar to a walk and let the movement of the gait move her hips in a slow, therapeutic motion. At one point, she closed her eyes and felt the late day sun on her face. Here's something you can't do in a car, she mused, as she concentrated on the feel of the sun and the movement of Sugar's smooth gait.

217

Just when she was ready to turn around and direct her thoughts to where they might have Christmas supper this evening, she felt something off in the way Sugar was walking. She took a few more steps down the trail until she was sure.

Crap. He was limping. It wasn't that easy to get back on him without a mounting block, but it was definitely too far to walk back to the barn on foot. Resigned, she slid off him and tucked the reins under her arm. She had no idea which foot was lame so she carefully lifted each one. Naturally, it was the last one she checked, but happily, it was just a small rock with no obvious damage to the tender frog that she could see. She pried out the rock with her fingers and positioned herself to remount. As soon as she had her foot in the stirrup, Sugar moved away, forcing her to hop alongside him on one foot.

"Whoa, Sugar," she said. "Knock it off. We've had a pleasant ride up to now so don't ruin it by being a jerk." She positioned her foot in the stirrup again and grabbed the pommel with both hands when the sound of a gunshot exploded in the woods near her. Sugar screamed and wheeled away from her. Thankfully, she wasn't wearing low-heeled shoes and her booted foot easily slipped out of the stirrup as he took off down the trail. She landed on her butt in the middle of the trail, the sound of the gunshot reverberating in her head. Before she had time to form the thought: *Hunters? on Christmas?* another shot rang out, this one kicking up dirt, leaves and pebbles a foot away from her.

Jesus God. Someone was shooting at her! Liddy scrambled to her feet, not bothering to straighten all the way up and dove into the bushes off the trail. Fear exploded in her. Her heart was beating so fast she lost all audible sensory perception. It was like she was acting in a totally muted world of color and agitation. *Had the gunshot made her go deaf?* She couldn't hear if the shooter was coming closer, she couldn't even hear if he was shooting again. The audio to her world slowly returned but only in the form of the sound of her heart beating in her throat— obliterating all other noise.

Trembling, she lay as still as she could in the muddy ditch by the side of the road. What seemed like minutes but was probably only seconds later, her hearing returned. She heard the birds overhead but nothing else. She did not hear bushes moving as if someone were stealthily approaching. She waited and tried to collect herself.

Someone had shot at her. Someone was still out there.

Tucker stood in the kitchen watching Haley mix up a batter using a cake recipe Liddy had given her. Her mother was on her way over to take Haley to a movie. It had been a surprise suggestion from Daisy and Tucker didn't think it was a half bad idea. It was a start, anyway.

"Did you know that, Uncle Tuck?" Haley had stopped the rotors on the Mixmaster.

"What, sweetheart?" he said. "Sorry, was off on my own planet for a minute."

"That Liddy said you get better results if you bake your cupcakes twenty five degrees less than any recipe tells you. So, if *Joy of Cooking* says bake 'em at three fifty, you know to set it for three twenty five. Weird, huh?"

"Yep," he said. "That is certainly odd."

"I mean, why don't the recipes just tell you the lower temperature to begin with, you know?"

"Certainly would make more sense."

"Okay, Uncle Tucker, I can tell you're not listening to me." Haley turned to look at him with one hand on her hip.

"I'm sorry, sugar," he said, shaking his head. "I've got this whole fire thing on my mind."

Haley gave her batter a last look and then came and sat down at the kitchen table. Tucker frowned. This was new. He sat down, too.

"Dennis burned the bakery," she said.

"Well, of course we don't *know*—"

"Okay, you can stop treating me like I'm eight, okay?" She reached out and touched his hand. "I know Dennis is a dick."

Tucker forced himself not to smile. He really shouldn't encourage such language, but he was finding himself very proud of the girl she seemed to be evolving into.

"And I meant to say when we were talking earlier... thank you for...for everything you've done for me."

"You don't have to thank me. I'm your uncle. Comes with the job."

"Well, anyway, I wanted you to know, okay?" She got up to return to her mixer. "And I knew about Dennis. I knew he was using and he was cooking crank, too."

Tucker tensed. He hated hearing how close to all that Haley had been, but he needed to listen.

"You have any idea where he might have gone to?" he asked.

"I haven't talked to him since I came to live with you. You know that, right?"

"I figured you hadn't," Tucker said. "But you still might know where he crashes or where he'd run to."

"Not really," she said as she scraped the batter into her two lined cake pans. "I know one thing. He was pretty obsessed with doing spoosh all day long…"

"Spoosh?"

"You know, zip, boo, crank?"

"Okay, Haley, honey, I got the picture."

"He told me once he had his own kitchen." Haley put the bowl and spatula in the sink and Tucker stood up.

"Did he say where?"

"No, I don't really remember…wait a minute." She turned to look at her uncle. "Oh my God! Remember that day you took me riding?"

"In October," Tucker said, already looking for his car keys.

"We rode right past it and I couldn't believe it was the place. Well, I'm not a hundred percent sure it is but it was just like he described it. A broken down house out in the middle of the woods." She turned to tamp down both cake pans by thumping them one by one on the counter. "He said he had a kitchen there. And by that, you know I don't mean…" She waved her hand to encompass the room she was standing in. But when she looked around, her uncle was already down the porch and gone, the front door slamming shut behind him.

Chapter 17

Liddy tried to listen to hear anyone moving around in the bushes or on the path. She was afraid to move. Afraid to go looking for Sugar, afraid to turn and run back to the barn. All she could do was lie in the ditch and hope the shooter would leave. It occurred to her, when she put it in those terms, that what she was really doing was waiting for the shooter to come and finish her off. She needed to do something to save herself.

All of a sudden she heard a noise not far off from her. Although she couldn't absolutely identify it, it sounded like the bolt of a shotgun being slid into place. The noise was the only thing to be heard in the woods, as if the person making it was utterly unconcerned with being heard. Liddy lifted her head and peered in the direction of the noise, trying to see movement, anything that would tell her where her assailant might be.

As she inched her way slowly up the side of the ditch and peered over the rim and down the path, she was astonished to see the ramshackle house she had seen before. She had no idea she had ridden this far into the woods and her stomach clenched at the thought of how far away from the barn she was. All at once, he stepped out of the shadows by the house and into the center of the path.

Liddy gasped, although she cursed herself for not guessing sooner. It was that Dennis kid, Haley's ex. He looked the picture of a twitching drug addict, standing in the middle of the path, holding a sawed-off shotgun and swaying drunkenly. She stayed perfectly still, afraid even in his addled state he would catch a glimpse of movement in her direction and start shooting.

"I know you're here, bakery bitch!" the boy yelled. Liddy resisted the urge to withdraw. She held her breath looking around wildly. *Could she wait him out? Would he come looking for her?* He giggled shrilly then grimaced and turned and aimed at the house. He fired the gun. Liddy watched the wood explode from the side of the house, throwing splinters in every direction. The boy took a step back.

"Oh, we got a friend what's showed up to help you!" he called. He had his back to her and she couldn't see what he was looking at. She thought about using the opportunity to scramble up onto the road, but once she got there she had no idea what to do. She inched forward to see what he was seeing. The bile jumped high into her throat when she saw Sugar, his reins dusting the ground in front of him, trotting down the path toward the boy.

The boy put the gun to his shoulder and watched the horse walk toward him.

"Come on, horsey-horsey," he called to it. "Hey, I'm gonna shoot your horse!" he yelled over his shoulder.

Liddy was on her feet in a flash, unmindful of the noise she was making. Whereas seconds before she had absolutely no idea of what to do, now she was working on pure instinct. Without taking her eyes off White, she grabbed a heavy branch off the side of the road and ran toward the boy and her horse as silent as an Indian.

"I'm gonna blow his fuckin' head off so you can bake it in a pie!" White screeched. "How's that? You can sell fuckin' dead horse in your—"

Liddy swung the heavy branch and slammed the kid square in the side of the head with it. He went down but the shotgun was still in his hands and he was fighting to point it at her from flat on his back. Liddy knew she didn't have enough time to bring her arm back for another swing so without thinking she stomped him hard on the stomach and twisted her body away from the muzzle of the gun. He shot into the trees, making Sugar shy violently and start to run. This time, he was heading in the direction he loved best—the barn. With not a second to spare,

Liddy flung herself out of his path as her horse steamrolled his way back to the barn—right through Dennis White.

Even over the noise of three ATVs, Tucker heard the gunshot. His gut flipped over.

We're too late, he thought in anguish. He was riding a three-wheel ATV with two of Baxley's finest. The path was too narrow for a police cruiser. Within seconds of the gunshot, Tucker saw one of the worst sights he would ever see in his life.

Liddy's horse was galloping riderless down the path. Tucker cut the engine, stood up on his ATV and held his hands up in front of the terrified horse.

"Whoa, whoa, Sugar," he said. "Whoa, boy, settle down!" He hopped out of the vehicle and grabbed the horse's reins. Sugar was still jumpy and white-eyed, but he stopped. Tucker hesitated long enough for the detectives to drive up beside him, which sent the horse into a new panic but this time he didn't bolt.

"Is it her horse, Tuck?" One of them asked. "Check to see if there's blood on him. Did you hear a gunshot?"

Before Tucker could answer, his eye caught movement down the trail. He tossed the reins over Sugar's head so he wouldn't trip over them and let him go. Worse came to worse, the horse would find his own way back to the barn. Tucker unsnapped his service revolver.

One of the detectives called out: "Drop your weapon! On the ground! Now!" Behind him, both men had drawn their weapons.

Tucker held up a hand. "Hold it, guys," he said. "Stand down."

It was Liddy. Stumbling down the path, looking like she'd just been dragged out of a tree by her hair, her riding helmet was looped over her shoulder by its strap and she cradled a short-barreled shotgun in her arms. When she saw the three men she stopped in the middle of the path, blinked twice and burst into tears.

Later, Tucker would remember it as one of the most endearing things he'd ever seen. The relief of seeing her whole and unhurt was so incredible, he didn't even care that the other two saw him grab her in a very unprofessional hug. He plucked the gun out of her hands and handed it to Stanton, wiped her tears away with his fingers, and kissed her solidly on the mouth.

"Whoa, Tuck," one of the men said, grinning. "We usually let Victim Services console the vic."

"Are you hurt? Did you come off him?" Tucker asked, running his hands lightly over her back and legs.

She took a long breath and put a hand out against his chest to steady herself. "Don't even begin to tell me, Tucker Jones, that you'll make me get back on him if I fell off." She put her hand to her head as if in a daze. "I dismounted," she said.

Tucker restrained himself from laughing. He pulled out his cellphone and called for someone to find the barn manager to locate someone to come and ride Sugar back. The two cops went ahead to find White. They radioed back that he wasn't dead but, between the branch up side the head and a well placed horse hoof on his spleen, he wasn't going to be causing trouble any time soon either.

"How did you know I was here?"

"I didn't," he said. "I got a tip on White's meth lab. I had no idea you would be here until I got to the barn and saw your saddle and bridle gone."

He used his fingers to turn her face to him. His eyes probed hers and there was a catch in his voice when he spoke. "It may be the most selfish thing I've ever done," he said. "But the way I look at it, I flat deserve to have you in my life."

"Even with all the cussin'?"

"Yeah."

"And the Catholic thing?"

"You're *Catholic*?"

They both started laughing.

"I guess it's only fair," Tucker said, still chuckling. "After all, I never came clean about why I never ate your cupcakes."

"You didn't eat my cupcakes?" Liddy's mouth fell open. How had she missed noticing that Tucker didn't eat her cupcakes?

Tucker shrugged. "I'm diabetic," he said. After the briefest of pauses, both of them started laughing again.

Within thirty minutes, Liddy was back at the barn with Tucker. An ambulance and four police cruisers waited in the parking lot of the small barn for White to be brought out of the woods on a stretcher. Tucker drove her to the Assisted Living Center that evening to collect her mother and took them back to his large sprawling ranch house. While Tucker spent more time on the phone with the police than he did toasting the Christmas miracles of the day with Haley, Liddy and her mother, it was still a wonderful night of good food and laughter and astonishing stories of how Liddy had disarmed White with a tree branch. Each telling became more colorful the more hot buttered rum she drank.

Even with all the events of the day, everyone retired late. It was almost as if the fellowship and holiday warmth was too good to walk away from, Liddy thought. Haley kissed both Liddy and Tucker goodnight and went to her room. Liddy's mother was already fast asleep in Tucker's big guest room.

While she had spent the evening with Tucker, he had been so involved with tying up loose ends of the episode with White—not to mention Meryl's involvement—that Liddy felt like she hadn't really spoken to him since they left the barn. When everyone else was settled, she saw him turn his phone to vibrate and retrieve a bottle of wine and two glasses in the kitchen. If she had any questions about where she would sleep that night, Tucker succinctly ended them when he led her to his bedroom at the far end of the house.

It was a large room with a ten-foot ceiling, a king-size bed and large, masculine wooden furniture. Double doors led to an adjoining bathroom. Liddy turned to face Tucker, raised up on tiptoes and kissed him but before he could put the wine bottle down and return the favor, she spoke.

"Jenna?"

"That's over."

Liddy sucked in her breath with a mixture of dismay and relief.

"She dumped me."

225

The smile began slowly on Liddy's face and she shook her head in wonderment.

"Seems our mutual friend, Riley," Tucker said, "made a very serious pass in her direction and Jenna decided...she was interested in receiving." He shrugged.

"They're a good match," Liddy said, nodding. "I saw that at the dance but I was so jealous of you being with her it didn't register at the time."

"So you were jealous, huh?" His crooked grin spread across his face, one hand on his hip.

"Okay. Hold that look and that thought," Liddy said, turning on her heel. "I'll be right back." She turned and went into the adjoining bathroom. After quickly showering and rubbing herself nearly raw with the rough towels hanging in Tucker's bath, she wrapped herself in a dry towel and peered into the bedroom.

He was, of course, fast asleep.

Happier than she could ever remember being, Liddy dropped the towel and slipped into bed with him. As soon as she slid next to him, her hand on his chest, he was awake. He turned to face her and kissed her face in the dark.

"Big day," he said.

"About to get bigger," she said with an impish grin.

He held her chin in his hand so see her face better. "You sure about this?" he whispered.

In answer, Liddy began pulling at his shorts. Literally shivering with anticipation and longing, Tucker still would have held off—even with Liddy naked in his bed—but she had discovered an urgency in her with Tucker that could not be put off.

"I'm not planning on being very ladylike with you tonight," she said, reaching inside the waistband of his boxers for the hard bulge between his legs.

"I'm not planning on being very ladylike with you tonight," she said, reaching inside the waistband of his boxers.

"Shut up," he growled, pulling her naked body on top of him. He kissed her hungrily, feeling the heat of her soft breath across his chest. He stopped for a moment and groaned as she kissed his lips, his neck, his chest.

"No quips," he moaned. "No smart talk. Just..." He moaned again as she lifted her hips off him and then back down onto him, supporting her body over him on the bed. She looked into his eyes as she moved her hips and suddenly her body shuddered with the first wave of her orgasm. Seconds later, he groaned and they fell limp together on the bed. He still held her tightly against him, both of them flushed and tingling with the heat and spent lust of their union.

"I thought we were going to try it slow this time," he said in gasps, staring at the ceiling.

She laughed, for once totally at a loss for words. After a few moments, he stroked her cheek with his thumb and she slowly opened her eyes. He smiled and she turned to him and kissed him, putting her hands on both sides of his face.

"Never letting you go," she said softly.

"I was hoping you'd say that," he whispered, leaning down to kiss her.

Epilogue

Six Months Later

Liddy turned in bed to squint at the bedside clock. Eight a.m. She burrowed a little deeper into the blankets and duvets that swaddled the king-sized bed. A shaft of sunlight escaped between the slats of blinds on the window.

How life can turn around, she thought. One minute you're poor and struggling to make and sell one lousy damn cupcake in a town that doesn't want you, and the next...

The door kicked open and he was there. He stood, his brown hair ruffled, his shirt open over his low-slung jeans. In his hands he was holding a large tray. She could see the steam drifting off the tall coffee mugs.

"Sorry," he said. "Couldn't get the door open any other way."

Liddy moved over to make room for him. He set the tray down then leaned over and kissed her. "Good morning," he said.

She loved the smell of him. It was the smell of maleness, a scent of something wonderful she couldn't name or put her finger on.

"Good morning. How long have you been up?"

He settled next to her and handed her a mug of coffee. "Long enough to create a full four-course breakfast for a girl who wears me out every night. And for whom I need to get her strength back every morning."

Liddy peered over at the tray. "Four courses?"

"Toast and jam," he admitted.

She laughed. "I love you, Tucker," she said.

He stopped the motion of the coffee cup to his lips and looked at her. A slow grin inched his way across his face. "I love you, too, Liddy," he said. He put his mug down. "Three thousandth time saying it calls for a kiss."

He touched her chin lightly and kissed her on the mouth.

Liddy fell into the sensation of the kiss, his warmth, his scent, the feel of his fingers on her face. When he pulled away, she looked into his brown eyes.

"Is three thousand the number of times we've said 'I love you' or is it the number of times, we've...?"

"Your guess is as good as mine."

"Can you believe we're here after all that's happened?" Liddy whispered.

"We're here because of all that's happened," he said, retrieving his coffee cup.

"We're here because of your wife."

He glowered at her. "*Ex*-wife. I should think you, of all people, wouldn't have trouble remembering that."

"Don't get grumpy on me, Tucker. But it's true. If it wasn't for Meryl being all psycho jealous about the thought of you and me getting together—"

"I'm not willing to give her credit for our being together," he said. "If anything, because of her...antics...it took longer."

"Longer, you mean, to sort out how we felt about each other?"

Tucker frowned and handed her a plate of buttered toast. "Some of us already knew how we felt," he said pointedly.

"I'll give you that," she said, taking a toast slice. "It's the part where you nearly married Jenna to demonstrate your love for me I have trouble with."

"Can we talk about something else?"

"Sure." Liddy took the coffee mug from his hand and set it down. Still holding his hand, she licked butter residue from his fingers. He groaned.

"In fact," she said, moving over next to him. She reached for him, "we don't have to talk at all."

Later, while Tucker ran errands, Liddy sat in the bed and sipped her now cold coffee. She reflected on how her life had changed since the shooting on the trail. White, addled from his years of drug abuse had become obsessed with the idea that Liddy knew of his meth lab in the woods. Convinced because of her connection with Tucker, that she would turn him in, he believed that killing her was the only way to protect his operation. As Meryl had insisted, the possum was all his idea.

Meryl, on the other hand, had been determined to drive Liddy from Infinity from literally the first day Liddy arrived in town. When she learned that there might be more than a friendship budding between Liddy and her ex-husband, she intensified her campaign to drive Liddy away. She did allow Tucker to buy Liddy's family jewelry back from her so that Liddy could return them to her mother in law. Liddy saw Meryl often around town. She still worked out of her realtor's office. She still called up Tucker from time to time on pretenses of needing his help or advice.

The legacy of the psycho ex-wife, Liddy thought. Once they have kids, or live in the same small town, even if the ex-wife goes nuts and tries to kill people, she'll still be there in the family portraits forever. *Note to self*, Liddy thought. *Tell Ben not to marry a sociopath.* Thinking of Ben, she smiled. He had gone back to Athens and was in the process of talking again about a future that involved not just his getting his four-year degree, but graduate school. He was officially back on track.

Haley had also found a track of her own. Her passion for the culinary arts felt authentic to both Liddy and Tucker and so Haley enrolled in a dual degree culinary school located in Baxley. She still lived with Tucker, and the combination of her excitement seeing her life go forward combined with the accomplishments she was performing every day in preparation for the school continued to add polish to a girl everyone had given up on but Tucker.

The daughter I never had? Liddy found herself thinking more than once. Whatever the relationship was, it was very good —for both of them.

Then there was Mama. Happy, snappy and telling the world she always knew that Tucker Jones was a fine catch. Liddy planned to move her in with them as soon as everything else settled down. And as soon as Mama could leave her tight coterie of cohorts and pals at the Assisted Living center.

Would things ever settle down? Did she really want that? Except for losing her personal effects, the bakery burning was not the worst thing that could happen. There were few people who thought it a great loss. The two stores on either side of the bakery were damaged to the point that they were able to benefit greatly from their insurance payouts. One of them went so far as to send Liddy a thank you note which Tucker assured her was not sarcastic but absolutely genuine. With the bakery gone and any hope with it of her ever picking up and starting again, her first impulse, she had to admit, was to leave Infinity.

That Christmas night they spent together—their first of many—Tucker Jones put a decisive end to that notion.

And as far as dreams go, and Liddy's in particular, Tucker pointed out to her something she should have seen all along. Because her dream had always been to open a cupcake shop, she didn't see that the business she really had was a catering business. When she finally recognized how her original dream needed to change to fit who she was now, she realized something she never would have believed a week earlier—she had already made her dream come true.

Her cupcake shop may have been tanking on every level, but her catering business was doing great.

She looked over at the chair flanking Tuck's side of the bed where his clothes from the day before were neatly folded, his belt coiled on top. He wasn't Bill. And that was fine. She still cussed and likely always would. He didn't like it, and likely never would. But what they brought to each other in every other way outweighed their differences. They had both already lived full lives before they met and those lives, in one way or another, would always be there in the background. This time around, it made what they had richer and deeper.

On top of all that, in one week, she would be back in Paris. While Tucker admitted he didn't share her fascination with the City of Light, he was only too happy to go there on their honeymoon.

Liddy walked into the kitchen, her glance falling on the refrigerator where a copy of their wedding invitation was attached by a magnet made to look like the Eiffel Tower. She traced the raised letters on the invitation with her finger and smiled.

No one would ever be able to convince her that some dreams don't come true, she thought as she touched the pair of Air France tickets right next to the invitation.

In fact, some of them come true in a way you could never imagine in your wildest.

Finding Infinity

About the Author

Susan Kiernan-Lewis lives in Atlanta and writes about horses, France, mysteries and romance.
Like many authors, Susan depends on the reviews and word of mouth referrals of her readers. If you enjoyed *Finding Infinity*, please consider leaving a review saying so on Amazon.com, Barnesandnoble.com or Goodreads.com. Go to Susan's website at susankiernanlewis.com and feel free to contact her at sanmarcopress@me.com.

Susan Kiernan-Lewis

Finding Infinity

Made in the USA
Middletown, DE
22 February 2019